More from Mark David Gerson

FICTION

The MoonQuest

The StarQuest

The SunQuest

The Bard of Bryn Doon

The Lost Horse of Bryn Doon (coming soon!)

The Sorcerer of Bryn Doon (coming soon!)

MEMOIR

Acts of Surrender: A Writer's Memoir

Dialogues with the Divine: Encounters with my Wisest Self

Pilgrimage: A Fool's Journey

SELF-HELP & PERSONAL GROWTH

The Way of the Fool: How to Stop Worrying About Life and Start Living It

The Way of the Imperfect Fool: How to Bust the Addiction to Perfection That's Stifling Your Success

The Book of Messages: Writings Inspired by Melchizedek

RESOURCES FOR WRITERS

The Voice of the Muse: Answering the Call to Write

The Voice of the Muse Companion: Guided Meditations for Writers

From Memory to Memoir: Writing the Stories of Your Life

Organic Screenwriting: Writing for Film, Naturally

Birthing Your Book...Even If You Don't Know What It's About

The Heartful Art of Revision: An Intuitive Guide to Editing

Writer's Block Unblocked: Seven Surefire Ways to Free Up Your Writing and Creative Flow

Time to Write

Write with Ease

Free Your Characters, Free Your Story

Write to Heal

Journal from the Heart

SARA'S YEAR

The Sara Stories

MARK DAVID GERSON

SARA'S YEAR

This is a work of fiction. Names, characters, businesses, places, events and incidents are either the products of the author's imagination or used in a fictitious manner. Any resemblance to actual persons, living or dead, or to actual events is purely coincidental.

First Edition 2015. Second Edition 2020.

Published by MDG Media International
2370 W. State Route 89a, Suite 11-210
Sedona, AZ 86336
www.mdgmediainternational.com

ISBN: 978-1-950189-20-5

Cover Photograph and Title/Section Pages Sketch:
Westmount Public Library (cc) Jean Gagnon
https://commons.wikimedia.org/wiki/File:Westmount_Public_Library_12.jpg
Adapted from the original image and used under Creative Commons License (CC BY-SA 3.0) https://creativecommons.org/licenses/by-sa/3.0/legalcode

More information
www.markdavidgerson.com
www.thesarastories.com

*To ask an author who hopes to be a serious writer if his work is
autobiographical is like asking a spider where he buys his thread.
The spider gets his thread right out of his own guts,
and that is where the author gets his writing.*
ROBERTSON DAVIES

*Imagination has given us the steam engine, the telephone,
the talking-machine, and the automobile,
for these things had to be dreamed
of before they became realities.*
L. FRANK BAUM

For my mother and my daughter

Death

1

"*Yis'gadal v'yis'kadash sh'mei raba.*" Swaying gently back and forth, Bernie Freed chanted the timeworn mourner's prayer in counterpoint to the doleful tolling of St. Luc's, its hulking mass shrouded in a fog that lent a Dickensian air to the century-old cemetery.

"*B'al'ma di v'ra khir'usei, v'yam'likh mal'khu—*" Bernie stopped with the echo of the final bell, his lips frozen in mid-syllable. For a moment he stared at the simple pine coffin at his feet, a raised Star of David its only adornment. Like him, it seemed to hover uncertainly. Would it slide into its tidy slot or would it do something else? Something unexpected? Bernie scratched his beard, tilted his head and waited.

Nothing.

A single shaft of sunlight thrust through the gray haze, dropping to the clump of damp earth just to the right of Bernie's highly buffed Oxfords. He gazed at the solitary shock of brightness, mesmerized.

Rabbi Fleischer prodded Bernie with a bony elbow. "*B'chayeikhon uv'yomeikhon,*" the old man prompted, a little too loudly, glaring up at the church. The massive stone building had no business being there. All those crosses and saints staring down at him gave him heartburn. St. Luc's Père Benoît felt much the same about the Jews on his doorstep: Dead or alive, they did not belong. Both old men were powerless against the accident of nineteenth-century real estate history that placed Catholic church and Jewish cemetery side by side as reluctant neighbors.

Bernie ignored the rabbi. Instead, he dropped to his knees. He touched the ground where the brief patch of light was already fading and pressed his lips to the casket's polished surface, ignoring the startled stares of his relatives. After a moment, he rose unsteadily, brushing away the three pairs of hands that stretched toward him. Eyes glistening, he opened his mouth as if to make a pronouncement, then shut it, saying nothing. He scanned the faces of his fellow mourners, his eyes resting for a breath longer on Sarah Swartz, his mother's oldest friend. He would swear later that she smiled and nodded. She would swear, equally insistently, that she did nothing of the sort. Regardless, he turned his back on coffin, rabbi and family, pushed passed his aunt and marched out of the cemetery.

"Bernie," Sadie Finkel hissed icily after her nephew. Tall and spindly, with angular features that matched her brittle temperament, the seventy-year-old spinster was the family matriarch.

Bernie heard his aunt but ignored her. Everyone in the family always deferred to Sadie. No one had dared defy her, until now.

Nine years older than Bernie's mother, Sadie had ruled Esther and her two brothers with uncompromising sternness from the moment of their mother's untimely death at age thirty-six. According to the family, Ruth had finally succumbed to some sort of slow poisoning, the result of too many long hours among the chemical dyes of the Park Avenue schmatta factory that had been her second home for more than half her life. Neighborhood gossip suggested otherwise. Was she stabbed to death at her sewing machine by Faygie Kaufman, whose hunchbacked husband, Yitzak, owned the factory and, it was rumored, most of his comely employees? Or was she shot by the same gun Max Finkel gave her to keep her safe on her late-shift return home through Montreal's antisemitic streets? Knife wound, gunshot or poison? Murder or suicide? A half-century later there was no way to know for sure, although Bernie bet that Sadie would know.

Whatever she knew about Bubbie Ruth, and she made it her business to know most things, Sadie had held the Finkel family together through and past the tragedy — not with loving kindness but with the iron fist of a grim despot. Ruthless, that's what she was. Bernie half-smirked at the unintentional pun as he stuffed his black yarmulke into his suit jacket pocket and strode past the clutch of idling limousines, out the cemetery gate and to the corner bus stop, just as a blue-and-white No. 124 shuddered to a halt in front of him.

As the bus lumbered past the Haitian groceries and Vietnamese dollar stores that were slowly erasing the neighborhood's Jewish past, Bernie leaned back into the worn leather seat and squeezed his eyes shut, wishing that Auntie Sadie and the rest of his crazy relatives could disappear as easily. Not his mother. Not Esther. But she was already gone. And not Sarah Swartz. No, not Sarah.

2

Sarah Swartz tucked one of the many loose strands of crinkly white back under her fraying funeral hat and watched Bernie leave the gravesite. With his short, dark hair, close-cropped reddish-brown beard and wire-rim glasses, he reminded her of a younger version of old Fleischer. A better-looking version, but no less grim. Fleischer had always been a humorless bastard. But Bernie… Did Bernie ever not look like the serious, conservative-suited accountant he had grown into? Maybe as a toddler. Maybe not even then.

She felt eyes drilling into her and turned back to the ceremony, meeting Sadie's steely glare with a shrug. "It's my fault your nephew walked out on his mother's funeral?" she wanted to ask. "More like it's your fault, you dried-up old prune."

Sarah stifled a smile. Maybe one day she would tell Sadie what she thought of her. After fifty years, it was probably time. She raised her eyes heavenward. *What do you think, Esther?* If Esther was watching, she would be nodding yes. "Do it," she would say. She might even be giving Sadie the finger from up there. She would be giving it to Manny, too, that spineless nogoodnik of a brother of hers, who could never find the backbone to stand up to their oldest sister. *Didn't then, still doesn't.*

Esther did. Once upon a time.

That was the Esther Sarah preferred to remember: the spunky teenager whose feisty single-mindedness threw Sadie into a choleric rage more times than she could count. That was the Esther who, when a vagrant grabbed her ankle as she and Sarah strolled up the Main, first ignored the filth-encrusted bum, then marched back a block and a half, Sarah huffing to keep pace, and delivered a sharp kick-in-the-gut to the astonished derelict.

That was the Esther who dared to dream — of a husband, of a college degree, of a life free of the poverty and housewifely drudgery that ruled so many St. Urbain Street lives. That was the Esther who fled Sadie's tyranny only to find herself locked into a different kind, one that spent decades eating away at her dreams until cancer finished the job.

"Oseh shalom bim'romav, hu ya'aseh shalom…"

Sarah hadn't noticed Manny take over the Kaddish from Bernie in a voice as whiny now as it was when he was twelve.

"Aleinu v'al kol Yis'ra'el v'im'ru amen."

"Amen," Esther's friends and family responded as the coffin creaked slowly into the ground.

Moments later, the gathering broke up. As its black-clad members melted back toward their cars, some exchanged disapproving whispers about "that poor Esther's son" while others stole glances toward neighboring gravestones as if expecting to see the prodigal leaning against one of them, nonchalantly smoking a cigarette. Like in a scene from a movie.

"Sarah?" Sadie hooked her clawed, arthritic hand onto Sarah's elbow. "You're coming to Manny and Dora's for the shiva, aren't you? Esther would want you there today, you know, especially after—" She tilted her head toward the cemetery gate.

Sarah knew what Esther would have wanted and it had nothing to do with Sadie, Manny or Dora. She knew, too, what that fifteen-year-old Esther would have done, and she wished she possessed half that long-ago teenager's chutzpah. Instead, she sighed, lifted her cane and let herself be nudged toward the lead limo.

Transformation

3

Bernie opened his eyes and gazed out the window, trying to ignore the ghostlike reflection that stared back at him. He loosened his black tie, razor-ripped before the funeral as symbol of mourning, and unbuttoned the top button of his white shirt.

"I'm crying," he whispered, surprised. He had not shed a tear in two days, not since the hospital room, not since his mother stopped breathing. He had no memory of the wail of the flatlined monitor nor of the clutch of medics who flew into the room in response. All he remembered was his mother's face, pale and at last untroubled. That and the wracking sobs he was startled to discover were his own.

He watched the spectral finger in the window touch a shimmering droplet before it disappeared into his beard, then another… and another. Over his shoulder, across the aisle, a twelve-year-old youth, also dressed in black, scrutinized him curiously.

Self-conscious, Bernie wiped his face with the back of his hand. He longed to turn and meet the boy's gawking stare. He didn't dare, in case the boy was not really there, in case what he was really seeing was his younger self.

What would he tell this boy, decked out in his bar mitzvah suit on his final visit to Rabbi Fleischer before the big day? How would he counsel him if he could? Would he urge him to stop being so afraid? As if anyone could switch off fear with a snap of the fingers. He couldn't. If he could, maybe he wouldn't have fled his mother's funeral. Or was his leaving the very act of fearlessness that Esther's eyes had begged him to undertake hours before they closed that final time?

Bernie's breath steamed up the bus window, obscuring both his reflection and the boy's and erasing the hazy Westmount graystones beyond them…the same foggy condensation that had shrouded the view out Esther's hospital window on Tuesday.

"Bernie," Esther rasped.

Bernie spun around, but his mother slept, her face more peaceful than it had been through the many months of chemo and radiation therapy that had passed since her diagnosis. Her hair tumbled onto her pillow in wisps of white silk and her skin was almost translucent. Her long, slender fingers rested lightly on her stomach, which covered a body now so wraithlike that it was barely detectable under the sheet. Even her breathing, so labored when she was awake, was calm and steady in slumber. As if she wasn't sick at all.

"Bernie."

He heard it again and moved closer. Esther's mouth didn't open; her eyes did, a slit.

"You're so much like me," they said. "I'm sorry."

"No," Bernie said aloud, not certain he had heard what he thought he'd heard, not certain she could see him or was aware of his presence. "Don't be sorry. You were—" His voice caught. "You are—" He swallowed his tears. "You are the best mother any son could ever wish for."

"I was so…so afraid for so long. There are so many things…" Esther moved her head so slightly that Bernie suspected that maybe his eyes as well as his ears were playing tricks on him. "Don't let Sadie…" Her eyes flickered shut.

He *had* let Sadie. So many times since Esther's cancer had imprisoned her in this hospital room, he had let Sadie.

He had let Sadie decide that Esther's basement-flat tenant must be evicted. "That renter will be too much for your poor mother when she gets home from the hospital." Never mind that Mona cooked and cleaned for Esther in exchange for much of her rent. "That's a sister's job," she insisted, closing up her dank, cluttered one-room apartment in Côte-Saint-Luc and settling into Esther's sunny guest room.

He had let Sadie phone Harold Coopersmith and had then let her invite him to his mother's hospital room. "The poor man has a right to see her. They're still married, for God's sake. For seven years, until— For those seven years they shared everything. He owes it to her to share this." That through much of their marriage, what his second stepfather had shared most was the back of his hand with Esther and his smarmy charms with a bevy of barely legal bimbos didn't matter. As far as Bernie could tell, what Harold owed Esther most was to stay as far away from her as possible. Sadie could not see that, or would not. After all, she was the one who had introduced them.

He also had let Sadie bully him into abandoning his plans to abridge the shiva mourning period from seven days to a less traditional three. "Your mother will turn in her grave, God rest her soul, when she sees how you are disrespecting her." Sadie's eyes blazed and her voice rose. "Disrespecting her," she shrilled. Bernie was fairly certain that if the Esther of a few years earlier would never have done anything so public to attract the disapproval of friends and family, the Esther whose body had only just been removed to the hospital morgue would have applauded her son's late-blooming chutzpah.

"Well," Bernie muttered as he stepped off the bus in front of the sandstone pile that was the Westmount Public Library, "Sadie, Harold, Manny and Dora can sit for all seven days and kvetch to all the shiva visitors about what a terrible son I am. I won't be there to hear it."

Bernie climbed the worn stone steps and crossed under a series of columned arches to reach his favorite sanctuary, a Victorian-style conservatory attached to the turreted library building. With its exotic plants and tinkling fountain, the jewel-like greenhouse set amid the mature oaks and maples of Westmount Park was a perfect retreat. Esther had introduced her son to it when he was seven. Then, park, library and conservatory had formed a convenient and welcome break from the Saturday afternoon bus trek home from the farthest reaches of French Catholic east-end Montreal, where Bernie's grandfather lay in a convalescent-hospital bed.

Esther always arranged their weekly outing so that Bernie could pick out a half-dozen books from the shelves and shelves of colorful kids' titles. Although they had no borrowing privileges in Westmount, a sympathetic staffer often let Bernie carry his selection into the conservatory. There, while Esther wandered the stacks or found respite among the greenhouse greenery, Bernie immersed himself in imaginary worlds so much more satisfying than his real-life one.

At closing time, mother and son strolled the few blocks west to Stella's Lunch, where they shared burgers, fries and cherry Cokes before continuing on to the final ride home — on the same bus transfer, if they timed it right.

The Westmount outings ended with Zeyda Max's death, and Stella's shut its doors soon after. Yet Bernie still found himself drawn to the wealthy Anglo community and its stately oasis.

Here is where his mother dropped him the day after his first stepfather went to prison. While Esther, Auntie Sadie and Uncle Manny were downtown conferring with lawyers, Bernie was sitting at the edge of the conservatory fountain, praying for a better life without Gerry.

When Bernie failed to get a date for his high school prom, he told no one. Instead, he sat in his rented tuxedo on a park bench across from the glowing conservatory. When the tower clock in nearby Victoria Hall struck one, he caught the last bus home.

Here, too, is where Bernie went to wrestle with his mother's announcement that she would be marrying Uncle Harold. As he paced angrily from one greenhouse room to the next and back, he tried to conjure up memories of his father. When he couldn't, he cursed himself for remembering so little, cursed Auntie Sadie for bringing Harold into their lives, cursed Harold for being such a slimy bastard and cursed God, in case there was one, for having taken his real father from him.

4

Sarah found Bernie sitting crosslegged on the floor in the kids' section, thumbing through an old copy of *Ozma of Oz* and focusing with particular interest on the classic illustrations by John R. Neill. His suit jacket lay crumpled on his lap and scattered around him in a multicolored heap were as many of L. Frank Baum's other Oz books as he had been able to locate: not only *The Wonderful Wizard of Oz*, but *Dorothy and the Wizard in Oz*, *The Marvelous Land of Oz*, *The Road to Oz*, *The Lost Princess of Oz* and *The Emerald City of Oz*. The sun streaming through the stained-glass window created a polychromatic halo around him.

Bernie looked up at the squat little woman he had known all his life. Sarah's hat was askew, her hair kinkier than usual in the clammy August heat and dried tears scarred her makeup. Her wrinkled, dandruff-specked black dress added to the rumpled effect. It didn't matter how much effort Sarah applied to her appearance, she always reminded Bernie of an older, female Columbo — as unconsciously disheveled as the Peter Falk character, and just as sharp.

He slammed *Ozma of Oz* shut. "Gerry made me get rid of it. All of them. He said they were too sissy for a boy."

It wasn't only the Oz series that Gerry had disapproved of. He also insisted that Bernie's dog had to go, a copper-colored cocker-terrier mix named Tik-Tok, after Dorothy's automaton companion in several of the books. Gerry claimed to be allergic to dogs. Tik-Tok's growling, bare-toothed hostility toward this new addition to the family suggested something different.

"Didn't you used to call Gerry the Nome King?" Sarah asked.

Bernie flipped through *Ozma of Oz* until he found an illustration of a round little man with a white beard and cruel eyes. "Gerry was exactly like the Nome King: short, fat, ugly and mean."

Sarah peered at the drawing. "Doesn't do him justice."

"Then there was Harold." Bernie shuffled through the stack of books until he found *The Lost Princess of Oz*. He opened it to a black-and-white rendering of a skeletal, sinister-looking figure with long, stringy hair. "Meet Ugu, shoemaker-turned-evil-sorcerer."

"Your mother sure knew how to pick them. All of them." Sarah chuckled. Her chuckle dissolved into a sigh. "Me, too," she added softly.

Sarah forced a smile as she brushed the top of Bernie's head, but her red-rimmed blue eyes were sad. In one way, her loss was greater than Bernie's. Sarah and Esther had discovered each other in the midst of the schoolyard chaos and cacophony that was their first day at Bancroft School. They had been inseparable ever since — at least as inseparable as growing up and multiple marriages would allow.

Even when World War II sent Esther's first husband, Morris, to a hush-hush, high-level Defence Department job in Halifax, Sarah and her husband were able to follow when Morris found Sammy a desk job. Nearly deaf in one ear, Sammy had been ineligible for military service. On top of that, his nascent Montreal dental practice was going nowhere. "A catastrophe" was how Sarah described it to Esther. So Sammy welcomed the excuse to leave town and start over somewhere else. Sarah, of course, was grateful to be able to stay close to Esther.

Not long after the war's end, both couples returned to Montreal and the new Jewish neighborhoods springing up on the north side of the Mountain. Even when, a few years later, both couples moved again, they were only five miles apart: Esther and Morris in a compact bungalow in well-to-do Town of Mount Royal and Sarah and Sammy in a tiny ground-floor flat on the less affluent side of Notre-Dame-de-Grâce.

Bernie reached for Sarah's hand. "How did you know where to find me?"

"After all this time, I shouldn't know where to find you? Who first told your mother about this place?"

Sarah's eyes glazed over. She wasn't looking down at Bernie and his tower of books. She was looking down at Esther and hers — hefty volumes of art reproductions featuring masters from Rubens and Rembrandt to Picasso and Chagall. For her part, Sarah was carrying an armload of George Eliot, Emily Dickinson and the Brontës. Esther flipped through the pages of one of her books to a mass of golden squares and cubes. *"Ma Jolie,"* she said, pronouncing it 'ma jolly.' '"Why don't we ever see this in art class?" she demanded. "This Pablo Picasso is a genius." She dropped that book and picked up another, then another. "Here it is," she announced. "A *Jewish* artist. Look at this." She stabbed the black-clad beggar floating over the Russian shtetl. "His name is…his name is…" She squinted nearsightedly at the caption. "Marc Chagall. Marc with a 'c.' That almost makes him like he's from Montreal." She thought about that for a minute. "No, that can't be right. That would make him French not Jewish."

Sarah bent down to join Esther on the floor, straightening up when a sharp pain shot through her right knee. She wasn't fifteen and that wasn't Esther. She was sixty-one, if just barely. She didn't feel like sixty-one, whatever that was supposed to feel like. Her arthritis rarely agreed.

"I'm too old to stand here like this and I'm too old to sit on the floor," Sarah said.

Bernie started to get up.

"No, no. Stay where you are." She leaned into her cane. "Did your mother ever tell you about your name?"

"Bernard was for my great grandfather, her grandfather."

"Baruch, yes. What about your middle name? Marc."

"She always said it was a name she liked."

"What about the French spelling?"

"To make me feel more like I belonged in Quebec?"

"Wait here." Sarah hobbled off, first to the fine art section, then to literature. Five minutes later she returned clutching a Chagall coffee table book and *The Autobiography of Alice B. Toklas*. "Your mother couldn't believe that there was such a thing as a famous artist who was also Jewish. Or a writer like Gertrude Stein who was more than Jewish; she was a woman. She couldn't believe it."

"Why have I never heard of this Gertrude Stein?" Esther demanded. "Why isn't she in the Baron Byng library? A woman, Sarah. And a Jew. Like us!" Her eyes shone. "I tell you this, Sarah Schumacher. I am going to

be an artist. And a writer. Me. Esther Finkel. I swear it to you right now on my mother's grave. And I'm going to create things more meshugena than this Marc Chagall and Gertrude Stein ever dreamed of."

"Marc. Chagall." Bernie's voice jarred Sarah back to the present.

"All her dreams," she said, "she put into you."

"It didn't happen."

"None of it." Sarah frowned. "In those days it was hard for girls. It was even harder for Jews. So maybe it wouldn't have happened, even without your Auntie Sadie."

"Auntie Sadie?"

"Sadie made sure it couldn't happen. Esther wanted to go to college, to study art. Max, your zeyda, alevasholem, might have said yes. But he never recovered from…from…you know. So he relied on Sadie. He listened to Sadie."

"And Sadie said no."

"Sadie said no. Sadie said girls don't go to college. Not Jewish girls. Not good Jewish girls. Sadie said girls like Esther get married and raise a family. Sadie said college is a waste of time and money. Especially for girls. Especially for good Jewish girls." She paused, remembering. "Sadie said no."

Bernie returned the Oz books to the shelf one by one and stood up. "Sadie always says no."

"You have to understand, Bernie. Your Auntie Sadie was jealous. Of course, she loved your mother, but she was jealous. Bitter. Spiteful, even. She wasn't twenty-five yet and she was already an alte moyd. An old maid. What could be worse for a Jewish girl than no husband or family?"

"Jealous? What do you mean?"

"Your mother was the pretty one. Your mother was the smart one. No one ever paid attention to Sadie, as much as she tried. But Esther…Esther always had the boys chasing after her. Half the boys in Baron Byng asked her out. The other half would have if they'd dared." Sarah half-smiled. "Esther could have chosen— No." She shook her head. "She chose who she chose." She touched Bernie's arm. "If she hadn't, you wouldn't be here."

Bernie stepped away and stared through the prison-like bars of the leaded window and into Westmount Park. He stared at the blue-and-white-clad nannies pushing prams along the path…at the kids swinging higher and higher in the playground…at life.

"If she hadn't, you wouldn't be here," Sarah's voice echoed in his head. *Not being here…maybe that would have been better…*

"…I'm sorry, Bernie."

Sarah was talking. Bernie turned from the window. His eyes were wet.

"I'm sorry about your mother. I'm sorry about your Auntie Sadie. I'm sorry about the whole farkakte mess. And I'm sorry you have to be in the middle of it. It isn't right. It isn't. None of this has ever been right."

5

"What are you going to do?" Sarah raised the china cup to her lips and watched Bernie through the curls of steam. She held the cup with both hands but didn't drink. A tuna salad — salade niçoise, they called it here — and a plate of french bread sat untouched next to her vacant saucer. Bernie had taken only one bite from his cheeseburger before shoving it aside. Melted swiss cheese congealed on the plate next to soggy french fries.

Bernie said nothing. He opened the Chagall book that Sarah had borrowed from the library. It fell open at *Self-Portrait with Muse.* He touched the androgynous artist figure and its angel-like muse, then stared past Sarah out to Sherbrooke Street, through the plate glass window that had once had "Stella's Lunch" stenciled onto it. Today it said "Café Bistro Chez Dominique."

What was he seeing? What was he remembering? What was he wishing? Sarah couldn't guess.

Dominique's had been Sarah's idea. Bernie had been reluctant to return to his empty apartment and it was already well past lunchtime.

"You have to eat," Sarah had insisted in her best Jewish mother voice, though she had no appetite herself. Curious about Dominique's — Bernie had not been since those early childhood days with his mother — he agreed. Sarah, however, was a regular, as she had been back when it was Stella's Lunch. Then, she didn't live within walking distance of the restaurant. Instead, she took a Sherbrooke Street bus from the NDG flat she shared with Sammy and their son, Morty. Then, this wasn't a trendy café with starched linen tablecloths and ambient lighting. It was a simple coffeeshop, its harsh fluorescent tubes glaring off gleaming chrome and Formica. Then, too, the background buzz was the all-English chatter of 1950s Westmount, not the bilingual buzz of a 1980s metropolis.

It was nearly as viscously muggy inside Stella's Lunch as out on Sherbrooke Street when Esther and Sarah pushed open the door. Only a trio of strategically placed table fans kept the coffeeshop bearable. With Labor Day already a few days' past, the city's sultry summer temperatures should have eased by now. They hadn't.

Stella mopped her glistening forehead with a handkerchief as she greeted her two regulars. She wore a coral-colored full apron over a crisply pressed white uniform, with a matching cap perched atop a tight chignon that was too blonde to be natural. A line of blood-red, her only makeup, scarred her full lips and leached onto her teeth.

"Bad news, girls," she said, gesturing toward a table by the window. "Your favorite spot's taken." She dropped her voice to a whisper. "They've been here for hours, all on a coupla cups of coffee."

"Just like us," Sarah giggled.

"Not like you at all," Stella countered. "I like you." She beamed. "And you order pie."

"Who couldn't order your pie? Who could resist it?" Sarah asked. She turned to Esther. "Don't say it."

"What? What shouldn't I say?"

Sarah patted her stomach. "Nothing. Nothing at all."

Stella eyed Esther, who never looked like she noticed the heat. In her sleeveless, light cotton dress — white with pastel print — and white, open-toed pumps, she looked as refreshed as if she had stepped out of an air-conditioned movie theater, not in from the hottest day of the month. Even her dark hair, its soft waves and curls coming together in a carefully casual, modified Italian cut, was impervious to the weather. Still, Esther Freed never looked "put together." Everything about her seemed natural, effortless, unaffected…until you looked in her eyes. Stella knew people. You couldn't run a restaurant and not know people. Most people wouldn't notice the ache in those deep chocolate eyes. Stella did. She didn't know why it was there, but it was. The girl's eyes were different back when she was a teenager, when she was a Finkel not a Freed. Then, they sparkled with anticipation. Now… Now it was as though there was nothing left to anticipate.

Sarah Kaplan was different. More than a head shorter than her friend, and considerably wider, Sarah always turned up looking like she had barely survived a cyclone: As hard as Stella knew she tried, something was always off. Her lipstick was crooked or the wrong shade. Her dress bulged in the wrong places or wasn't properly pressed. As for her shoes, they never worked. She wore flats when the outfit called for heels; she tottered awkwardly on heels when flats would have been more appropriate. And her hair. No matter how Sarah tried to style it, it always looked to Stella like a rusty, overused Brillo Pad: kinky with flyaway strands that refused to be tamed. The oppressive humidity only made it more unruly. Sarah may have looked peculiar, but she had the kindest heart Stella had ever encountered, always reaching out to help when someone, even a stranger, was in distress. That heart also hid some secret ache. Stella was sure of it. Maybe, she thought, it was their pain that bound them together.

"Hey Stella," a voice boomed from across the restaurant. It belonged to a tiny man whose operatic bellow belied his scrawny appearance.

"That's enough, Stanley," Stella snapped. Yet her eyes were laughing as she turned back to Esther and Sarah. "Ever since that darned *Streetcar* movie, every bag of bones thinks he's Marlon Brando."

"Hey, you hens. Cut out the cackling!"

Stella rolled her eyes and sashayed to his table. "Sit where you like, girls," she called over her shoulder.

"Let's sit at the counter," Sarah said. "We never sit at the counter." She plopped onto a stool at the end closest to the window, where a diminutive Christmas tree strung with tinsel and sparkly ornaments and dusted with artificial snow glittered merrily under the coffeeshop's bright lights. "I hate putting it up every year and I hate taking it down nearly as much," Stella had explained to them years before. "So now I do neither. At Stella's, it's Christmas all year round."

Stella licked her stub of a pencil then held it expectantly over her order pad. "What'll it be, girls?" A strand of hair came loose as she turned to glance into the kitchen. She combed it back into place with her pencil.

"A slice of your apple pie and a Sanka, please. Sarah?"

"Tea and pie, thanks."

"Apple or lemon meringue?"

"Apple," Sarah quipped. "I'm on a diet."

Stella laughed. "Sure thing." She tucked the pencil back behind her ear, stuffed her pad into a capacious pocket and pulled two giant sugar-dusted slices from the pie case. A few minutes later, she returned with two cups, two pots of hot water, a teabag and a sachet of Sanka.

"So, what did Dr. Callendar say?" Sarah asked, as she added three cubes of sugar to her coffee. "You said you'd tell me as soon as we got here."

Esther returned her fork, still speared with a hunk of pie, to her plate. "Stella?" she called.

"What is it, dear?"

Esther pointed to an empty table in the corner by the kitchen. "Do you mind if we move over there?"

"Course not. Let me go wipe it down."

Sarah and Esther followed her to the table, carrying their cups and plates.

"Girl talk, huh?" Stella asked, giving the table a cursory swab.

Esther stared silently into her cup.

Stella hovered for a minute, shrugged and vanished into the kitchen.

"What is it, Esther? Are you going to have a baby or not?"

"Yes, but—"

"Yes? Oh, Esther!" Sarah leapt up as quickly as her stout frame would let her and clapped her hands. "Mazel tov."

Stella pushed her head through the swinging kitchen door. "Need anything, girls?"

"No, Stella. Thanks." Stella disappeared. "Sit down, Sarah. Please. You're making a scene."

"I shouldn't be making a scene when my best friend is having a baby?"

"Yes, but—"

"Yes-but, yes-but. What's with the yes-buts? You're having a baby or you aren't having a baby. Which is it?"

"Oh, Sarah." Esther burst into tears. "I wish it was that simple."

#   #   #   #   #

"Nothing's ever simple, is it?"

"What?" Bernie turned his attention back to Sarah. "Did you say something?"

Sarah shook her head. "Where were you just now?" She returned her teacup to its saucer.

"Nowhere. That's what it feels like. I came from nowhere and I'm going nowhere." Bernie paused. "How could I walk out on my own mother's funeral? What kind of son am I? What kind of person am I? Maybe Sadie's right about me."

"Narishkeit. Sadie's never right about anything. Certainly not about you."

Bernie flipped through the Chagall book and stopped at one of the many paintings of a Russian shtetl. This one depicted a man in a heavy overcoat. He was carrying a cane and a beggar's sack, and he seemed to float over the village. *"Over Vitebsk,"* Bernie read. "His work is sure strange. It's like he's living in a dream…like he's painting all the dreams he's living in."

"Let me see."

Bernie passed the oversized book across the table, careful to not knock over his Coke. Sarah pulled her glasses from her purse. They sat at the tip of her nose as she studied painting and caption.

"I haven't seen it since—" She peered over her glasses at Bernie. *"Over Vitebsk,"* she repeated. "How strange. It has to be the same one."

"Same as what?"

"As Esther liked. She said the man looked like your grandfather." She leaned into the page and poked at the figure with a pudgy finger. "I didn't see it then and I don't see it now." She jerked her head up. "Wait. What did you just say? Something about dreams?"

"Like he's living in a dream?"

"Yes. No. About his painting."

"I don't remember."

"You have to." Sarah's voice rose. She pushed her chair out. It made a loud scraping noise on the floor and the young couple at the next table pretended not to look. She carried the book around to Bernie and thrust it onto his lap. "Look again. It's important. You can't know how important it is."

Bernie looked up at her curiously then back down at the painting. He stared at it silently for a moment. "It's like he's painting—"

"The dreams he's living in," Sarah finished the sentence, a smug grin on her face. "Yes. *Yes!*"

"What is it? What's wrong?"

"Nothing's wrong. Everything's right." Sarah shuffled back to her seat, made a point of pushing it in quietly as she glowered at the couple and took a sip of tea. "Ahh. That hits the spot. It's as good here as it's ever been. I should know."

"Well?" Bernie tried to look annoyed. He couldn't help but smile. Sarah could be such an imp. If she weren't Jewish through and through, he would swear she was part leprechaun.

Sarah wanted to reach out and touch his face. This was the first time she had seen him smile today. He had such a nice smile. Like Esther's.

"Like Esther," she said in a half-whisper.

"You're a crazy old bat," he said, laughing. He hadn't laughed in days. It felt good. "You know that, right? What *are* you talking about?"

She raised her teacup to take another sip. "What you said about Marc Chagall and dreams. Esther said almost the same thing, almost the same exact words, that day at the library." She dropped the cup back onto its saucer with a loud clank. "Have you ever tried to draw?" she asked.

"Never. I hated art in school. Everyone made fun of me. Even Mr. Buchanan, the art teacher. He said I drew like I was still in kindergarten. So, no, I can't draw." He turned the page back to *Self-Portrait with Muse*. That could have been her. That could have been Esther. "What happened?"

"Life happened. Sadie happened. Your father happened. War happened. In that world in those days, there was no room for dreams. Not for any kind of dreams. Not for anyone. For sure not for Esther." *Not for me, either.*

6

Sarah Schumacher was never much interested in art. But books! Of course she had read I.L. Peretz and Sholom Aleichem, staples in every Yiddish-speaking home. Unlike her parents, though, Sarah was born in Canada and spoke English first. It was natural for her to want to read the literary greats in the language of her country. She had already added Jane Austen, Edith Wharton, George Sand, Daphne du Maurier and Virginia Woolf to the mostly male staples of her high school English class and was always looking for something new, especially if it was written by a woman. She had her nose in a book in every spare moment: before getting out of bed in the morning and long after her official bedtime at night. She could even be seen walking the ten blocks to and from Baron Byng with her schoolbag in one hand and an open book in the other.

Most kids ignored her. That was okay. Sarah was used to being on her own. Rare in an immigrant family, she was an only child. Her older sister had died before she was born, her younger brother was stillborn and her mother could no longer bear children. Just as rare, Sarah generally ate supper by herself, an open book propped up against a milk bottle or water jug. Only on Fridays and Saturdays did the family eat together, for Shabbas. Every other night Gertie Schumacher waited to have dinner with Mendel, who rarely staggered home from Yitzak Kaufman's coat-and-dress factory before nine. It wasn't that Sarah didn't love her father or the candle-lighting rituals and special meals that marked the beginning and end of the Sabbath, but she didn't look forward to them. She preferred weeknights, when her sole dinner companions were the exotic women and men of Longbourn, Manderley, Middlemarch and Fifth Avenue

— many introduced to her by Elaina Drew, the eccentric librarian who could have stepped from the pages of some of the same novels she urged on the equally eccentric teenager.

Where most members of the Baron Byng staff, whatever their age, seemed ancient to their students, Elaina Drew's actions and appearance were at odds with her years. She wore her silver hair long and loose a third of the way down her back, tied at the tip with a scrap of glitter-dusted gauzy fabric. Every day, a different matching scarf floated, Isadora Duncan-like, down her back. Her shapeless, unbelted dresses hid what may once have been a willowy figure but, now shockingly ungirdled, moved in jellylike counterpoint to its colorful coverings.

Barely two months into the school year, Elaina's first at Baron Byng, it became clear to her that her library could never keep pace with Sarah's insatiable literary thirst. Ignoring all rules and protocol, she slipped her library card to the fifteen-year-old, swore her to secrecy and sent her four miles, two streetcars, a bus and myriad worlds away — to the genteel, tree-lined streets of Westmount and its stately public library.

When Sarah stepped off the green-and-yellow bus that first time and crossed Sherbrooke Street to the library's park-side entrance, she gaped at the building in disbelief. Sure, her part of Montreal was crammed with old buildings, but this one was different. None of the buildings she knew sat in a park and none was this, well, tidy. Even the clack and clank of the traffic behind her seemed muted and orderly compared to the chaos and cacophony of the Main and the hurly burly of downtown.

She stared up the twelve stone steps to the library's arched entryway. Did she dare pass under the stone angel that stood guard above it? Did she dare step into the revolving door? If she did, she was certain that she would be the first Jewish teenage girl to set foot in this building. Maybe the first Jew. Miss Drew assured her that Jews lived in Westmount but she didn't believe it. Were Jews allowed to live in Westmount? She doubted it.

"Tongues in trees, books in the running brooks," she read on the sandstone frieze as she tentatively climbed toward the door. Shakespeare, Miss Drew had told her when describing the building. From *As You Like It*, she said. They would be doing Shakespeare in English class, but not *As You Like It. Hamlet* or *Macbeth,* probably. Maybe she shouldn't wait. Maybe she should add Shakespeare to her reading list. She would ask Miss Drew.

All thought of Shakespeare and Elaina Drew dissolved when Sarah stepped into the high-ceilinged lobby. Light streamed down from clerestory windows and across the floor from tall leaded panes, illuminating decorated arches painted a milky cream and rows upon rows of walnut shelves crammed with books. Sarah had never seen so many books in one place. The Baron Byng library was "adequate." Miss Drew's description. But this? She wandered between the bookcases, aisle after aisle, trailing her finger along the leather bindings and paper dust jackets, inhaling the slightly musty smells of volumes old and new, wonder struck not only by the number of books but by all the people — mostly men, but some women — who had written them all.

What would it take to write a book? How much would you have to know to fill all those pages? To fill all those pages with words that others would want to read? With stories that no one had ever thought of before?

She pulled a book from the shelf and opened it at random.

"I may say that only three times in my life have I met a genius and each time a bell within me rang and I was not mistaken, and I may say that in each case it was before there was any recognition of the quality of genius in them. The three geniuses of whom I wish to speak are Gertrude Stein, Pablo Picasso and Alfred Whitehead."

Gertrude Stein? Miss Drew told me to look for Gertrude Stein.

Holding her finger in place as a bookmark, Sarah shut the book to see its title. *The Autobiography of Alice B. Toklas* by Gertrude Stein.

Sarah dropped to the floor, scrawled the paragraph into her copybook, made a note to look up this Pablo Picasso and Alfred Whitehead, then flipped to another page.

"About six weeks ago, Gertrude Stein said, it does not look to me as if you are ever going to write that autobiography. You know what I'm going to do. I'm going to write it for you."

She copied that, too.

"Gertrude Stein had been going to the opera every night, and going to the opera also in the afternoon, and had been otherwise engrossed and it was the period of the final examinations, and there was the examination in William James's course. She sat down with the examination paper before her and she just could not. 'Dear Professor James,' she wrote at the top of her paper, 'I am so sorry, but really I do not feel a bit like an examination paper in philosophy today,' and left. The next day she had a postal card from William James saying, 'Dear Miss Stein, I understand perfectly how you feel. I often feel like that myself.' And underneath it he gave her the highest mark in his course."

Sarah chortled and, remembering where she was, stopped before the librarian could hush her.

If only William James taught at Baron Byng. I never feel like writing exams.

"*By* Gertrude Stein?" Esther asked incredulously the following Saturday. She pulled her cloth coat tight against the late-autumn chill and shoved her bare hands into her pockets. Montreal streetcars were not heated. "That doesn't make any sense. How can someone write someone else's autobiography? That isn't how it works."

Sarah retrieved her well-thumbed copybook from the school satchel she always carried with her instead of a purse. The worn leather bag, a hand-me-down from her cousin Barney, always carried her two most valued possessions: whichever book she was currently reading and the notebook-cum-diary in which she jotted down her thoughts, feelings and favorite quotes. "'I am going to write it simply,'" she read aloud over the clatter of the streetcar, "'and as Defoe did the autobiography of Robinson Crusoe. And she has and this is it.'"

"I still say that that isn't how it's supposed to work," Esther maintained.

"Wait until you see the book. Wait until you see the *library*."

"Terminus," the driver shouted. "Everybody out. Tout le monde descend."

The girls stood shivering in the cold damp of a gray November, waiting for the No. 4 bus that would carry them the rest of the way, into Westmount.

"Sadie's going to kill me if she finds out."

"That never stopped you before. Anyhow, it'll be worth it. I promise. Besides, she won't find out." Sarah pulled a small card from the satchel and waved it in Esther's face. "I was saving this to show you when we got there, but—"

Esther yanked the card from Sarah's gloved hand. "What is it?" She held it up to her face. "Oh, no. Where'd you get it? *How'd* you get it?"

Sarah grabbed it back. "It's okay. Miss Drew gave it to me. It's her library card. She said we could each take one book out, as long as we promise to give both books back to her next week so she can return them."

"We can take books *home?*"

"Yup."

"From the *Westmount* library?"

"Uh-huh."

"Sadie will definitely kill me." She grinned. "I can't wait."

7

"What books did you take out that day?" Bernie asked Sarah. "Do you remember?" He flagged Dominique for a coffee refill.

Dominique glided over with a steaming carafe. In her early fifties, the café owner towered over most of her customers at what could have been an ungainly six-foot-three. Yet she was not at all awkward. Rather, she carried herself with the easy grace of the dancer she had once dreamed of becoming. She topped up Bernie's cup and turned to Sarah. "More hot water?" she asked.

"No— Yes, please. Thank you, Stella. More lemon, too, please." Sarah shook her head to clear the past. "Did I say Stella? I meant Dominique." She pronounced the French name the English way, with the accent on the first syllable. "Some days…"

"I know, honey."

"You even look a little bit like your aunt."

"There aren't many who come in here these days who remember Aunt Stella. I'm glad someone does." Dominique smiled.

"Your smile. That must be what it is. When you smile, it's easy to see Stella standing here." She turned to Bernie. "Do you remember Stella at all?"

"Not really. It was twenty years ago."

Sarah patted Bernie's arm. "This is Esther's son, Dominique. Bernie."

Dominique dropped the carafe onto the table and grabbed Bernie's hands, squeezing hard. "I'm so sorry about your mother, Bernie. She was a beautiful lady."

"Thank you," Bernie mumbled.

Dominique released Bernie's hands. He flexed them a few times.

"She talked about you all the time. Right, Sarah? All the time," Dominique continued before Sarah could answer. "She was so proud of you, you know." She scrutinized Bernie's features, reached toward his face, then pulled back before touching it. "You look just like her. Just like Esther. Don't you think so, Sarah?" Suddenly, she noticed Sarah's empty cup. "Your hot water," she exclaimed, swiveled on her white sneakers and fled back to the kitchen.

Sarah waited until Dominique had half-run back with an overflowing stainless steel teapot, a saucer of teabags and a bowl of lemon wedges and then moved off to take care of other customers.

"My father took his tea like this," Sarah said. "With lemon. In a glass. So long ago." She dropped the bag into the empty teapot, poured hot water from the second teapot over it and stirred. She then squeezed a lemon slice into her cup, stirred the pot again and poured. Only when she had taken a few sips did she speak again.

"You asked about the books."

Bernie nodded.

"It was hard to choose. You can't imagine how hard it was to choose. So many books we had never seen before. So many we might never see again anywhere else. This might be the only chance we would have. Ever. And we were allowed only one each. What if Miss Drew never let me borrow her card again?"

"Did she?"

"For a few months. Until Sadie found out where Esther was going and put a stop to the narishkeit, as she called it. That Sadie," Sarah said, her voice hardening as she remembered. "She didn't only kvetch to my mother about me. That would have been bad enough. She called the school and complained to the principal about Miss Drew, tried to get her fired. She was a piece of work, your Aunt Sadie, even back then." Sarah opened *The Autobiography of Gertrude Stein* and riffled through the pages.

"You took the Gertrude Stein," Bernie said

"I had to. She was a famous Jewish writer, like I wanted to be." Sarah closed the book. "I haven't read it since. I've hardly thought about it since." She traced the title with her finger. "This doesn't look anything like the one the library had all those years ago. Then, it wasn't only words on a cover. Then—" she closed her eyes. "Then, there was a picture. A photograph. Black-and-white, of course, and out-of-focus, like they were in those days. They were both in it, I think. Gertrude Stein and Alice B. Toklas." She paused. "Strange," she said softly, her eyes still closed, "I remember when she died."

"Gertrude Stein?"

"Alice B. Toklas. Gertrude Stein died right after the war, and I was busy with other things." Sarah opened her eyes and pushed the book aside. "Morty had just been born..."

Bernie remembered Morty, barely. At the time they would have called him retarded, if they were being polite. Most of the time, they weren't being polite. Today, they would have been kinder. Today, they would have said he was autistic or had Down Syndrome and sent him to a special school. Back then, from what he was not supposed to hear when he was a still a boy, it was all Sarah could do to keep him out of some kind of institution. That's what Sammy Kaplan wanted, and Sammy Kaplan always got what he wanted. Except this once.

Sarah's reverie ended. "It was a bad time with Sammy. It was always a bad time with Sammy, especially when Morty was alive. This was worse." She gazed into her teacup for a few minutes before whispering, "This time he hit me."

I look up from the lunch dishes, out the kitchen window. It's an early spring. Too early. Shirtsleeve weather today could mean snow tomorrow. Probably will. That doesn't stop Sammy. Sammy's sure that spring is here for good, which means that the grass needs mowing, even though the last patches of snow only melted away last week. And Sammy's always right.

Morty knows better. Morty knows that this week's weather is foolishness, that winter will roar back two, three, maybe four times before it's done with us for another year. That's why he's outside, too, sitting on the damp grass in the middle of the backyard staring up into the sun.

How he loves the sun. He was born into the wrong climate, was my Morty. He shouldn't have been a Canadian baby. He should have been born in Florida or Arizona or Mexico, somewhere where the sun never stops shining, somewhere where he could gaze up into that hot, bright light every day all year round.

That and Mozart.

Mozart and the sun are the only two things that make Morty happy...if "happy" is a word I can use with him. Even Mozart and the sun don't make him smile, never mind laugh. He never laughs. Even as a baby, my Morty wouldn't laugh when you tickled him. He would just stare at you, the way he still just stares.

I know he must blink. Everybody blinks. But the way Morty looks at you, it's as if he doesn't. He hardly ever says anything or shows any emotion. He never really cried, even when he was little and hurt himself. But the way he looks at you…it's like he's looking into your soul and knows everything there is to know about you, especially the things you would never tell, especially the things you yourself don't know you know.

It makes Sammy crazy when Morty looks at him like that. It makes him crazier when Morty won't look at him at all. He thinks Morty is ignoring him. He thinks Morty is just a bad boy. He's not a bad boy. He's different. I wish for his sake he wasn't different, but he is.

Sammy thinks hitting fixes everything. It doesn't, and it won't fix Morty. Not that he's broken. He's just different, like I said. I finally got Sammy to stop spanking him. It wasn't easy and Sammy wasn't happy about it. I think maybe he still spanked him when I wasn't around.

Lucky for Morty, he's too big to spank now. He's as big as Sammy and at least as strong. Why wouldn't he be? He'll be twenty before you know it. That has to make Sammy mad. And Sammy mad is never a good thing. Sammy mad is always a bad thing.

Sammy pushes the mower into the backyard, pushes it straight toward Morty. I bang on the window — to get Morty to move, to get Sammy to stop. But Morty is staring at the sun and Sammy won't stop. Nothing stops Sammy. Especially not Morty.

I run outside. It doesn't matter that I'm in my slippers and housecoat. I can't think about what I look like right now.

I race to my son, to place myself between him and his father.

Sammy stops the mower at my feet. "Move."

"No."

"Then get your idiot son to move."

"Leave him alone, Sammy. Morty isn't hurting anyone."

Sammy pushes the mower onto my slippers. "I have to mow the lawn."

"What lawn?" I pull my feet free and kick at the mower. "The grass isn't growing yet and you're out here mowing."

"What do you know from grass and lawns? I say the grass needs mowing and I'm going to do it." He shoves me out of the way.

"Get up, stupid," he hisses at his son, my son. "Get up and get out of here."

Morty ignores his father. For him, I think, only the sun is real. Only the sun's voice talking to him is real. Nothing else is real. Nothing else matters. No one else matters.

Again I step in between Sammy and Morty. "I told you before: Don't call my son — our son — stupid."

"Your son, not mine. No one like that can be any son of mine."

"If you think that, you're the one who's stupid."

Sarah never saw the fist coming.
It was the first time. It wouldn't be the last.

8

"He hit you?" Bernie didn't know why he found it so difficult to believe. He always thought Sammy was a nasty son of a bitch, so that's not what surprised him. Sarah taking it: That's what surprised him. But, then, he was also surprised that his mother hadn't thrown Harold out long before she did.

"It was the next day, I think. The day after he…" Sarah's voice trembled. She took a few sips of tea to collect herself. "I picked up *The Star* and there was her obituary. Alice B. Toklas's. It was March. A Wednesday. Nineteen sixty-seven. It's funny how I remember that. I can't remember where I put my glasses five minutes ago but I remember that." She stared out the window and her voice dropped. "I read that obituary and I remembered. I remembered Miss Drew and the Westmount Library and that book." She turned back to Bernie and picked up *The Autobiography of Alice B. Toklas*. "This book." She stroked the cover. "And my dreams. I remembered my dreams, Bernie." Sarah reached into her purse for a handkerchief and dabbed her eyes. "I remembered my dreams."

The restaurant door swung open to a whoosh of traffic noise.

"I wanted to call your mother that day like I did every day," Sarah continued when the door had again shut off the outside world. "But I didn't. If I did, I would have had to tell her, and I couldn't. I couldn't tell her…"

And when it happened to Mom, she couldn't tell you.

"I couldn't tell her about…"

"About Sammy?"

Sarah nodded. "Jewish men don't beat their wives. Only goyim do that. That's what everyone said. That's what everyone believed."

"It wasn't true. It isn't true."

"No." What would have been worse, Sarah wondered: knowing that Sammy was the only one, or that he wasn't. Then, he had to have been the only one. How could he not be? No one talked about things like that. No one dared. So no one knew any different.

"Anyhow, she had tsuris of her own, did Esther. That was the year Gerry was arrested, that gonif. He—"

Should she say? About Gerry and Sadie? She looked away. What kind of sister sleeps with her brother-in-law? *With Gerry, for sure. With Harold, too, I wouldn't be surprised.*

"What is it?"

No, not today.

"That was the year that gonif was arrested," she repeated. She stuffed the handkerchief back into her purse and opened the book.

"'It is hard living down the tempers we are born with,'" she read. "'We all begin well.'" She snapped the book shut. "Esther wanted it, too."

"Huh? What?"

"Back at the library. The Westmount Library. Isn't that what we were talking about?"

"Yes, but—"

"Esther wanted every book in the library, so of course she wanted this one, too." Sarah chuckled. "In the end she picked an art book. A modern art book. What was in those days modern." She laughed again. "I don't remember the book, but I remember that it didn't have a lot of pictures and the ones it had weren't all that good. 'You don't want one with more pictures?' I asked. Your mother said it was the only one she could find that had pictures by both Picasso and Chagall. Those were the only two artists she really cared about, she said.

"We made a pact that day, on the ride home, me and your mother. I would drop the 'h' from Sarah and I would be Sara Shumacher, the first world-famous Jewish Canadian writer. I thought my name looked more exotic that way, with no 'h.' There was no Mordecai Richler yet. Or Irving Layton. Or Leonard Cohen. So I would have been the first. And the first woman. Sara-with-no-h Shumacher." She giggled. "It sounds silly now, but we were serious…as serious as two fifteen-year-olds could be in 1937."

"Not silly at all," Bernie said softly.

"Maybe I would win a Pulitzer Prize, like that Josephine Winslow Johnson had just done with *Now in November*…only she wasn't Jewish. Or Canadian. We talked like that. Can you believe it? Meshugena.

"Your mother also wanted to be the first world-famous Jewish Canadian writer. She had ambition, that one. But she wanted to be a world-famous artist even more. So we decided that I could be the writer if I would let her be the artist.

"It was an easy decision. Being an artist didn't interest me. Not at all. But being a writer… Now *that* would have been something. That would have been *something.*"

"What happened?"

Sarah said nothing. She gazed out the window. For the briefest instant she thought she caught a glimpse of two teenage girls waiting at a streetcar stop, animatedly exchanging dreams.

"What happened? I still have the 'h' in my name and your mother's dead. That's what happened."

Sarah scraped her chair back. It grated across the tile floor. "I have to go," she announced brusquely.

Bernie jumped up. "You have to? Are you sure? Let me put you in a taxi."

"No, from here I can walk. It's only a few blocks."

"It's more than a few blocks. Let me at least walk you home."

"It isn't necessary." Sarah started to push herself out of the chair but it was as if her knees suddenly refused to support her, as if decades of disappointment had sapped her of all strength. She collapsed back into her seat. "Maybe it is," she muttered. "Necessary," she added.

Bernie waved for the check.

"Never mind checks," Sarah said when Dominique reappeared. "I think maybe I need another cup tea first. Would that be okay, you think?" She looked first at Dominique, who slid the slip back into her order pad, then at Bernie. "I need to rest a few minutes more."

"Of course."

"You don't have to wait…"

"Where am I going to go?" Bernie asked. "To Sadie and her shiva circus? To pretend that I can stand being in the same room with Ugu Harold? To pretend I like Uncle Manny and Auntie Dora?

You're more family than they could ever be. Of course I'll wait for you. Besides, I'm still not ready for an empty apartment." He noticed Dominique staring at him expectantly, pen poised. "Oh, another coffee, Dominique, please."

"You got it." Dominique turned to Sarah. "You look like you need a slice of pie. I've got strawberry rhubarb. Fresh out of the oven."

Sarah smiled weakly. "You are a devil, Dominique Ryan."

Dominique turned back to Bernie. "Two?"

"She makes the best pies," Sarah said. "Better even than Sara Lee."

Dominique beamed.

"Fresh out of the oven?" Bernie asked.

"Still warm."

Bernie grinned. "Two, then."

"With vanilla ice cream?" Dominique asked, her eyes twinkling.

"Of course."

"Sarah?"

"I don't know…"

"It's from St. Aubin, like always."

"St. Aubin?" Bernie asked. "We used to go there as a special treat when I was a kid. Better make mine two scoops, Dominique."

"Done. What about you, Sarah?"

"A devil, that's what you are. Okay, St. Aubin ice cream for me, too. But only one scoop." She patted her ample stomach. "I have to watch my figure."

"I'm sorry for acting like that, Bernie," Sarah said after Dominique had deposited two dinner plates on the table, each heaped with a quarter pie's wedge and three generous scoops of vanilla ice cream.

Bernie shoveled a hunk of pie and ice cream onto his fork. "When?"

"A minute ago, when I tried to leave but my legs wouldn't let me." Sarah closed her eyes as she savored a delicate morsel. "Heaven." She sighed with contentment. "You see," she said, opening her eyes, "I never told anyone about what happened with Sammy. Not your mother. No one. Not even Jack. Not until now. It was hard. Hard to remember and hard to tell."

"Mom never told you about Harold, did she?"

"About Harold? What about Harold?"

"What did she tell you when she threw him out?"

"I told him he had to leave, Sarah. Finally, I told him he had to leave." Esther returned her cup to its saucer. Her eyes were wet.

"About time," Sarah barked, surprised by her own vehemence. "Was it that secretary again? That Yvette?"

Esther glanced nervously around Dominique's. No one should overhear this. "If it was only just Yvette," she said.

"What do you mean?" Sarah's voice rose.

"Shh," Esther hissed. "Keep your voice down. I don't need the whole world to know my failures." She looked around again. Dominique started walking toward them. "No," Esther mouthed, shaking her head.

Dominique turned away.

"Your failures?" Sarah asked incredulously. "What do you mean your failures?"

"It's the wife's fault. It's always the wife's fault."

"Was it your mother's fault when that Kaufman went after her… and everyone else in that factory?"

Esther dropped her head into her hands. "I don't know, Sarah. I don't know anything. All I know is that it wasn't only Yvette. It was Kaufman all over again. It was every shiksa in the building. Maybe outside the building, too."

"That bastard."

Esther picked up her coffee cup. Her hand was shaking. She set it back down without taking a sip. "Now the bastard's gone." She started to cry.

"Good riddance."

"Yes. Good riddance. But…"

"But what? No buts. Not with that mamzer." Sarah placed her hand on top of Esther's. "You'll manage? You need help?"

"I'll manage, Sarah. Thank you. The house is mine, and Morris's father left me a little money last year. I'll manage. For money, I'll manage. For the rest…"

"The cancer?" Sarah asked.

"Nothing bad for now."

"Gott tsu danken."

Esther leaned in toward Sarah. "The cancer," she whispered. "Do you think...?"

"Do I think what?"

Esther said nothing.

"You'll be fine, Esther. Don't worry."

"It isn't that. It's..."

"What?"

"Do you think that's why Harold... Because I'm sick?"

Sarah snorted. "What Harold is doing with those girls has nothing to do with you. He was a bum before the cancer. He was a bum before you married him. Cancer or no cancer, he's a bum. Like I said, good riddance."

"Thank you. I needed to know." Esther leaned back into her chair and picked up her cup, this time with both hands. Despite what she had told Sarah, despite what she had told Bernie — Harold, too — the cancer news was not good.

"Mom always hated it when I called him Ugu," Bernie said. "Until she threw him out. Then she started calling him Ugu, too." He scooped up a final forkful of pie, now swimming in a sea of melted ice cream. "What else did she say about Harold?" He held the fork over his plate, waiting for Sarah's reply.

"There should have been more? What else was there to say? He was drek. Worse than drek."

Bernie hesitated. Should he say? Did he have the right? He let the final morsel of pie melt in his mouth.

"What more?" Sarah pressed. "What could be worse?"

"There was more," he said slowly. "Like with you and Sammy..."

"What do you mean, like with me and Sammy?" She clapped her hand to her mouth. "No. You don't mean...?"

Bernie nodded.

"She never said..."

Bernie said nothing.

"Like me," she whispered. "Just like me." She burst into tears. After a few minutes, she added, "At least your mother threw him out. I didn't throw Sammy out. I couldn't. I wouldn't have known how. I wouldn't have dared. And who would have believed me about...about what he was like?"

"Anyone who knew Sammy would have believed you."

"It's a horrible thing to say but thank God he died."

"It isn't horrible at all. He was horrible."

Sarah smiled weakly. "If only—"

"What?"

"If only my Morty didn't go first. I wish I could have had more time with him. I wish my Morty could have had some time, any time, without Sammy." She finished her pie in silence.

Dominique delivered more coffee and tea. "You're okay, honey?"

"You're a treasure, Dominique. You know that? A treasure. There's no better pie anywhere in Montreal. Not one. Don't let anyone ever tell you different."

Dominique kissed Sarah on the top of her head. "There's no better customer." She turned to Bernie. "She's the best, Sarah is. Just like your mother." Her voice cracked. "I'll miss her." She turned back to Sarah. "Now don't you think about going anywhere, Sarah Swartz."

"What? And give up your pies? Not a chance." She scraped the last of the ice cream and pie onto her spoon and licked it clean. "Wherever I'm going, and it's probably downstairs not upstairs, I know they don't make pies like this. So I'm not going until you go, Dominique. Just promise me that when it comes time, you'll remember to pack your pie tins."

"I promise." Dominique grinned. "For today, the pie and ice cream's on the house. Next time, too." She touched Bernie on the shoulder. "For you, too, hon. In honor of your mother." Then Dominique strode off, before either of them could see the tears welling up in her eyes.

9

Sarah and Bernie sat in companionable silence, each lost in thought, both thinking about Esther.

"Did I tell you the last thing Esther said to me?" Sarah asked at last. "The very last thing?"

Bernie shook his head.

"You were still at work. Manny and Dora had come and gone. It was only me and Esther. Like in the old days…but not like the old days at all." Sarah raised her cup to her lips and closed her eyes to the steam.

The hospital room is still, so still, even with the door to the corridor open and nurses hurrying past. It's like there's maybe a cocoon around us, Esther and me, like there's no one else in the world…like there's no other world except for this one.

She sleeps. That's all she does now, all she ever does. She never moves. Even her chest hardly moves anymore, she's so thin. Like a skeleton in a hospital gown, she is. Like she has already left me. Like she is already dead.

Dead.

Such a hard word. So…so final.

If I squint just right, she isn't an old lady on her deathbed anymore. She's fifteen. We're both fifteen. We're waiting at the streetcar stop and we're so excited about the future that we're dancing. Dancing!

What happened to us, Esther? What happened to the dreams? What happened to Esther Finkel and Sarah Shumacher? To Sara-without-an-h Schumacher? We were going to do such great things. To be such great things. Nothing could stop us. That's what we said. That's what we believed. That's what we promised. And now…nothing. Less than nothing. Here we are in the future and it's too late for you and it's too late for me.

Esther stirs. Her eyelids flutter...open. She squeezes my hand. Not strong but for her, strong. Strong for someone who isn't going to see another day. You can tell. I can tell.

She squeezes again, harder.

She tries to speak. All that comes out is a wheezy breath.

I lean in, my ear so close to her mouth that I can feel it move against my skin.

"Do you know what she said?"

"What?"

"She said, 'It's not too late, Sara-without-an-h. It's never too late.' Then her eyes closed and she never spoke again. She didn't, did she?"

"Not out loud," he whispered.

Sarah cried softly, and Bernie could feel the tears he had held back since his bus ride from the cemetery forcing themselves out.

"It's *not* too late," Sarah whispered, and she clutched the Gertrude Stein book to her bosom.

Bernie wiped his eyes. "What does that mean? What will you do?"

Sarah pulled the book away from her chest. "Nothing." She let it drop onto the table. "Of course it's too late. I'm an old lady. Like Esther, it will soon be time for that last piece of Dominique's pie."

"You're wrong, you know." Bernie said gently.

"What? I should be like Grandma Moses, you mean?"

Bernie laughed. "Well, yes."

"You want maybe I should be Bubbie Sarah?"

"Why not?"

"Why not? Because there are already plenty world-famous Jewish Canadian writers out there." She waved a hand toward the window. "No one needs another one, especially not an alteh machashaifeh, an old witch." She blew her nose loudly. "Never mind me. What about you?"

"What about me?"

"How old are you, Bernie? Twenty-one? Twenty-two?"

"Twenty-seven."

"Same difference. What are you doing with your life?"

"What do you mean?"

"You hate your job, yes? Pushing around farkakte numbers for a farkatke government."

Bernie studied the soggy crumbs on his plate. "I'm very good at what I do," he responded without enthusiasm.

"I'm sure you are, Bernie. That isn't what I asked."

"No. It isn't." He crushed a crumb with his thumb, then another, then another. "Could Mom really have been a good artist? A great artist?"

"You're changing the subject."

"Like you did," he retorted. "Well, could she have?"

"Anne Savage thought so."

"Anne Savage? Who's Anne Savage?"

"You don't know from Anne Savage?"

"Never heard of her. Who is she?"

"What don't they teach in school anymore?" Sarah gathered her things and pushed herself up. Her legs cooperated. "Come," she said. "We're going. For real, this time." She stabbed him with her cane. "Back to the library. Before it closes."

Bernie waved a twenty-dollar bill at Dominique, tucked the Chagall under his arm and chased after Sarah, who was already hobbling out the door.

"What's the rush, all of a sudden?" Bernie asked. "The library's open for hours still."

"Good. We have plenty of time." Sarah didn't slow down. "I'll tell you about Anne Savage when we get there."

10

After half a block, Sarah maneuvered herself onto a bench. "I'm not sixty anymore," she said in a grim voice, but her eyes twinkled. "I'll give my arthritis a rest, then we can be on our way."

"Take your time."

"Time's something that isn't so abundant anymore."

"Don't be silly, Bubbie Sarah." Bernie poked her playfully. "You're just getting started."

"Maybe. Maybe not." Sarah waved her cane at the twin Victorian townhouses opposite the bench. The staircases and much of the nineteenth-century graystone facade had been knocked out, replaced by a street-level entrance and an expansive display window filled with pretzel-like sculptures and wild, colorful abstracts. A stark black-on-white sign spanned the building under its top-story windows, proclaiming it as Galérie Cinq Arts.

"This gallery," Sarah said, "it's brand new. A couple of weeks only. I haven't been inside yet." She stared past the curtain of glass at all the strange pieces. Strange…and wonderful. "You want to go in? It looks open."

Bernie followed her gaze. Chagall was odd enough. But this? The pieces might as well have come from another planet, they were so alien.

Sarah regarded him curiously. "Esther would have loved it," she remarked thoughtfully. "Anne Savage, too, I think."

Not for the first time that day, Bernie felt as though he had never known his mother. She felt nearly as foreign to him as the artwork on the other side of the window. "You were going to tell me about Anne Savage," he said.

"At the library." Sarah eased herself up and peered into the gallery. "You sure you don't want to go in?"

"I want to hear about Anne Savage."

"When we get there in…one…two…three…" Sarah counted on her fingers. "Five blocks. Four and a half, really."

They walked in silence, at a more comfortable pace now, past boutiques and cafés and toward the leafy elms and maples that lined the more residential stretch of Sherbrooke Street near the library.

"I hate accounting," Bernie blurted as they waited for the light to turn green at Roslyn Avenue.

Sarah raised her eyebrows. She said nothing until the light changed and they had crossed. "Of course you do," she whispered.

"We have the results of your vocational test, Bernard." Cedric Fish squints across his cluttered desk, shoves aside a stack of reports and slides a single sheet of paper across the coffee-spattered surface toward Bernie. "It's, ah, interesting." He squints again and his right eye twitches. There's a reason kids call the school guidance counselor "fish-eyes."

Interesting? What does that mean? Bernie reaches for the document but doesn't pick it up. It probably says the same as the others. He did not want to take this test, the third since the start of his final year at Mount Royal High. But his mother has urged him to do it. She doesn't insist. His mother rarely insists. Yet she always manages to ask for things in a way that Bernie finds hard to refuse.

"You have to decide what you're going to do, Bernie. If you don't know what you want, these tests can help you find out. Besides, you have to pick a major for next year."

Bernie once hoped to become a lawyer like his father. He doesn't have the grades. He will never have the grades.

"They don't call it a major at Vanier, Mom. They call it a concentration."

"A concentration, then."

"I don't want to go to Vanier. All my friends are going to McGill."

"We've been through this before. All your friends' parents can afford McGill. You know Gerry left us with nothing." Esther looks around sadly. The rug still shows indentations where some of her favorite pieces once stood. Her mother-in-law's mahogany breakfront, along with all its fine-china contents. The dining room set that was a wedding present from Morris's grandparents. The car is gone, too, now. She didn't choose well,

did she? First Morris. Poor Morris. Then Gerry. Poor Esther. Maybe this Harold Coopersmith that Sadie wants her to meet will be better.

"Thank God the house is mine, Bernie, or who knows what we might have to do. Go live with your aunt and uncle, maybe." She shudders. "I know you want to be with your friends, but Vanier is free. You'll go to Vanier for your two years of that CEGEP thing. After that, we can see. For now, you need to take that test, to see what your maj— concentration should be. Okay?"

The first test suggests accounting and engineering.

The second test suggests accounting and optometry.

He looks down at the results of the third test. Beneath its chart of indecipherable computations is a single, blunt sentence: "Based on your answers, you would be well-suited for a career as an accountant or funeral director."

Funeral director?

"Not that accountants are bad," Sarah continued. "My cousin Barney was an accountant. He loved being an accountant, and everyone loved Barney. At least they loved having an accountant in the family, especially in April." She laughed, then turned serious. "You don't love it."

"I hate it. I hate it and I hate my job. And I hate it that everyone thinks I can fix their taxes because I work for Revenue Canada."

They walked on.

"I don't think I realized until now how much I hate it…how much I've probably always hated it."

"So?"

"So what?"

"So you're an accountant. That's today. You can be something else starting tomorrow. Why stay an accountant if you hate it so much?"

"What else am I supposed to do with an accounting degree?"

"Throw it away."

"What do you mean throw it away?"

"What I said. Throw it away. Throw it away and start over. That's what tomorrows are for."

They turned up the driveway to the library and stopped at the steps. Sarah took Bernie's right hand. "Look at your hands," she said.

"What about my hands?"

"Cousin Barney has short stubby fingers, perfect for a pencil and an adding machine. But yours… Look at them." She took the Chagall book from him and held both his hands up to his face. "These are artist's hands, just like your mother's."

"You're wrong." He pulled his hands free and stuffed them in his pocket. "I may not be cut out to be an accountant, but one thing I know for sure: I'm not an artist. Remember Mr. Buchanan?"

"What Mr. Buchanan?"

"My high school art teacher. I told you about him at Dominique's."

"Feh. What does a high school art teacher know about art? Unless she's Anne Savage." She started up the stairs. "Come," she called back to Bernie. "It's time you met her."

11

"There." Sarah pointed her cane up at a large canvas that hung above the rich walnut shelving in the fine art section.

"*Quebec Farm*. Anne Savage. ca.1935," read the tiny brass plaque set in the picture's simple frame.

Bernie had seen this painting many times, many more than he could count — all those Saturday afternoons all those years ago with his mother. On those occasions, when he'd gone looking through the library for Esther, this is where he often found her, with Anne Savage and the art books. Now he knew why.

Yes, he had seen *Quebec Farm* many times. Until now though, he had never really looked at it. The painting was almost voluptuous: A woman in a white blouse and navy skirt, seen from the rear, bends over a flower patch at the edge of a farm. Immediately beyond her, a farmhouse with a steeply pitched roof is set back from a road that winds off into distant, breast-like hills.

"Meet Anne Savage," Sarah said.

Bernie saluted the painting. "Okay, we've met," he said. "Who is she?"

"Let's go sit down."

Bernie followed Sarah out to the conservatory.

"No, not here," Sarah said when Bernie started to sit down in the main plant room. Its humidity pressed on her even more claustrophobically than had the August mugginess they walked through to get here. She continued back to the more open fountain room, cooler for the running water, her cane clackety-clacking on the black and white tiles.

Sarah installed herself on a wood-slat bench and gazed into the fountain. For a while, she said nothing. The tinkling sound could have been the giggles of teenage girls on their first day in art class. The rippling water was like a veil separating August 1984 from September 1934. First it was just clear water flowing over green ceramic. Then the fountain floor melted into long-ago institutional walls and she was back in Baron Byng on her first day of high school.

"We didn't know she was a famous Canadian artist when we walked into her art class that first day, me and Esther," Sarah said at last. "She was just Miss Savage, our art teacher. Just like Miss Conover was our nobody-famous English teacher. We didn't know anything for weeks and weeks, until Freda Kimmel's mother heard her on the radio. Next morning we all knew. All of a sudden she wasn't just our Miss Savage anymore."

"Freda Kimmel? The crazy dean of fine arts at Concordia? You and Mom went to Baron Byng with her? I remember her from when I was in the business school. She wanted to force us all to take art classes."

"Maybe that would have been a good thing," Sarah said softly. "For you." Sarah stared again at the green of the fountain floor in silence. "It was your mother that asked," she said, still focused on the water.

"Asked what?"

"Your mother raised her hand in class that day. It had to have been later in November. Maybe December. She didn't raise it so much as wave it. She was always so excitable in high school."

Anne Savage noticed the ponytailed girl with eyes nearly as dark as her hair. She was easy to notice. Most of the girls in her classes were enthusiastic, although whether it was for a love of the arts or an indifference to their academic subjects, she could never be sure. But Esther Finkel? Esther was different. She had a spark…and a spark of talent. This girl would amount to something. She was certain of it.

"Yes, Esther."

"Miss Savage…"

"What is it, Esther?"

Esther swallowed hard. She had to know. She had to. "Are you *the* Anne Savage?" she asked.

Anne laughed. It was easy to laugh with this girl. Not at her. Never at her. With her. On one hand she was so serious. On the other, she never seemed to take herself too seriously. "Well," she replied, "I am *an* Anne Savage. It's not an uncommon name. I'm certain there's more than one."

"Not one who's famous…who's a famous *artist*."

The room buzzed.

"I don't know about famous…"

"But you are," Freda piped up from the back of the classroom. "My mother says you are. She heard you on the radio."

"That's settled." Anne smiled broadly, and the corners of her eyes and mouth creased and crinkled. "If Freda's mother says I am *the* Anne Savage, the notorious Anne Savage from the radio, then it must be true." She pulled her worn copy of *Art Appreciation for Today* from her desk drawer and opened it to the day's lesson, groaning inwardly at its faded reproductions of the approved classics and its even duller text.

"Open your books, girls," she called out. No one paid attention. Her girls were too busy chattering amongst themselves about the celebrity in their midst to pay that celebrity any heed.

Anne rose to her feet and clapped her hands. "Enough of that. Settle down. We have work to do." No work would be done, though, not until Anne promised to bring some of her work to class. Her girls insisted, Esther loudest among them.

"Your mother had chutzpah in those days. Not me. I wouldn't have asked like that. But she wanted to be sure, your mother did. I think maybe she already knew she wanted to be some kind of artist. Knew but didn't know."

"What do you mean?"

"She knew here." Sarah tapped her chest. "It was Anne Savage who helped her know here." She tapped the side of her head.

"How?"

"Have you ever been inside Baron Byng?"

"It isn't a high school anymore. It closed a few years ago. It's a community center now. Sun Youth."

"I know. But when it was Baron Byng, were you ever inside?"

"Not even outside. Why?"

"Then you never saw the murals."

"What murals?"

"Anne Savage's murals. Esther's murals. Your mother's murals. Walls and walls of them."

"Wait. You're going too fast. What are you talking about? What murals?"

It started simply enough, a week after Miss Savage's art class discovered that she was *the* Anne Savage and *the* Anne Savage decided that *Art Appreciation for Today* was not a textbook for that day…or any other day. Anne slammed the book shut and shoved it to the side of her desk, the side nearest the wastebasket. One more push and… *No. You do not throw books away, Annie Savage, no matter how tedious and archaic they are.* Instead, she slid it underneath the previous week's test papers. At least she didn't have to look at it. No one should have to look at it. Or in it.

What now? Anne stared at her girls.

Her girls stared back at her, waiting. Anne ran her fingers through her prematurely white hair and muttered something under her breath. The girls sitting closest to her in the front row would later insist that it was a swear word, but none of their classmates would believe them. Miss Savage was too elegant and refined to use bad language, they countered. She stood halfway up then dropped back into her seat with a thud and glowered at nothing in particular.

The girls glanced warily at each other. Was Miss Savage angry? She never got angry. Well, hardly ever. Had one of them done something wrong? It couldn't be. There was no "wrong" in art. That's what she always told them.

"I—," Anne began. She knew her girls were waiting for her to say something, to do something. Yet for the first time in her thirteen years of teaching, she did not know what to say, what to do. All she knew was that she could not continue to teach what she had been teaching from a book that couldn't have been more relevant to the study of art had it landed on her desk from the moon. She loved her students and was passionate about art, both creating it and teaching it. But there was no passion in the curriculum, even less in *Art Appreciation for Today.*

She looked around the classroom, at faces now more confused than expectant. She scowled at the spottily filled low-rise shelves against the back wall, shelves that should be overflowing with real books about art. She stared out the wall of windows to her right, to the grim sterility of a St. Urbain Street that looked grittier than usual on this gray morning. Her gaze returned to the classroom, to bare walls painted the same bilious green as every other wall in this school and probably every other school in the city and, in that moment, an idea formed in her mind. A radical idea, one that Principal Simon would either love or hate. You could never tell with Principal Simon.

"He loved it." Sarah smiled at the memory. "A few days later when we walked up to Room 214, there was a handwritten sign tacked to the door. It said, 'When you enter this classroom, you are artists.' Inside, the room was a mess. You can't imagine how big a mess. The janitor had pushed all our desks together in the middle. The floor by the walls was covered with burlap. There were brushes and paint cans everywhere. Everywhere." Sarah closed her eyes, transported back fifty years. "So many colors," she sighed. "You've never seen so many colors in one place. She even had smocks for us, Miss Savage did. She was already wearing hers."

"Paint," Anne ordered. "Paint anything. I don't care what. If we decide we don't like the result, we can paint over it another day. But when we're finished in this room, I do not want to see an inch of this…this…excuse for green. Not an inch of it." She slapped her hand against the wall. "Ever again."

Sarah opened her eyes. "So we painted and painted and painted. It was a real mishmash those first few days. Nothing but globs and blobs." She grinned. "It would have fit right into that new gallery back there on Sherbrooke." Her voice grew animated. "Once the green was all gone, Miss Savage had a new idea, a better one. We would paint a mural. A real picture. Right there on the wall of Room 214. Or maybe that was her plan all along." Sarah shrugged.

"What could we paint? We kept telling Miss Savage that we knew nothing from painting…that we couldn't paint…that we didn't know how to paint. She kept saying that we knew everything we needed to know…that we could. That we would. We would get marks for it, too, she said."

"So you painted the wall?"

"We did more than paint that wall. When we finished one wall, we painted the other walls. When we finished Room 214, we moved out into the halls…into other classrooms…into the cafeteria…into the gym. We painted and painted and painted. Not only us. Not only Miss Savage's girls. Boys, too. Teachers, too. Not all the teachers. Some thought it was all mishigas. Craziness. But Mr. Simon loved it. So we kept at it. And after we graduated, it went on. Every year, more murals until there was hardly any of that drekky green left anywhere."

"And Mom?"

"Your mother was a talent. Such a talent. She started off rough, like the rest of us. But soon she was painting like you can't believe. Such bilder. Such pictures. And so different. She had— What do you call it?" Sarah paused. "A style. That's what it was. She had a style. I was barely a wall-painter. Your mother was an *artist*."

"An artist," Bernie echoed softly.

"She didn't think she was very good. Because she was different. Because of her 'style.' Miss Savage thought she was good. *Knew* she was good. Wanted her to go to art school, even."

Bernie opened the Chagall book to *Self-Portrait with Seven Fingers*. "That's why she was so excited to see those art books in the library that first time," he said, stroking the artist's palette in the print.

Sarah nodded.

"What happened?"

"What always happened," Sarah replied bitterly.

"Auntie Sadie."

"It was your grandfather who told Esther it wasn't right for her to go to art college. It was your grandfather's voice; it was Sadie's words."

"Please, Papa." Esther reached for her father's hand and looked pleadingly up at him from her place by his feet. This spot, on the floor next to his favorite armchair, had been Esther's favorite since before she could walk. Then, she would crawl over to the paisley-patterned chair, wrap her arms around Max's muscular leg and hug it with all her infant strength. Now, the chair's upholstery was worn and fading, like Max Finkel himself. His clothes hung loosely on a frame that had shrunk in on itself, and his dark eyes were set so deeply in his pale, haunted face that in the dim light of the Finkel front room they looked like empty sockets. He was only forty-seven; he looked sixty-seven.

Max squeezed Esther's hand but she knew his heart wasn't in it. His heart hadn't been in much of anything since her mother died, however she died. That was almost ten years ago; it could as easily have been a hundred. However much Esther strained — until her head hurt, she strained — she couldn't remember anything about Ruth Finkel. Even the photograph, a serious pose up at the Lookout on the Mountain, the city spread out behind her, seemed foreign. Taken the summer of the year she died, it sat where it had always sat, in a place of honor on the table next to the sofa, its silver frame kept polished to a high sheen by Sadie. It might as well have been someone else's mother, or a picture cut from a magazine. The woman staring soberly at her from the past was a stranger. The only mother Esther had known was Sadie, who was more tin-pot dictator than loving parent. Sadie acted like she was deferring to their father. Esther knew different. Esther knew that every important decision in that shabby third-floor flat was her older sister's.

That was why she waited until Sadie was out of the house to make this final appeal. No one knew where Sadie had gone. It was foolishness to go out on a day like this. Not only was it New Year's Day — where was there to go on a New Year's morning in Montreal? — it had been snowing relentlessly for two days. As often as Manny trudged out with his shovel, the storm continued to outpace him, and Esther imagined Sadie muttering dark curses as she maneuvered her way down the icy corkscrew staircase to the empty, snow-blanketed street.

Inside their cramped Clark Street home, the stalwart efforts of a pungent oil heater couldn't expel the damp chill of a harsh winter. Esther and Nate wore their heaviest sweaters, ill-fitting pullovers handed down from Jewish Family Services. Manny never shed his coat, another charity castoff, after coming in from his latest battle with the snow. And Max kept the bright orange scarf Sadie had knit for him wound tightly around his neck.

"Teacher's college, maybe, Esther. Maybe." Max stroked her hair. "But art school? What kind of Jewish girl goes to art school? Art school is for shiksas. Good Jewish girls don't go to art school. Good Jewish girls find husbands and take care of those husbands. Good

Jewish girls have sons who grow up to be doctors and good Jewish husbands themselves. You're a good Jewish girl, shaineh maidel. You are, aren't you?"

"Yes, Papa." Esther's eyes teared up, as much for her father's answer as for the shadow he had become.

"Okay. So we can stop this talk about art and art school?" He picked up the photo of Ruth and wiped the glass with his sleeve, staring longingly at it as he continued. "You know your mother wouldn't like it, may she rest in peace. Your mother would want what all Jewish mothers want for their daughters: a good Jewish boy from a good Jewish family and a house full of grandchildren."

Who knew what her mother would have wanted? Esther doubted that even Sadie knew; it was Sadie who repeated that maxim about Ruth the most often — every time Esther or one of her brothers attempted something of which Sadie disapproved, which was nearly all the time.

Max stared into the picture for a few minutes more then replaced it gently on the table, sliding it half an inch to the left, a quarter of an inch to the right and a smidge back until it sat precisely as it had before he picked it up.

"What about that young man who keeps coming around to see you," Max asked, "that Morris Freed?"

"What about him, Papa?" Esther turned toward the window and pretended to look through the sheer curtains and out at the storm. She didn't want her father to see her crying.

"He comes from a good family, that Morris. You like him, maybe?"

"Maybe."

What was not to like? Morris Freed was handsome, with his dark hair, dark mustache and dark eyes. It was the eyes that Esther noticed right away, almost before anything else — eyes that took her in with an embrace that made her feel warm and tingly all over. The look was more than friendly, she told Sarah, but not...well, not unsuitable.

No, nothing about Morris was unsuitable. After all, he was a college graduate. From McGill, yet. Even with the Jewish quota, he got in, and graduated. Maybe he wasn't a doctor. But he was a lawyer. And everyone always ends up needing a lawyer, at least that's what Sadie said. Maybe she was right. Maybe this one time she was right.

Esther shut her eyes and let herself be transported to the Freed family home in Outremont. In *Outremont*! Who knew that Jews lived in Outremont? Or in such a big houses? And on streets with trees and grass.

"Sadie says he's a good boy, Esther. Is he a good boy?"

"He's a good boy, Papa."

But did she love him?

"Sadie made your mother's life hell," Sarah continued. "Like in the Cinderella story with the wicked stepsister. Only there was no stepmother and Sadie wasn't a stepsister. She was a real sister. She was blood. And she was mean. All her life, she's been mean."

"Don't I know it."

"I know you do, and not just from today." She pursed her lips. "It's not a surprise Esther married your fath— Morris. She thought she loved him. I know she did. But how could she know what love was, from such a family?" Her anger exploded into a sharp bark of a guffaw. "I should talk. I didn't do a whole lot better than she did." She grew serious again. "Well, not the first time. Not with Sammy. But with Jack… My Jack was a prince. I wish your mother could have let herself have a prince like my Jack instead of all those frogs. Schmucks. All of them. All exc—" Sarah stopped herself mid-sentence. She glanced at Bernie. Had he noticed?

If I keep slipping like this, I will have to tell him. I will have to tell him everything. What do you say, Esther? Does he have to know? Does it help him to know? He's been hurt so bad. I say forget the past. I say he doesn't need any more—

Suddenly, she noticed that Bernie was standing and talking. What was he saying?

"—back inside the library?"

"What is it Bernie?"

Bernie grinned. "You aren't listening, Sarah. Where were you? Back in art class?"

"Back somewhere. Lots of somewheres today. What were you saying, dear?"

"I want to take another look at the Anne Savage painting."

"Good idea."

"Are you coming?"

"No, no. Go look. I'll sit here and wait. I get to see it all the time."

Sarah's eyes were puffy and her lids could barely stay open. She set her elbow on the arm of the bench and leaned her head into her hand.

"Are you okay?" Bernie asked. "Do you want me to stay here with you? Do you want me to take you home?"

"I'm fine, Bernele. I'm tired is all. It's been a day." She sighed. "Go."

"You're sure?"

"I'm sure." For an instant, Sarah saw Bernie the day he was born: Pudgy and apple-cheeked, with tufts of surprisingly coarse blond hair that refused to be tamed. And wailing. So loud he was wailing, in staccato sobs as if he was being snatched from his mother's arms instead of hugged tightly within them. Then there was Esther. How could anyone look so beautiful after the ordeal she had just been through? The labor, of course, which dragged out for a torturous day and a half of trying to push out a tiny infant who seemed reluctant to emerge. The nine months before, too.

Sarah had gone with Esther to the doctor a few weeks after he confirmed the pregnancy. For days, she had been having cramps that felt like she imagined labor would feel. They would come in sharp bursts, stop, then come again. While Dr. Callendar tapped, poked, prodded and peered, Sarah watched from a hard chair in the examining room. Esther had insisted. His nurse stood primly to the side, casting bearish glares at Sarah.

Twenty minutes later, she and Esther were back in the consulting room, the nurse having disappeared back into her lair.

"Everything looks normal, Mrs. Freed," the doctor pronounced. "You're probably anxious. It happens sometimes."

The expected smile of relief was delayed for less than an instant, and Sarah wondered whether Dr. Callendar also noticed the hesitation. That lightning flash of panic in Esther's eyes was one that Sarah would catch throughout the next days and months. One minute Esther would be extolling the virtues of this child-to-be of hers. He — it had to be a he — would be the greatest artist-writer-doctor-lawyer-statesman-philanthropist who ever lived, and her eyes would shine brightly with joy and pride. In the next, her voice would continue, drained of its warmth, and the look would return: an amalgam of shame and terror. No one who didn't know her as well as Sarah did would catch it. Not even Morris. Sarah couldn't miss it.

For ten days after the visit with Dr. Callendar, she didn't dare ask Esther what it was all about.

Then she did.

12

Bernie gazed up at the Savage canvas, letting his eyes trace first the sweep of the artist's brushstrokes, then the sweep of the road. That road couldn't help but capture his attention…and imagination. Where did it go? What would it reveal up in those hills? What would it reveal beyond them? Where would it carry him if he dared to step onto it? His mother hadn't dared. Not Sarah, either. Not in the end.

You tried, Anne Savage. I know you did. What happened? Was it just because of Zeyda Max and Auntie Sadie? Was that all it took to demolish Mom's dreams? Was there more you could have said? More you could have done?

He tried to imagine this woman who had taught his mother, who had encouraged her. What had she been like? How had she managed to become an artist? Born when she was, it must have been harder for her…even without an Auntie Sadie.

"Young man?"

Bernie turned. A matronly figure, gray-haired in a gray wool suit and starched, high-neck blouse, stood next to him, also studying the painting. Her brass name-tag read "Evelyn Waugh, Librarian." Bernie quickly looked away when she noticed him staring.

Evelyn laughed. "Don't be embarrassed. Everyone stares. I don't know what my parents were thinking."

"Maybe they liked Evelyn Waugh's writing?"

"When I asked, they said they'd never heard of him. They liked the name is all. Who hasn't heard of Evelyn Waugh? *Brideshead Revisited*? I shouldn't have been surprised. Mater and pater Waugh have never cared much for books, except by the yard as wall decoration. Now that they've seen *Brideshead Revisited* on television, they think they were so very clever all those years ago." She grinned a toothy grin. "Mine's *EH-vul-yn*," she pronounced, "not *EEV-lyn*, like the writer. It's a perfect name for a librarian, don't you think?"

"I guess."

Evelyn returned her gaze to the painting. "It's something, isn't it?"

"She taught my mother you know, Anne Savage did."

"Did she?" The librarian looked back at the handsome young man next to her. So serious in his dark suit. So sad. "Anne Savage taught many people. She taught Mordecai Richler, you know."

"I didn't know."

"Freda Kimmel, too." She pointed to a nearby abstract. It was twice the size of *Quebec Farm* and consisted of spiky, serrated silver shards with blood-red tips flung randomly around an inky pool of ooze. "You know Freda Kimmel?"

"Concordia Fine Arts."

"The dean now, yes. But she was quite the enfant terrible in her younger days, almost as famous in her own way as Anne Savage. She donated that to us last year. Frankly," she added in a conspiratorial whisper, "I like the Anne Savage better. Much better." Evelyn leaned in toward Bernie. "Don't tell her I said that."

Bernie smiled. "Not a word."

"Freda comes in now and again. I think she wants to make sure that *Silver Shards* — that's what she calls it — that *Silver Shards* is still hanging here. Maybe when she dies we can take it down." She covered her mouth. "I should never have said that. Poor Freda."

Bernie stared at *Silver Shards*, trying to salvage some glimmer of understanding from it. But it was like the pieces in Galérie Cinq Arts. He didn't get it. He was glad to know he wasn't the only one. "It is pretty awful."

"Maybe your mother knows Freda, if they went to Baron Byng around the same time."

"Knew her." Bernie looked away. "My mother died. Tuesday."

Of course. That explained the black suit and the nick in his tie, which she only now noticed. "Oh, dear. I am sorry."

Bernie shrugged. "How do you know so much about Anne Savage?" he asked, breaking an awkward silence. "Did she teach you, too?"

The librarian laughed a deep throaty laugh, attracting disapproving glares from a nearby gaggle of blue-rinsers. "Oh, my, no. That was never my part of town. This is. Westmount. I have lived here all my life."

"So how do you know…" He looked back up at the Savage.

"Anne Savage was a Montreal legend. She inspired many, many people, not only at Baron Byng. We were lucky to get this painting." She tilted her head toward the Kimmel and grimaced. "Not so lucky with that one." She laughed again then turned to go. "It was lovely talking to y— Wait. Would you like to know more about Anne Savage?"

"Yes. I think so."

"I thought you might. Can you wait here a moment?"

Bernie nodded and returned his attention to the painting, to the woman who had followed her dreams but never managed to get his mother to follow hers.

"Here."

Bernie hadn't noticed Evelyn's return. She thrust a book into his hand: *Anne Savage: The Story of a Canadian Painter*. The cover featured a painting of three girls looking into a bucket, with a typical Québecois pitched-roof house looming up behind them. "It's called *Strawberry Pickers*."

"I like it."

"I do, too. I understand that she didn't often paint people, so this is unusual."

It wasn't the people or the house that drew Bernie to the painting on the book cover. It was the hills, barely noticeable in the distance. He compared the picture with *Quebec Farm* and its hills. Both sets were like "beyond the rainbow" hills, images of yearning, potential and promise.

"Would you like to borrow the book?" Evelyn asked.

"Yes. No. I can't. I'm not a library member."

Evelyn pulled him toward the circulation desk. "Not a member? Impossible. Let me fix that for you right now. Do you have something that shows your address? You live in Westmount, don't you?"

"That's it. I don't. I live in TMR." He placed the book on the counter.

"I see." She paused. "I would tell you to look for it in the Town of Mount Royal Library, but there are not many copies of this book around." She studied the young man again. Evelyn Waugh had worked at the Westmount Library for thirty years and seen all types pass through its doors, from vagrants to cabinet ministers. All it took now was a quick glance at someone's eyes and hands and she knew immediately whether he could be trusted. Unfortunately, that also explained why she was still *Miss* Waugh.

"If I let you take it, will you promise to bring it back?" she asked.

"Uh, yes," Bernie replied. It suddenly occurred to him that Sarah could borrow the book for him. Before he could say anything, though, Evelyn pulled the book's card from its rear pocket with long-practiced fluidity and replaced it with a date-due notice. She slipped the card into her pocket.

"See that you do, Mr...."

"Freed. Bernie Freed."

She smiled warmly. "Nice to meet you, Mr. Freed Bernie Freed."

He took the book. "Thank you."

"It's important, isn't it."

"I'm not even sure why," Bernie replied, "but yes."

13

Sarah closed her eyes and let the sound of the fountain wash over her. What a day it had been. Bernie. Esther. So many memories. All buried that morning. Or were they? A funeral was never easy. Not at her age. Not when it was the funeral of her oldest friend.

What happened to you, Esther? What happened to us? How did we choose so badly so often about so many things? And Bernie. He's chosen badly, too. He isn't an accountant. You know he isn't an accountant. How did you let him become an accountant? It's not too late for him, is it? But me. Is it too late for me? Is it, Esther? It must be. I'm so tired…

Sarah's breath deepened. Her head dropped to her chest. Her purse slid to the floor, echoing loudly in the glass-and-tile greenhouse. As she jerked awake, *The Autobiography of Alice B. Toklas* slid out. She leaned down to pick it up, leaving her purse where it had fallen, and opened to the first page.

"'I was born in San Francisco, California,'" she read half-aloud. "'I have in consequence always preferred living in a temperate climate but it is difficult—'" She stopped. "It *is* difficult."

"What is? What's so difficult?" Frank Littleton strode to Sarah's desk and peered down into her exercise book.

"Writing," Sarah sighed. "It's so hard."

"Then you're doing it wrong," her English teacher offered gently.

"I never know where to begin."

"Begin anywhere."

"That doesn't make any sense. You have to start at the beginning. That's what beginnings are for." Sarah looked up at her teacher. "Aren't they?"

Tall and blond with wavy hair, a trim mustache and tortoise-shell glasses setting off sparkling, sea-blue eyes, Frank Littleton could have stepped straight out of a Hollywood picture and into Room 308. To the adolescent girls of Baron Byng whose lives revolved around the brash, dark-haired sons of Jewish immigrants, their English teacher was rare and exotic. Most had a crush on him.

"Are they?" he asked. "Are you sure?"

"What do you mean?"

"You say you have to start at the beginning, Sarah," he continued. "Why?"

Sarah thought for a minute. "Because…because…because all books start at the beginning."

"That's where they start for you when you read them. What makes you think that that's where they start for the writer?"

Frank returned to the front of the class. "How many of you think like Sarah, that you always have to start whatever you're writing at the beginning?" A sea of hands shot up. "Okay, then. Here's your homework: Write me a composition that starts anywhere except at the beginning. Start in the middle or start at the end. Start wherever you want, however you want. Just start and see where it takes you."

"Anywhere?" Sarah asked incredulously.

"Anywhere," Frank replied.

From the back of the classroom, a scruffy teen leapt to his feet. "We can really start at the end, Mr. Littleton?"

"Sure, Tommy."

Tommy Shatz dropped back into his chair, smirking.

"But," Frank added, "you can't hand in a composition with one sentence followed by 'the end' and expect to get a passing grade."

Tommy's grin faded.

That night for the first time, Sarah wrote without struggle. Instead of trying to figure out where her story began, she dove in and started, without thinking about it. Also for the first time, the story almost wrote itself. That story for Mr. Littleton's assignment led to another and another and another, written not for class but because she wanted to. Sarah had never experienced such freedom, had never had so much fun. Now, a pencil and open copybook were as likely to share dinner with her as a library book.

A few weeks later Sarah marched into the offices of *The Bugle*, Baron Byng's ultra-militant student newspaper, known by lesser radicals at the largely Jewish school as *The Bagel*, and demanded an assignment. She would be the next Kit Coleman, the pioneering Toronto newspaperwoman that Mr. Littleton talked about in class. He even brought in old copies of *The Toronto Mail*, where Kit Coleman had been a columnist for years. Why, Kit Coleman was in Cuba during the Spanish-American War for *The Mail*. A woman war correspondent! Who ever heard of such a thing?

It didn't take long for Sarah to realize that she was no Kit Coleman. The more newspaper stories she read and wrote, the more they all seemed too much the same. Besides, they all started at the beginning, and that was something she had yet to master. She would have to find her own way, with a little guidance from Mr. Littleton and with examples from all the library books she was reading. Somehow, she *would* find her own way. Somehow, she would be a writer.

"Somehow," Sarah whispered, her eyes wet with tears of failure. "What happened to my somehow?"

"Somehow what?" Bernie sat next to her, scooping up her purse from the floor as he did.

Sarah wiped her eyes. "Somehow," she began but didn't know how to continue. "Somehow," she repeated, paused then went on, "somehow I think I should make you dinner. You shouldn't have to eat alone tonight, of all nights." She pushed herself up off the bench, then lowered herself back onto it. "You haven't changed your mind about going to your Uncle Manny and Auntie Dora's for the shiva, have you?"

"Maybe tomorrow. Probably not. For sure not tonight. Tonight, I was just going to go home."

"Like I said, you shouldn't be alone. That's what shiva is for. When you have a family that's really mishpochah, that is. Not like yours, God forgive me for saying." Sarah stood. "Come. You'll come with me to my apartment. I shouldn't be alone, either." She sat down again. "It's only…"

"What? It's only what?"

"It's only that I'm a terrible cook. Shreklekh." She laughed. "What kind of Jewish wife and mother is a terrible cook? Sammy hated my cooking. Morty never cared what he ate. Jack— No one was supposed to know this because a husband doesn't cook. But Jack?

He would put the fancy chef at the Ritz-Carlton to shame, he was that good. So, here I am inviting you for dinner and I'll probably poison you. Now your mother, she could cook."

"What if I cook dinner for you?" Bernie asked.

"You can cook?"

"Maybe. It depends what you have in your fridge."

"What do I have? Not much. Some eggs, I have. Some cheese. Some tomatoes. A challah. Some butter. Maybe a few cans of vegetables. You see what I mean? The world's worst balabusta."

"Do you keep kosher?"

"Feh. Not in years."

"Do you have a salami?"

"A salami? Of course, I have a salami. Who doesn't have a salami?"

"Good. I can make you my specialty: the Bernie Freed omelet, with salami, cheese and tomatoes, and whatever else we can find. How does that sound?"

"Batamt. Delicious. Better than anything I could cook for you, not ever in a million years."

The only staples Sarah lacked, at least as far as Bernie was concerned, were wine and dessert, which is how Bernie found himself retracing his steps toward Dominique's. He had offered to first walk Sarah the three blocks to her apartment. She refused. Nor would she consent to a taxi.

"I'm an old lady?" she huffed. "Is that what you think? And you: All of a sudden you're some kind of Boy Scout that you have to escort little old ladies across the street? You think I can't make it home on my own? Wait until you're my age, Mr. Bernie Freed, Mister Poor Excuse for a Boy Scout. I can get to Kensington Avenue just fine on my own, thank you very much." She grinned and kissed him. "You're a good boy. Thank you for offering."

Bernie laughed. "I'm not any kind of Boy Scout. After three weeks in Cubs, I refused to go back. I may be the only dropout in scouting history."

"Good for you. How old were you? Seven? Eight?"

"Something like that. Anyhow, I've never helped a little old lady across any street. Little old ladies can make their own way across the street." He gave Sarah a gentle shove eastward, in the direction of her building.

"A dropout, you say? See? You were a rebel even then. Maybe even an artist. What kind of artist wears uniforms and follows rules?"

"I told you: I'm no artist."

"We'll see," Sarah stated in a tone that brooked no argument. "Yes, we'll see."

He wasn't an artist...or was he? He was an accountant. Or was he?

14

Galérie Cinq Arts's bright lights spilled onto the patch of sidewalk in front of the renovated building. Bernie peered into the window. How could he be an artist when he couldn't begin to make sense of what he was seeing? He started to walk away, stopped and turned back. He touched the brushed aluminum door pull, then dropped his hand. Again, he started to move away. Again, some inexplicable force drew him back.

Like iron filings to a magnet, he thought. "More like a moth to a flame," he muttered darkly as he pulled the door open and stepped across the threshold. A chime sounded. No one appeared.

Esther would have loved it. Anne Savage, too.

Bernie looked around. "What is there to love? Just a lot of blotches and splotches."

It was a real mishmash. Nothing but globs and blobs. It would have fit right into that gallery back there on Sherbrooke.

"True enough," Bernie said silently. "It is a mishmash."

He found a backless stainless steel bench, its seat pocked with swiss cheese-like holes, set in front of a massive painting: a rough, thunderbolt-like streak of scarlet slicing through a blue-green oval. The rest of the canvas was bare other than a precisely drawn upside-down triangle in brilliant yellow in the upper left-hand corner and the artist's cramped signature in the lower right. A label next to the piece read, "Erik Donnekin, *Untitled*, 1984."

"Not even a clue in the title," Bernie grumbled. He stared uncomprehendingly at the canvas for a few moments more then dropped his eyes to the Anne Savage biography that Evelyn Waugh had let him borrow from the library. It sat next to him on the bench, on top of the Chagall book. He flipped it open, hoping for some magical key that would explain all that he was seeing, feeling and experiencing on this increasingly peculiar day. Instead, he saw an old black-and-white-photo. "One of Anne Savage's art classes at Baron Byng," the caption read.

It was a poor reproduction, not crisp enough for him to make out whether any of the eighteen teenaged girls pictured might be Esther Finkel or Sarah Schumacher. Half the students were hunched over the drawing paper spread over their desks. The other half focused on a costumed model posing on a chair perched atop a long wooden table. Overseeing the scene from the back of the classroom and barely visible amidst all the busyness was a white-haired Anne Savage.

Bernie took off his glasses and pressed his nose against the photo, trying to get a sense of this woman who had so influenced his mother…who had, perhaps, been so disappointed by his mother. Unfortunately, the halftone dots revealed little detail. More revealing was the classroom wall behind Savage, completely obscured by paintings of Pierrots and ballerinas and by shelves crammed with classical busts.

"Are you an Anne Savage fan, too?" The sonorous masculine voice so startled Bernie that he dropped the book onto the concrete floor.

"Sorry. I didn't mean to sneak up on you."

A paint-stained hand scooped up the book and dropped it back onto Bernie's lap before he could reach for it. The hand shot out to shake Bernie's. "Hi. I'm Erik Donnekin."

Bernie took the hand and looked up. The model's face that greeted him was classically Nordic, with high cheekbones, a ski slope-straight nose and clear skin, smooth but for a light stubble. His blue eyes were darker than any Bernie had seen before, piercingly insightful and with long lashes a few shades darker than his silky, blond hair. His smile was luminous.

"I-I," Bernie stammered. "Bernie. Bernie. Bernie Freed. You're Erik Donnekin?" He pointed to the canvas. "You did that?"

"You don't like it, do you," Erik replied, pretending to be offended.

"No, I mean—"

Erik dropped onto the bench next to Bernie. "It's okay. My mother doesn't like it, either. 'It's just a bunch of blobs,'" he mimicked with a pronounced Scandinavian inflection.

"Everything okay out there, Erik?" a Québecois-accented voice called from the back. "Is it a customer?"

"Don't shout into the gallery, Pierre," a second man's voice, unaccented, chastised no less quietly. "It isn't professional." A brief, unintelligible verbal skirmish later, the second voice repeated Pierre's questions.

Erik scrutinized Bernie with mock seriousness. "You aren't a customer, by any chance, are you?" he asked.

"A customer? I don't think… I mean I didn't… I—"

"I don't think so, Jeffrey," Erik shouted back. "Go back to your dinner." He paused. "Don't forget to leave some for me. And don't let Pierre drink all the wine." He turned back to Bernie and reached for the book. "May I?"

Until that moment, Bernie hadn't realized how tightly he was clutching it. "Yes. Yes. Of course." He released the book into Erik's hands. Artist's hands, Sarah would probably say. "You know about Anne Savage?"

"I saw one of her paintings at the Art Gallery of Nova Scotia a few years ago and fell in love with her. She's great, isn't she? Not at all like the Group of Seven. But, then, they were all men. There's something so feminine about her work. You must have seen *Quebec Farm*, right? At the Westmount Library?" Erik stopped abruptly and blushed a deep shade of pink. "Everyone says I talk too much. I do, don't I."

Bernie said nothing. Erik's race of words had left him breathless. Besides, he didn't know what to say. Erik intrigued him and at the same time left him edgy and unsettled.

Erik shoved the book back into Bernie's hands, noticed the Chagall book and opened his mouth to speak; he also loved Chagall. Instead he rose silently and backed away. "I shouldn't have disturbed you."

"No, wait," Bernie croaked. "Please."

Erik stopped.

"Your painting."

Erik raised one eyebrow expectantly.

"It's not that I don't like. It's that I—"

Erik looked at his canvas then back at Bernie.

"It's that I don't get it." He stared down at the book on his lap, which, again, he was gripping so tightly that his knuckles were white. "I'm not real smart when it comes to art."

Erik loped back to the bench and plopped down next to Bernie.

"Art's not about smart. Art's all about heart," he recited. "That's what Mr. Graves always said. He was my art teacher at Horton High."

Bernie looked at him blankly.

"In Wolfville. Nova Scotia? Where I'm from. Mr. Graves was my Anne Savage. Only he wasn't famous like Anne Savage. Or as talented. It's because of him that I became an artist. That's why I went to NSCAD." He pronounced it EN-scad. "The Nova Scotia College of Art and Design. In Halifax. Now I'm finishing up my MFA at Concordia." He pointed to *Untitled.* "You're trying to figure it out, aren't you? Don't."

"Don't?"

"Don't. There's nothing to figure out."

"Now I really don't understand."

Erik tilted his head to the right, scrunched his right eye shut and sat like that for a few minutes while Bernie twisted his thumb.

"How about this?" Erik asked, straightening out. "When you see a beautiful scene in nature, do you try to figure it out?" Before Bernie could reply, Erik leapt back in. "No. Of course, you don't. Or a sunset. Or a beautiful woman. Or a baby. Or a cute puppy. You don't think it. You *feel* it. That's what art is: It's feeling. It's emotion. It's intuition. Mac taught me that. Eventually." He giggled. "I was a slow learner."

Bernie looked at him questioningly.

"Mac. Marc-Allan Cameron. One of my profs at NSCAD. He's also a great abstract artist. His work's in the MOMA. In New York. I thought maybe you'd heard of him."

Mac. NSCAD. MOMA. What language is this guy speaking? Bernie tapped the book on his lap. "I never heard of Anne Savage until a couple of hours ago."

"No. Really?"

"Really." Bernie looked at Erik's painting again, then down at the book cover. "At least with Anne Savage, I know what I'm seeing: strawberry pickers. It's obvious from the picture and it says so in the title. Same with a sunset or a puppy or a baby."

"Doesn't matter."

"Of course it matters. It has to matter."

"Nope." Erik grinned. "You're dying to know what I mean, aren't you. Of course you are. Here's the thing: Even if you know it's a sunset or a puppy or a baby you're seeing, you aren't responding to that sunset or puppy or baby from your head. Sure, you label it from your head. But you respond to it from your heart and from your gut. You aren't thinking it. You're feeling it."

Bernie did not look convinced.

"Look at my painting," he ordered. "I don't care if you like it or not— Well, that isn't really true. I do care. But let's leave that for right now. Look at it," he repeated. "Don't think about what it is or whether you like it or whether you'll hurt my feelings if you don't. If I can deal with my mother not liking it, I can deal with you not liking it. If you don't like it, that is…but I'd still rather you did."

Bernie stared at the painting.

"You're trying to analyze it. Don't do that. Just kind of look at it as if you were hurrying by and stopped because it caught your eye. Let it catch your eye."

Bernie softened his gaze. His turned his head slightly.

"That's it." Erik watched him closely. "Now, never mind what it is or isn't. Never mind what it looks like to your brain. Does it remind you of something? Anything?"

It did, of a cupid's arrow piercing a heart. But that was silly. He couldn't say that.

"There is no wrong answer," Erik prompted gently, reading Bernie's thoughts. "It isn't like math. *Every* answer is right."

Bernie shook his head. *That's why I became an accountant. In accounting, only one answer is ever right.*

"Okay. We can come back to that. Do you feel anything when you look it at that way?"

He did, and it was not pleasant. It felt like someone was pounding on his chest with a hammer while someone else was pouring acid into his stomach. Beads of perspiration popped out on his forehead and he felt nauseous. He rose shakily to his feet, looking for something to hold on to. There was nothing. He knew that if he moved any more quickly, he would throw up. "I have to go," he announced hoarsely.

"Oh," Erik said, unable to mask his disappointment.

"I—" Bernie sighed. "No. I mean, I do have someplace to go, but…"

"But this is scaring you."

Bernie nodded and sank back onto the bench.

"Good."

"Good?"

"Art can be scary. It can make you feel things you don't want to feel. It can make you think things you don't want to think. It can even make you believe things you don't want to believe. It can do all that without you understanding what the fuck is going on." He paused. "That's just for the artist."

Bernie laughed weakly. "You don't know what it is, either."

"I *think* I know what it is, not that I knew even that when I was painting it. All I did was paint what wanted to be painted."

"Huh?"

"Never mind. Let's just say that I feel more about what it might be than I think I know what it is. The bottom line is that what I think and feel is only the tip of a ginormous iceberg. And that iceberg is—"

"Everything it really is."

Erik jumped up and clapped his hands. "I knew you'd get it! I knew you would."

"A heart," Bernie said softly. "A cupid's arrow piercing a heart."

"Really?" Erik couldn't believe what he was hearing.

Bernie frowned. "I thought you said there was no wrong answer."

Erik walked up to the painting and traced the thunderbolt with his finger. He turned back to face Bernie. "No one has ever said they saw that before, and…" He again turned away, this time to hide the tears that were welling in his eyes. He pulled a red-and-white bandana from his front pocket and wiped his eyes before turning around.

"And?"

"And that's what I was feeling when I painted it. Thank you."

"For what?"

"For getting it. For sharing my tip of the iceberg with me."

15

Sarah watched Bernie go. As he crossed at the next intersection, she strained to see if a bus was coming. None was. She waited a few minutes longer then turned back into the library and conservatory. She had lied to Bernie. She was too tired to walk those few blocks. Yet it wasn't right to take a taxi for such a short distance. Perhaps she should have let Bernie help her home, but it had always been difficult for her to accept help. She had even been reluctant at first to take Miss Drew's book recommendations all those years ago. Her mother always said she was too proud. She was probably right. *It's only getting harder the older I get. What will I do when I'm really old?* Sarah shrugged and settled back onto her recently vacated bench. A few minutes' rest and she would be good for the walk.

Sarah closed her eyes and again let the tinkle-plash of the fountain carry her back in time, fifty years back in time, to a different tinkle-plash: the sound of her mother washing dishes. It was Sunday morning and Gertie stood over the kitchen sink, softly humming a minor-key melody as the water dribbled over the dirty Shabbas dishes. Sarah sat at the freshly scrubbed kitchen table, reading. Always reading. That was the morning she knew that more than anything else in the world she wanted to be a writer. Not a Kit Coleman journalist. A writer. A book-writer. An author. Something in what she was reading that morning triggered a desire so primal that she gasped — in delight at the realization and horror at what her parents would say. Gertie and Mendel loved that she read, loved that she valued her education as much as they valued it. An education was important, even for a Jewish girl destined for marriage and family. How else would she be able to carry on an intelligent conversation with her doctor husband? How else would she instill the importance of an education into her children? Her sons?

Which book had she been reading that changed everything? How odd that she should remember the experience, not the book. It wasn't even the book. It was a single sentence in that book, a single sentence that awakened in her something that no Jewish girl had a right to have awakened. Today, yes. Then? No.

She had tried to honor her dreams, to honor and follow them. She and Esther both. So hard they had tried. If only she were fifteen today. If she were fifteen today, no one would try to stop her from becoming that great Jewish Canadian woman author she had once longed so passionately to become, had once been so determined she would become. Yes, her parents might have tried to discourage her. "Who can make a living as a writer?" they would have asked. Or, "Who do you think you are? Margaret Atwood?" A fifteen-year-old today, she could fight back. She could shout, "It's 1984. A woman can be anything she wants to be. Look at Barbara Frum, right there on TV every night for all of Canada to see. And Bertha Wilson. A Supreme Court judge!" But in 1934? In 1934 Barbara Frum wasn't born. In 1934 it was the Depression. In 1934 the best thing Jewish parents could do for their daughter was to make sure she made a good marriage, to a professional.

What did I do? I married Sam Kaplan.

She opened her eyes and laughed bitterly. "He looked good on paper," she said to the Kentia palm in the corner. "He wasn't a doctor or a lawyer, but he was a dentist. A *professional*." She pronounced it with a rolling "r" and Yiddish inflection, the way Gertie would have said it. Did say it.

The Kentia palm stood there.

"It started out fine," she continued, still addressing the plant. "The marriage did. I'm pretty sure I loved him. I'm pretty sure he loved me. And he flattered me. Oy, how he flattered me." She turned to the ficus in the opposite corner. "I needed flattery. Look at me. I'm short. I'm fat. I'm not much to look at. I know I'm sixty-one, but I wasn't any taller at eighteen. Or thinner. Or prettier.

"Sammy paid attention to me. A handsome boy paid attention to me, when not even the mieskeit boys would. No, he didn't read. No, he didn't take my dreams of becoming a writer seriously. But he wanted to marry me, and a girl had to get married. What else was a girl to do in those days, if not get married?

"To be honest," she turned back to the palm, "what I wrote was strange for a girl my age. 'Mature,' Mr. Littleton called it. I know he thought it was odd. But he never tried to get me to change…or stop, like Sammy tried to get me to stop.

"'You need a baby,' Sammy said at first, right after we were married. He was right, of course. A Jewish wife needs a baby. And a Jewish mother has no time to write, not with a baby like Morty who was so…so different.

"Once Morty was born, Sammy wasn't so flattering. Once he saw what Morty was like, Sammy wasn't flattering at all. Or nice. It didn't matter then. Then, there was no time to be a writer."

Sarah pushed herself up on her cane. If she didn't get home soon, Bernie would get there before she did.

As she approached the ficus on her way out, it seemed to ask reproachfully, "And after Sammy? What about after Sammy?"

She smacked the plant with her cane. "Then," she retorted, "it was too late."

Was it? She asked herself the question as she climbed down the library steps to the street. She asked it again as she made her way east on Sherbrooke. She asked it a third time as she pulled open the wood-framed glass door into her apartment building. She asked it one last time on the elevator ride up to the top floor.

"No," she answered as she fumbled to get her key into the front-door lock. But whether she was answering her own question or refusing to answer it was unclear, even to her.

16

Bernie stared at the racks of Bordeaux wine in the SAQ liquor store, all glinting with scarlet pinpoints from the fluorescent strips overhead, each point of light flashing either Erik's painting or Erik's face at him. He couldn't decide which made him more uneasy. All he knew was that when he finally left the gallery and stumbled to a payphone to call Sarah with an excuse for his delay, he had never been so scared…not since those two thugs roughed him up on the way home from high school one night long ago. He had never been a fighter, had no idea how to defend himself. What Jewish boy did, unless he was a Maccabee or an Israeli soldier? And Bernie was neither. So all he could do was cover his face and take it, before limping home with a bloody nose that no one was allowed to see. He was scared then — of getting badly hurt, for sure. He was more scared that someone would find out that he had been beaten up, that someone would find out that he was a sissy.

This was scarier, though he couldn't think why. He couldn't think it and was afraid to feel it because if he did, he might identify it and understand it, and that might be more terrifying still. Bernie reached blindly for a bottle and carried it to the register. That was the first time he looked to see what he had picked: a Saint-Émilion.

Perfect. Didn't he read once that Émilion was a hermit-monk? *What I wouldn't give to go into hiding right now. From myself. From what I'm trying not to think. From what I'm trying not to feel.*

The clerk bagged the bottle and handed Bernie his change.

"Merci." Bernie stuffed the coins into his pocket and stumbled out the door.

Next stop: Dominique's, two blocks away. Sarah had called ahead and a blueberry pie was waiting for him, baked, Dominique boasted, with fresh-picked wild berries from Quebec's Saguenay-Lac-Saint-Jean region.

Bernie wasn't sure he could face Dominique, let alone Sarah. What would he say? What could he say, when he didn't know what he was feeling. Whatever it was, it wasn't only about the art; that was disturbing enough. It was about Erik. Erik Donnekin who had suddenly gone shy and awkwardly slipped a business card into Bernie's hand as he left.

Bernie retrieved the card from his wallet. It bore the same color scheme as *Untitled* and said, simply, "Erik Donnekin, artist," along with a Westmount phone number and post office box. "No," he said to the card and dropped it into a trashcan. A half block later he ran back to retrieve it, even as he couldn't imagine any scenario that would prompt him to call the number on the card. Maybe he could hang around outside the Greene Avenue post office and pretend to happen to bump into him? "You're an idiot," Bernie said aloud and held the card aloft over the next trashcan, unsure whether to let it drop inside.

"So, Bernie, do you have a girlfriend?" Sarah's question had popped up, seemingly out of nowhere as they walked from the library to Dominique's earlier that day — lifetimes ago, it felt like. It was an innocent Jewish-auntie question, asked as much as a matter of form and to break the tension of the day as from any deep-seated inquisitiveness.

"Uh, no," Bernie replied. "Not right now."

"Not right now?" Sarah wanted to know. "Or not ever? You don't mind me asking, do you?"

"I guess not." He did mind. But how could he say so? "Not 'not ever.' Also not now."

"Are you a homosexual?" she asked, now with genuine curiosity.

"I—"

"Wait." Sarah tugged on his arm, pulled him to a stop in the middle of the busy sidewalk. "Before you answer, I should tell you that if you are, it doesn't matter. Maybe to some. Not to me. You know Jeffie Golden? Your Auntie Dora's sister's son? The notary?"

Bernie nodded.

"He's a homosexual. 'Gay,' they call it now?"

Bernie nodded again, increasingly uncomfortable.

"You couldn't ask for a nicer boy. Well, he's not a boy anymore. He's your age. Maybe a couple years older. You know what I mean. And my Jack's brother's sister-in-law's boy. Howie. You've met Howie? No. Probably not. You have to meet Howie. Everybody loves Howie. I think maybe he is, too. Not that I would know. How would I know? Not that you can tell. Who can tell? I just feel it. You know?"

"I—"

"Wait. One more thing. If you are, that is. And you don't have to be. Believe me, you don't have to be. But if you are, you have to know that your mother wouldn't have minded. She might have felt guilty, like it was her fault. Jewish mothers are like that. I should know. I always felt Morty was my fault. Sammy always thought so, though the doctors said again and again that it was nobody's fault the way he was. And if you can't believe doctors, who can you believe? But we aren't talking about me." She poked Bernie with her cane. "It's you we're talking about. It's Esther we're talking about. Your mother." She paused to put her thoughts into words. "Listen, Bernie. Whatever you are or aren't, your mother wouldn't have loved you any less. I know— I knew my Esther and that's more than a feeling. That I *know*. So before you tell me anything, yes or no, you have to know that."

Sarah waited. "So? Not that you have to say anything…"

"Let's walk," Bernie said.

They continued for a block in silence. As they passed Librairie Westmount, Bernie did his best to ignore the bookstore's window display: a pyramid of books featuring a single, disturbingly relevant title, *A Blessing on My Head: Gay, Jewish and Proud*. He prayed that Sarah wouldn't notice.

She didn't. "Am I being too nosy?" she asked, continuing her inquisition. "Jack always used to say that I was too nosy. Tell me what you want to tell me and don't tell me anything else. Okay?"

"Okay." Bernie forced out a laugh. "But you aren't letting me get a word in to tell you anything."

"Jack used to tell me that, too, always. God rest his soul. So I'm not saying nothing." She clapped her hand over her mouth.

"You could always get me to tell you anything, Sarah Swartz. You know that? I bet Jack told you the same thing."

Sarah winked.

Bernie turned serious. He stole a glance back toward the bookstore. "I can't tell you—"

Sarah dropped her hand. "Of course you can't. I should never have asked."

Bernie lifted her hand and covered her mouth with it. "Will you let me finish already? I can't tell you because I don't know. At least I don't think I do."

Erik was gay. Bernie was certain of it. Was he, Bernie? Was that why he was feeling so, well, queer? He grimaced. Puns were his weakness. He loved puns. Everyone in his humorless government office hated them. They were all so serious, so uncompromisingly earnest. But who makes jokes about income tax? Not Revenue Canada bureaucrats, that's for sure. *How did I ever end up at Revenue Canada, of all places?*

It was true. He was no accountant. Especially not a tax accountant. Especially not a boring tax accountant, working in a boring office filled with boring people. But an artist? He was no artist. He was sure of that.

Or was he?

"Erik's an artist," he said aloud.

Erik again. Why so much Erik? He's just a guy who picked me up in an art gallery.

"Picked me up? Is that what happened?" He reached into his pocket for Erik's card. *It isn't there!*

Bernie swiveled around to retrace his steps. *Of course it isn't there. It's in the trash. Shit. Maybe I can get it out.* Only then did he realize that he still clutched the card in his other hand.

"You really are an idiot, Bernie Freed. All he wants to do is talk to you about art. That's all he wants."

And if he wants more?

He stopped in front of Librairie Westmount and stared at the books in the window. "Gay, Jewish and *proud*?" he asked. "Is that even possible?" He studied the giant poster that soared up behind them, a larger-than-life photograph of the author. With his dark, curly hair, laughing eyes and magnetic smile, Ray David Blackman was as arrestingly handsome as he had always been...as he was the last time Bernie saw him, the last time Bernie spoke to him.

#   #   #   #   #

"I have to talk to you, Bernie."

"Sure, Ray. What's up?"

Ray turns away. He can't look Bernie in the eye and pretends to look out the window. He and Bernie are sharing a padded bench in the stark, mezzanine-level lounge of Concordia University's massive monstrosity of a main building.

"What is it? What's wrong?"

Ray's mouth moves. No words come out. Then they do. "I-I'm gay," he says tentatively, so softly that for a moment Bernie can't be sure he heard right.

Then he is sure and he's just as sure that it must be some kind of joke. Ray has never been much of a kidder but…

Ray forces himself to look at his oldest friend, and the minute Bernie sees Ray's face, he knows it's no gag. But it's not true. It can't be.

"You were on the high school football team," he argues. "You box. You go mountain-climbing. You go skiing. You're so athletic, so…masculine. How can you be gay?"

"Mountain-climbing has nothing to do with being gay, Bernie."

"I know, but…" Bernie shakes his head.

"I have a boyfriend, Bernie. We're getting an apartment together. On St. Marc. We move in next week."

"It isn't possible," Bernie whispers.

"I've wanted to tell you for a long time. I didn't know how…and I was afraid…" His voice trails off.

Now it's Bernie's turn to look away. He watches the relentless river of traffic surging west along de Maisonneuve Boulevard toward St. Marc and Ray's new apartment building. "I can't believe it," he says. "I don't believe it."

"Is it so horrible?"

"No, it's okay. I guess. I don't know."

There's more, but Ray hesitates, not sure it's the right thing to say or the right time to say it. He swallows hard and decides that it has to be the right time. If he doesn't say this to Bernie now, he never will.

Ray forces himself to keep his eyes on Bernie. "There's something else." He touches Bernie's hand.

Bernie flinches but doesn't pull it away.

"Maybe I shouldn't say it."
"What?" Bernie turns his head slowly back to meet his friend's gaze.
"I think maybe you are, too."
Bernie jerks his hand free. "Me? You're crazy."

"I'm not gay, Ray," Bernie declared to the poster. He pulled Erik's card from his pocket and ripped it in half, then in half again. But instead of dropping it and letting the pieces scatter on the breeze, he tucked them carefully into his wallet. "I'm an idiot," he repeated.

Bernie continued toward Sarah's, refusing to think about Ray or Erik or art or sexuality. He tried instead to think about his mother. *I buried my mother this morning and all I can think about is this guy and art and sex and what I'm going to do when I grow up…if I grow up.*

He let an image of his mother form in his mind's eye. It was of her two days earlier, dying. That is not what he wanted to remember.

He rewound the tape of his memory. Now she was in the bathroom, her wig askew with wisps of silky white poking out the sides, vomiting up the morning's chemotherapy. No. Not that memory, either.

He rewound some more. A lot more. Years more.

"Bernie? Is that you?" Esther's voice called out from her darkened bedroom.

"Yes, Ma. Did I wake you?" It was late, later than Bernie usually returned home from his single night class, and he had tried to sneak in unnoticed. But Esther's antennae were no less finely attuned than when he was a kid. She always knew when he came in, whatever time it was. "I need to get my own place," he muttered. *One more semester, then a job…then freedom.* Not only from his mother but from that piece of Ugu shit she had married. Where was Harold tonight? Probably out shtupping another one of his secretaries.

"How come you're so late, Bernie? You're always home earlier than this."

"Class ran late," he lied. "After, I went out for coffee with a few of the guys from school." Another lie. Professor Whittaker would stop mid-syllable if the clock ever struck eight while he was blathering on about nothing in particular instead of about twentieth-century marketing. *More like nineteenth-century marketing.* Most nights, though, Whittaker's lecture finished long before the class's official end-time.

And coffee with guys from class? It would never happen. A more tedious bunch he had never encountered. *They would probably say the same about me.* No, he had walked up and down Stanley Street in front of Le Rocambole, the only gay bar in town he knew about. He wouldn't have dared go in, of course. And why should he? He wasn't gay. But after what he had seen in the washroom at the Y a few weeks earlier… Well, he could say that he was just curious. Intellectually curious. *Yeah, right.*

The Concordia business school was housed in the aging Norris Building, a dowdy 1950s relic that straddled the block between Stanley and Drummond streets and whose corridors linked up with the decades-older YMCA that had originally constructed it. No less dingy than its newer neighbor, the Downtown Y's worst-kept secret was its notorious first-floor men's room, where a daylong orgy of male-to-male sexual exploits trumped all other uses of the facility. Bernie rarely crossed from the Norris into the Y, so he knew nothing of the bathroom's reputation when nature called more insistently than usual one day and the Y's washroom was the closest at hand. When he pushed open the door into a maelstrom of half-naked grunting and moaning, he was as stimulated as he was disgusted, as fascinated as he was repulsed.

He never opened that door again, although he found himself wandering by it many times in the days ahead. Then one evening after class, he left the Norris through the Stanley Street exit and strolled, as casually as he could manage, the few doors south to Le Rocambole. It was early on a weeknight and gay Montreal's downtown nightlife was hours from springing into action. But Bernie couldn't know that. He paced up and down Stanley and circled around and around the block, hoping to see someone he recognized while dreading the possibility that he might. He saw no one. When he checked his watch as he rounded Peel and de Maisonneuve for the umpteenth time it was 10:30. He crossed the street to the Metro station and caught the train home.

Being gay has got to be about more than bars and sex at the Y. Doesn't it? Bernie dropped onto a bench, fully aware of the irony of his location: directly across Sherbrooke from Le Boulevard des Arts, the neighborhood's trendy artists' supply store. He pulled out his wallet and reconstructed Erik's card on his lap and their gallery encounter in his mind. What did it all mean? Was it possible that he was attracted to Erik? Bernie had never been much interested in girls, though he had gone through the motions over the years. But his rare dating experiences and rarer sexual flings always left him in mind of Peggy Lee's "Is That All There Is?" He always assumed that he was not particularly sexual or social. What if that weren't true? What if there were something more? What if he was refusing to see it? If that was true, could he face it? Could he accept it? Could he accept himself? Sarah could. Sarah said his mother would have. Could *he*?

17

The four-story brick-and-stone apartment building at Sherbrooke and Kensington was already forty years old when the newly remarried Sarah, now Swartz, moved in with her new husband, Jack. Yet The Whitehall had lost none of its luxury cachet over the decades. Black walnut doors, frames, cabinets, wainscoting and trim — all kept oiled and brightly polished — accented suites of bright, spacious, high-ceilinged rooms. Never more than an indifferent cook, Sarah was less enraptured by the recently modernized kitchen than by the three (*three!*) bathrooms with their updated plumbing and upgraded fixtures. But what seduced her most were the air conditioners, one in each room for Montreal's sultry summers, as well as the working fireplace in the living room, which she still sometimes insisted on lighting year-round. "Imagine: a fire you don't need for heat," she had exclaimed, recalling the poverty of her childhood and the penny-pinching of her first marriage. In the early years, she also insisted that Esther and all her other friends visit often, less for social reasons then because it was so much fun to buzz them in with this, her first intercom.

Sarah's new home was only a few miles east of the NDG flat she had lived in for nearly twenty years, but it might as well have been in another universe, what with the blue-rinsed widows on either side of her and the Englisher-than-English lawn-bowling club across the street. Not that Kensington Avenue was entirely alien, culturally speaking: Shaar Hashomayim, one of Canada's largest synagogue complexes, was right next door. Better yet, her new home was only a few minutes' walk from her beloved Westmount Library. And now that she was a Westmount resident, she could borrow books whenever she wanted, for free.

These days it took Sarah a few minutes longer to make the trip between home and library on foot. Fortunately, if she was too tired to walk it, two stops on the No. 24 bus would get her there in a flash. These days, too, there was no Jack. Their marriage had lasted barely nine years before his sudden death left Sarah a widow a second time.

Now, her best friend was also gone. More than either of her husbands, more even than her son, who died so young, Esther Finkel Freed Rosenbaum Coopersmith had framed much of Sarah's life. For more than half a century, Esther was her closest confidante, always around when she needed a shoulder to cry on or had a joy to share. In all that time, Sarah kept only one secret from Esther and, in the kind of irony that only occurred in literature, she now knew that Esther had kept the same secret from her.

Wearier than she had felt in years, Sarah shut the door behind her and collapsed into the overstuffed sofa. *Maybe it's getting time for me to go, too.* She shut her eyes and let the coolness of the air conditioning wash over her.

"Don't you dare, Sarah Shumacher. Don't you dare think about going anywhere." Esther's voice. "There's a whole new life waiting for you. Right where you are. Right here."

Sarah's eyes shot open. "Esther?" she whispered and scanned the room for the ghost she was certain must be present. Her eyes lit on a grainy black-and-white snapshot that sat framed in a place of honor on the mantelpiece, next to a color photo of her and Jack on their honeymoon. She rose creakily and made her way to the fireplace. Before picking up the photo, Sarah knelt and lit the logs and kindling that she always kept primed and ready, regardless of the season. Then she picked up both photos, turned up the air conditioning and installed herself in the flowered easy chair next to the fireplace.

She laid the picture of her and Esther on the antimacassared arm and gently caressed the round, wrinkled face of her Jack. Jack lacked Sammy's strikingly good looks. He also lacked the rarely concealed anger that always simmered so close to the surface with Sammy, especially once Morty was diagnosed as "different." Like Sarah, Jack was short and well-padded. Unlike Sammy, he was an enthusiastic fan of her writing.

"Why aren't you writing anymore, honey bunch?" he asked when she had mustered the courage to confess her long-lost dreams. He continued to ask until she reluctantly bought herself a Smith-Corona portable at Eaton's and even more reluctantly began to peck at it. Yet there never seemed to be time.

A retired high-powered lawyer with an equally high-powered investment portfolio, Jack loved to travel. In those nine years, Sarah experienced a world she had never expected to see. She and Jack started small, if a luxury compartment on the *Canadian* could be called small. For Sarah, who had never ventured west of Toronto, north of Ste. Agathe's Jewish cottage country or south of New York's Catskill resorts, traveling the Canadian Pacific Railway's transcontinental train all the way to Vancouver was a major expedition. It paled compared to Jack's next surprise: first-class passage for two on the still-new *QEII* from New York to Southampton, followed by a leisurely rail tour of England and the Continent. For that odyssey, Sarah and Jack were gone from Montreal for four months. More trips followed that one, each more exotic than the last: Sweden, Norway and Denmark...Israel, Cypress, Greece and Turkey...Japan, Taiwan and Hong Kong...Australia, New Zealand and Fiji.

Jack had been in the midst of calling in favors from his External Affairs contacts in Ottawa and his Secretary of State contacts in Washington to organize a trip for them to the USSR and Eastern Europe ("it's important to see where we came from") when a drunk truck driver jumped the median on the Décarie Expressway and slammed into his Buick Riviera. He was killed instantly in the fiery crash.

Sarah brushed away a tear.

"So, I've been gone six years, honey bunch. You can't say you have no time now." Jack's voice. It was so real. As much time as they had spent away from Montreal, everything about this apartment reminded Sarah of Jack. He had given her a free hand, and budget, to decorate and furnish it. That was no problem; their tastes were so similar. They both preferred comfort over style, and everything about the place was soft and easy, warm and comfortable. If the apartment had been too big for the two of them — it was bigger than her whole flat in NDG, for God's sake — it was even bigger for one now that she was alone. Still, as long as she was here in apartment 411, Jack was here with her. And as long as Jack was with her, she couldn't leave. She wasn't going anywhere, except maybe to join him. Maybe sooner instead of later.

"Don't you dare, Sarah Shumacher." Esther's voice again.

Sarah looked around warily. "I'm going crazy," she said aloud. The clock on the mantel chimed seven. "I should get up and get ready. Bernie will be here any minute." She didn't move. "I am not Sarah Shumacher," she retorted defiantly to Esther's ghost or, more likely, to her own craziness.

"You're right. You're Sara-with*out*-an-h Schumacher."

"I'm Sarah Swartz," she shouted into the empty apartment. "Sarah *with* an 'h.'"

"Oh?"

"I have to call Dominique. About the pie. Bernie's probably already there." She placed Jack's picture on the chair's other arm, made her way into the kitchen and dialed Dominique's number from memory. She had barely hung up when Bernie phoned to say that he was running late.

"Me, too," Sarah replied without explanation.

She looked into the dining room with disgust. Living alone, she always ate in the kitchen. The dining room table and chairs were cluttered with the detritus of the single life. Sighing, she began to clear it all away.

18

"Sarah!" Bernie called out and banged on the door to apartment 411, harder this time. He had buzzed her from the lobby then slipped in behind a resident without waiting for the intercom. "Sarah? Are you in there?"

A moment later, the door swung open...to a madwoman.

"I found it!" Sarah exclaimed. "I found it!" She was waving a sheaf of typewritten pages and doing a little dance. Her cheeks and forehead were smudged with dirt. Her hair was wilder than when he had left her, and strands of white dangled over her left ear and covered her right eye. She looked like a lopsided sheepdog.

Bernie couldn't help but burst out laughing, the anxieties of the previous hour dissolved by the absurdity of what greeted him. The scene inside the apartment was even more bizarre. Sarah was not the best of housekeepers. Her cherrywood furniture was nearly always coated with a fine layer of dust, and there were generally dirty dishes soaking in the kitchen sink. Yet the apartment was always neat...well, except for the dining room.

Now, however, the dining room was immaculate, but the living room had been overrun by more than a dozen cardboard cartons — all opened, some overturned — and piles and piles of paper. Gazing down on the disaster from a decorative marble pedestal, like some humming, forty-nine-eyed god, was a green portable electric typewriter, its cord snaking under the flotsam and jetsam to a wall outlet.

"I found it," Sarah repeated, grinning, and dropped onto the only spot on the sofa free of papers. She shoved the rest onto the floor and patted the seat next to her. "Find some place for the wine and pie — in the dining room, maybe — and come sit. There's something I have to show you."

Speechless, Bernie dropped his books next to Sarah and did as he was told.

"What is all this?" he asked when he returned.

"Sara-without-an-h Schumacher," she replied.

He raised his eyebrows questioningly. "And that?" he asked, poking at the papers still clutched in Sarah's fist.

"Good Jewish Girls Don't."

"Good Jewish girls don't? Don't what?"

"Don't do anything they want to do. Good Jewish girls don't become artists. Good Jewish girls don't become writers." Sarah chuckled. "Good Jewish girls don't play street hockey against the boys."

Bernie scrutinized his mother's oldest friend with concern. Had Esther's death been too much for her? Had she finally snapped?

"You think I'm meshugena, don't you?"

Bernie said nothing.

Sarah waved her hand toward the dining room table. "Go open the wine, boychik. You know where the corkscrew and glasses are?"

Bernie nodded.

"Pour us two glasses. Two *big* glasses. I have a story to tell you. About not-so-good Jewish girls."

19

Anne Savage studied her girls. Usually cheerful and eager to get on with the day's artwork, today they stared at her stony-faced, their mouths set in grim defiance. Especially Esther Finkel.

Anne was proud of their determination. She wanted to smile encouragingly and cheer them on. But their mutiny was directed at her and her authority, as well as at the Principal's, so it probably wasn't a good idea. "Principal Simon's decision is final," she said as sternly as her nature would allow.

The girls groaned.

"I know it doesn't seem fair—"

"It isn't," Esther called out.

"Esther," Anne rebuked.

"I'm sorry, Miss Savage, but…"

"No buts, Esther." Anne's tone was firm. Inside, she rejoiced at the girl's spunk. Chutzpah, they would call it in this part of town. "I know it doesn't seem fair that the boys get to go up to Mount Royal, to the cemetery, to sketch and you can't."

The girls nodded vigorously.

"If you settle down, I will tell you some good news."

"We can go, too?" Esther asked, her eyes lighting up.

"It's different good news, but it's still good news."

"Oh." Esther looked down, crestfallen.

"I talked to Mr. Simon and he's agreed to let me take you over to Fletcher's Field tomorrow. Just you girls."

The old man, his bald head shiny with perspiration, bent over his handcart and pushed a worn leather boot onto the pedal. As he pumped harder and harder, singing off-key in Yiddish, the whetstone wheel began to turn and whir, more and more quickly. The old man picked up a broad carving knife from the cart's small wooden shelf and set its blade to the wheel. He flexed his wrist with a practiced motion, making certain that every inch of the cutting surface touched the wheel for precisely the right amount of time. The polished steel caught the mid-afternoon sun and glinted brightly. The cart shuddered. Blade against stone screeched with an earsplitting whine. And the two teenage girls coming up on the old man and his cart, slapped their hands against their ears and ran screaming down St. Urbain Street until they were well past him.

"I hate that sound," Sarah exclaimed when they were out of earshot.

"Me, too," Esther agreed. "It's almost as bad as Miss Forsythe." She giggled. Estelle Forsythe was their French teacher. Cats scrapping in the lane behind her house was easier on the ears than Miss Forsythe's shrill squeak of a nervous tee-hee.

The girls turned east onto Villeneuve then north onto Clark.

"The cemetery would have been more fun," Esther grumbled. She had already forgotten about the peddler and was griping about Miss Savage's announcement.

Sarah agreed. Fletcher's Field was okay. But a cemetery! All those dead people. She was sure they could have helped her with the Jewish Montreal ghost story she was trying to write, inspired by all the Edgar Allan Poe she was reading.

"Wait!" Esther stopped suddenly. She turned to face her friend. "You know what I say to Mount Royal Cemetery and the boys and Mr. Simon? I say feh. *Feh.* That's what I say. To Miss Savage, too. Because I have a better idea. A much better idea. You won't believe how much better an idea."

20

"That's how we ended up across town at the Jewish cemetery that Sunday, by Esther's mama's stone, Esther with her sketch pad and me with my notebook." Sarah gulped down the last of her wine and picked up her papers. "That's where this story was born. That picture, too." She pointed her empty glass at the armchair by the still-blazing fire.

Bernie poured Sarah a second glass and retrieved the photo.

"We stopped at Stella's on the way back. I had my camera and Stella snapped a picture of us. You sure you haven't seen it before?"

"I guess I never noticed it." Bernie studied the photograph of the two teenage girls perched on stools at Stella's counter, grinning into the camera. "Mom looks so different. You both do."

"Of course we do. That was almost fifty years ago." Sarah laughed.

"That isn't what I mean. You look, well, happy...as though..." Bernie groped for the right words. "As though the world was yours and nothing could stop you."

Sarah took the photo from Bernie and gazed into it wistfully. "That's what we thought."

For an instant, Sarah felt the same frisson of excitement and derring-do she had experienced at Stella's that long ago afternoon. They hadn't exactly tricked Sadie into letting them go to the cemetery on their own. Yet how could Sadie argue with Esther wanting to visit her mother's grave?

"Wait until next Sunday," Sadie had urged. "Next Sunday I can go with you." She had not made it to the cemetery in a few weeks and was feeling guilty.

"I want Sarah to see Mama's grave," Esther replied not entirely ingenuously, "and she can't go next weekend. Please?"

Sadie tilted her head to the right, to the left and back again, as she always did when pondering another of Esther's unreasonable requests. If it stopped to the left, it was a yes; to the right would inevitably be a no. "Make sure you come straight back," she said sourly.

Well, they hadn't, had they. Nor did they spent all their time at Ruth's grave. It was their first stop and their last, but in between Esther wandered off to the oldest part of the cemetery, where some of the weather-faded stones dated back more than sixty years, quick-sketching headstones, foot stones and wrought-iron gates, even the Gothic bell tower of St. Luc's poking through the early spring's skeletal canopy of mature oaks.

Sarah, meanwhile, found a comfortable spot on the grass and leaned her back against "Rosalie Friedman, died 5th Aug. 1915 aged 72 yrs." As she closed her eyes and let the afternoon sun burn away the early spring chill, she tried to conjure up her ghost story idea. It refused to come. Instead, she saw a vision in her mind's eye. It had nothing to do with cemeteries, gravestones, Edgar Allan Poe or Esther's dead mother. It was of six twelve-year-old girls playing street hockey against a boys' team on St. Urbain Street. The whole neighborhood had come out to watch, lining the sidewalks on both sides of the road. Most of the cheering was for the boys because, as nearly everyone in this immigrant neighborhood noted, tsking loudly, good Jewish girls don't chase a ball around the street with a stick, especially against good Jewish boys.

Sarah saw it all, as if it were playing out in front of her like a movie: two girls, Sophie and Pearl, who wanted to join the boys' team but were rebuffed; Rosalie, a teen athlete who adopted them and their cause and helped them recruit more girls; the months of coaching that ultimately transformed a motley collection of girls into the indomitable Team Esther, named for the Biblical queen; and the final game, which proved with no possible argument that good Jewish girls can, will and *do*.

It was more than a vision. It was a story. A story she *had* to write. She pulled her copybook and pencil from her satchel and touched it to the page: "Autumn was already dying into winter when Sophie Birnbaum and Pearl Mutter strode up to Paul Epstein and announced, 'We've come to play.' The thirteen-year-old boy could not believe his ears. 'No way,' he exclaimed and turned his back on them, but not before he sneered, 'Good Jewish girls don't play street hockey.'"

Sarah had already scribbled a third of the story into her copybook when Esther found her and told her it was time to go. She had even scrawled a title at the top of the first page: *"Good Jewish Girls Don't."*

"I couldn't sleep that night, I was so excited," Sarah said, "so I wrote more on the story." She waved the papers at him.

"That's the story?" Bernie asked. "That's what you wrote in the cemetery?"

"What do you think? I had a typewriter with me in the cemetery, and an extension cord?" Sarah laughed. "I lost that first draft a long time ago. Or maybe Sammy threw it away." She shrugged. "This is the last draft I worked on. I typed it out from memory not long after I got me that contraption." She indicated the still-humming type-writer. "That's about all I ever used it for. That's when I changed the names." She grinned sheepishly. "Sophie and Pearl became Sarah and Esther. And Rosalie became Anna."

"Why Anna?"

"Anna Leonowens. *Anna and the King of Siam* Anna."

"You mean *The King and I?*"

"That, too. You know about Anna Leonowens?"

"From *The King and I.* Is that what you mean?"

"It is and it isn't."

"I don't understand."

"You will." Sarah pulled Bernie to his feet. "We have to eat. I'll tell you more while you make your famous omelet. And you'll tell me what happened after the library that took you so long."

Bernie averted his eyes. "I told you on the phone. I ran into an old friend."

Sarah gripped Bernie's chin tightly in her right hand and pulled his head toward her. "Look at me, Bernie Freed. You think I'm stupid? You think I haven't known you since before you were born? You think I can't tell when you're hiding something? You'll tell me?"

"But—"

"You'll tell me." She let go his chin.

Bernie nodded, resigned. "I'll tell you."

21

"I can't believe you aren't coming." Esther glanced at her watch and rose from the kitchen table. "Are you sure? I could wait and we could go another time. I know you want to see it as bad as I do."

Sarah maneuvered herself to her feet. Not that she could see her feet. Only six months pregnant, she was already so big that she was sure the Dionne quintuplets' fame would soon pale next to that of the Kaplan sextuplets. Or septuplets. Or octuplets. The doctor insisted she was having only one. She didn't believe him.

"You leave Halifax in, what, six weeks, seven weeks?" Sarah asked.

"Something like that. I can't wait to be gone from here. We've already started packing. Who knew we could collect so much in a couple of years?"

Sarah frowned at all the clutter in her dreary flat. A year after the end of the war, housing was still hard to find in Halifax. Decent housing was even rarer. "You would think a place so small wouldn't have room for all this chazerai…and for all this dust," she grumbled. "I don't want to start to think about packing it all."

"If you would start now, I'd help you."

"You've always been the organized one. Me? I can wait until I'm not carrying all these little Kaplans with me every time I take a step."

Esther gathered her coat and purse. "I hate to leave you here."

"It won't be for long. The minute all these babies show their faces, Sammy and I will be right behind you and back in Montreal where we belong. After I pack, of course."

"I meant today. I could send the taxi away and stay."

"Don't be silly, Esther. Movies only play for a week. Who knows when there will be another time. Go."

Esther touched her friend's belly. She was thrilled for Sarah. Who wouldn't be? After two years of marriage it was time. It was time for Esther, too. After all, she was married six months longer than Sarah, and still no babies. It had to be her fault. Wasn't it always the wife's fault?

"Your time will come, Esther," Sarah said softly, then winced. If this was what pregnancy was like, how had the human race survived this long? "I know it will."

Sarah waddled with her to the door. A black DeSoto sedan hugged the curb.

"It's not your fault, you know. Don't let anyone ever tell you that it is." Sarah kissed Esther on the cheek.

"I'm sure you're right," Esther said, trying to sound convinced. She hugged Sarah gently and hurried down to the cab. "I'll tell you all about it," she called back to Sarah before the cabbie shut the door. "I promise."

"Where to, ma'am?" the driver, a young woman Esther's age, asked. Patty MacGregor, her ID tag said.

"The Capitol Theatre."

"Yes, ma'am."

Esther leaned back in the seat. It pleased her to be able to take taxis again. During the war and through the first months after it ended, Morris urged her to take the streetcar for anything that wasn't urgent. Only now, as some of the country's wartime restrictions were starting to ease up, would he agree to a cab for something as "trivial" as the movies.

"I've missed taxis," Esther said as the car pulled away.

Patty smiled at her passenger through the rearview mirror. "I'll miss driving them, ma'am, but the boys will be needing jobs again now the war's over."

"True," Esther conceded. "It's still too bad you have to give it up."

Fifteen minutes later, they pulled up across Barrington Street from the Capitol, just as the bells of the church next door marked the hour. The movie palace marquee read "Irene Dunne. Rex Harrison. Linda Darnell. *Anna and the King of Siam.*"

Esther thrust a few bills into the front seat. Patty began to count out change but Esther shook her head. "No," she said. "Keep it."

"Thank you, ma'am." Patty beamed. "Next driver will be a man, more than likely."

"Next driver will be in two hours," Esther responded, "so maybe not."

Patty laughed. "Okay. Time after that." She flicked on the roof light. "Like I said, I'll miss it. Still, it's only right."

"Maybe," Esther said half to herself as she closed the door. "Maybe not."

A light November drizzle started up as she waited for a pair of Birney streetcars to pass. Then dodging traffic, she crossed the slickening paving stones to join a queue that snaked north on Barrington and around the corner onto Salter. "I will never get used to the weather here," she muttered, pulling up her collar and wishing, not for the first time, that she had remembered to bring an umbrella.

"You're getting wet," the man behind her in the movie line said with a light Scottish burr.

Esther ignored him and kept her eyes trained in front of her. She heard him open his umbrella.

"Excuse me," he said. He tapped her shoulder.

Sure, everything was looser and freer with the war: soldiers, sailors and airmen from all over Canada and beyond, all taking every liberty imaginable — and some not so imaginable — with single women, despite what everyone insisted was the English reserve of this small city. Why had they ever come here? After Montreal, it was like living in a gray, gloomy, overcrowded village. Thank God for Sarah. Thank God she was here, too. If it hadn't been for her… Now, Sarah was pregnant and she was not. Because of that, here she was at this movie matinee by herself, while some lizard of a soldier was trying to pick her up.

Esther spun around, her eyes on fire.

"Look here, mister—" Her mouth snapped shut. This was no ill-mannered serviceman. This was a gentleman. A few years older than she, probably in his late twenties, he was dressed smartly in a dark suit and tie, open coat and charcoal fedora and was…well, she had never seen anyone like him. It sounded clichéd to say that he took her breath away. But he did. She found herself gulping for air, then felt her face flush.

"Are you all right, miss?" He noticed her left hand, which was clutching at her throat. "Ma'am?" He reached out to steady her. She grabbed his arm with her free hand.

"I-I'm sorry," Esther gasped and turned redder. "I don't know what's wrong with me." But she did know what was wrong. Until that moment, she had never believed in love at first sight. She wasn't even sure she believed in "true love," even on second or third sight.

She had been convinced that she loved Morris. That's why she had married him. No, that wasn't true. He had dazzled her. His family had dazzled her. His family's wealth had dazzled her. And living at home with Sadie kept growing into more and more of a nightmare. She fled as soon as she could, as soon as Morris asked her to marry him. And now— It made no sense and it was also ridiculously hackneyed, but she had fallen in love with this stranger who had spoken only ten words to her.

It wasn't only his looks, though he was a million times better-looking than Sarah's Sammy, who should have been a movie star, he was that gorgeous. This man— He was talking to her but all she could see were his lips moving. And what lips. Not full, not thin… somewhere in between, forming a slightly crooked smile.

She wasn't that much shorter than him, so how come she felt so tiny standing next to him? It was like she was one of the little people she had seen when Manny took her to the Midgets' Palace on Rachel Street when she was eight, like she was gazing up at a giant — a lightly freckled giant with bright, hazel eyes and hints of auburn poking out the sides of his hat.

Oh, God. Now she felt like she had a fever, like she was on fire all over…especially in places she had no business being on fire. Not in public. Not with a stranger.

The line was moving. He was still talking. She thought he was suggesting that they sit together so he could make sure she was okay. She rummaged in her purse for her wallet. He pushed her hand away. He pulled a billfold from his suit coat and thrust a banknote at the gum-chewing blonde in the kiosk.

Esther loved coming to the Capitol. It was one of the few experiences that made Halifax bearable. Since arriving in mid-1944, she had come nearly every week. Here is where she prayed for Dorothy McGuire's safety in *The Spiral Staircase*, cursed the malevolent

Charles Boyer in *Gaslight*, giggled at Cary Grant's antics in *Arsenic and Old Lace* and envied a Judy Garland lucky enough to live somewhere she loved in *Meet Me in St. Louis*. While the rest of Halifax picked up after the city's ugly VE Day riots, Esther mourned the fact that she couldn't go to the movies: The Capitol, along with much of Halifax, was shuttered for a week.

Sarah joined her occasionally, when Sammy would let her; Morris, less often. He labored long hours at a grueling job about which he could share little, even after the war's end. Once home, he was rarely in a mood to go out again.

For Esther, the Capitol was about more than movies and the escape into another world they offered her. When she stepped into the baronial lobby, then into its even more magnificent auditorium, she could almost imagine herself back on downtown Montreal's St. Catherine Street, in its Capitol or Palace or Loew's. She could almost be home in Canada's greatest city, instead of stuck eight hundred miles away in a provincial capital teetering at the farthest edge of the country.

Today, Esther didn't notice the theater's plush opulence. She didn't need its counterfeit dreams. She was living in a fantasy of her own, and it was discomfitingly real.

"My name is Marc-Allan Cameron," her companion said as they took their seats at the front of the mezzanine, and he shook her hand firmly. "My friends call me Mac."

"Mac," Esther repeated dumbly. She whispered her name in reply.

"Like the queen?"

Esther nodded.

"You carry yourself like a queen," he said.

Esther's face turned as scarlet as the velvet curtains covering the screen. She was grateful when, seconds later, the lights dimmed, the curtains parted and the Twentieth Century-Fox drumroll, fanfare and searchlights pushed Marc-Allan Cameron aka Mac from the forefront of her muddled mind.

Yet Queen Esther, as he now thought of her, remained at the forefront of Mac's mind. As the credits flashed across the screen and through the next two hours, Mac was hard-pressed to focus on Irene Dunne. Instead, he kept stealing glances at the woman — the *married* woman — next to him, more beautiful than a hundred Irene

Dunnes. She did carry herself like a queen: nearly as tall as his six feet with a bearing that was proud and sure though not haughty. She hadn't smiled; she was too flustered. *Because of me, I hope.* But he knew that when she did, it would be a smile so infectious that it would leave him grinning like a fool and stammering like the shy Glasgow schoolboy he had once been. He looked at her hands, the right covering the left on her lap…covering her wedding ring. With fingers that long and slender she must be a musician…or an artist like him. *Let her be an artist. Then we'll have something to talk about.*

"Stop," Bernie ordered, choking on his omelet. He chugged down the rest of the wine in his glass.

Startled, Sarah looked up from the photo of her and Esther. She had carried it to the dining room table and been staring into it, as though those two teenagers needed to hear this story more than Bernie did. She had barely touched her dinner. "What is it, boychik?"

"Did you say Marc-Allan Cameron?"

"Sure I did. You heard me."

"Could there be more than one? In Halifax?"

Sarah set the photo on the table, face down. "Why? Maybe. Cameron's a common enough name. Down there, for sure. What are you talking about?"

"This Mac guy. Did you say he was an artist?"

"So? He's a famous artist now. You've maybe heard of him?"

"Does this Mac teach at…at an art college? An art college in Halifax? Ensc— N-something?"

"Now you're scaring me, Bernie." Sarah grabbed at her glass, nearly knocking it over. "You know about Mac?" She, too, took a big gulp of wine. "Your mother didn't already tell you about him, did she?"

"No." Bernie drew out the word.

"I didn't think she would. So how do you know about Mac?"

"Maybe you'd better finish your story."

"I think maybe you need to tell me yours first."

They stared at each other stubbornly, neither willing to budge.

"What happened at the end of your 'Good Jewish Girls' story?" Bernie asked, ending the stalemate. "Did Team Esther win?"

Sarah got up from the table and went into the kitchen. She

returned a few minutes later with the omelet pan. She scraped most of what was left onto Bernie's plate, saving a few forkfuls for herself. She started back toward the kitchen, then touched the bottom of the pan to make sure it was cool and placed it on the hardwood floor by her chair.

"In my story," she said, "Team Esther won. It was close. They won by a single goal. That was the story I wrote. In the other story, the story that Esther and I lived, it was different. It wasn't such a happy ending." She paused. "What about your story? How is it going to end?"

Bernie stabbed a piece of salami and skated it around his plate. "I don't know. I don't know anything." He put the fork down. "What about yours? Mom's story is over, but yours isn't. What about your story? How is yours going to end?"

Sarah looked back into the hurricane-disaster that was the living room and at the now-silenced Smith-Corona. "Me neither, Bernie. I don't know, either."

Daylight had faded, and the lights illuminating the backside of the Tudor Revival hulk that was Westmount City Hall leached through the partly closed venetian blinds, projecting an eerie glow into the apartment. Bernie and Sarah sat in the darkening room, each lost in thoughts not ready to be shared. Neither touched what remained on their plates.

"If I tell you how I know about Marc-Allan Cameron and why I took so long to get back here, will you finish your story and tell me why you think Mom would ever have told me something so personal?"

Sarah topped up her wine and Bernie's. "I don't know that she ever would have told it to you. Probably not. But, yes. Of course."

The auditorium had largely emptied by the time Esther and Mac rose, descended the grand staircase to the lobby and exited onto Barrington Street. Clouds and drizzle had fled, replaced by the rare golden glow of a waning afternoon. Without saying a word, they turned onto Spring Garden Road and strolled up toward the Public Gardens.

A bustling oasis of brilliant color and lush greenery from late spring until early fall, the century-old formal garden was deserted and starkly desolate in early November, its walkways empty of people, its trees and shrubbery stripped of their leaves and its exuberant floral displays either dead or dying. That did not matter to Esther or Mac as they passed through the Gardens' ornate ornamental gate a few blocks later. All that mattered was that they were holding hands, neither knowing how or when it had happened.

Then Esther noticed another couple ambling toward them and she panicked. She could not make out their faces from this distance, but what if she knew them? What if they recognized her? *I should pull my hand free right now and go home. Never mind "go home." I should run home. I should run as far away from Mac and Halifax as I can get, back to Montreal…farther, maybe. I should not be here with this man, like this. It isn't right. Good Jewish girls don't.* Good Jewish girls don't? She smiled, remembering Sarah's long-ago short story, and clung more tightly to Mac's hand.

"What is it, Queen Esther?" Mac asked, the first words either of them had spoken since the start of the film. *I was right about her smile.*

Esther said nothing and kept walking, past the couple. Strangers. *What is there to say? What is there to tell? I know him inside out and he knows me the same. It's crazy but it's true. We'll walk as long as we can, like this. After, I'll get in a cab, go home and never see him again.*

However, when twilight had dissolved into night and Esther and Mac found themselves back on Spring Garden Road, seeming to have walked every paved path in the Gardens multiple times, mostly in silence, she knew she would have to see him again. Mac wanted to set up a time for them to meet the following day. Esther said no. Nothing about this could be planned.

"If it's meant to happen, it will happen," she said. "It's in God's hands." They hugged, she let him kiss her, she picked up a taxi from the stand outside the Lord Nelson Hotel and she was gone.

God must have been keeping a close eye on the couple over the next days because no plans were needed. Instead, wherever life took Esther while Morris was at work and Sarah was immobilized by her pregnancy, she ran into Mac: at the train station seeing off a navy cousin who had finally been demobilized, on a stroll through the Halifax Common, in the middle of Halifax Harbour on the Halifax-Dartmouth ferry. They even found each other back at the Capitol for one of the final screenings of *Anna*.

Esther never managed to get enough of Anna Leonowens. Ever since she had chanced on Margaret Landon's *Anna and the King of Siam* book in the weeks before she and Morris left Montreal for Halifax, she had been hooked on Anna's story, sharing it with Sarah, who became equally obsessed. Here was a woman who had defied convention to live the life *she* chose to live, not the life that was expected of her. Sure, she was forced into it by circumstance, widowed with a young son. That only seemed to spur her on. Then after her adventures in Siam were over, Anna found herself in Halifax, like Esther. Only not like Esther at all. Anna was the moving force behind the women's suffrage movement here and behind the creation of what was now the Nova Scotia College of Art. Anna was always true to her husband, the dashing officer who had died on a tiger hunt. And Esther? Esther gave up on her dreams of being an artist, instead marrying a man she was betraying, right here in Anna's Halifax.

Good Jewish girls don't.

When she said goodbye to Mac after that second *Anna* screening, she vowed she would never, ever see him again. Who knew what they had in common? She didn't. Always a talker — a chatterbox, Sadie always said, not kindly — Esther rarely spoke in Mac's presence. Nor did Mac say much to her. Neither appeared to be at all curious about the other. It was enough that they were together. Mostly, they simply held hands and walked.

Well, that would have to stop.

22

Esther pulled the day's *Herald* from her coat pocket. The headline read, "United Nations Votes to Establish in NYC; Rockefeller Donates 18 Manhattan Acres for New HQ."

"What does Morris say about this United Nations?" Sarah asked.

"He says it could be a good thing. A real good thing."

"Better than that farkakte League of Nations?"

"It couldn't be worse, he says."

"I suppose he should know."

They sat at a rickety wooden table in Sarah's tiny, cheerless kitchen, the swing rhythms of Kay Kyser and his Orchestra offering the sole bright note with a rendition of "Ole Buttermilk Sky." Sarah had moved the tabletop Philco onto the kitchen counter the previous week. Until then, it sat on the floor in a corner of the Kaplan living room, itself not much bigger or brighter than the Kaplan kitchen. But the springs in the hand-me-down sofa had come unsprung, and Sarah could no longer lift her growing bulk from it. She spent most of her time in the kitchen now.

If Morris and Esther's West End house wasn't any more spacious or better built, it was new, one of hundreds thrown up after 1940 to ease a wartime housing shortage that was only getting worse with the influx of returning soldiers. Victory homes, they were calling them. Even so, Sarah and Sammy were luckier than many. Their narrow, nineteenth-century row house was clean and structurally sound. Not everyone in Halifax could say the same.

"After all this time, you still don't know what Morris does over in his important government building?" Sarah asked. "By the harbor, right?"

"That's the one." Esther shrugged. "Who knows if he'll ever be able to tell me what he does."

"If he can't tell you, it's got to be important. If it's that important, he maybe did something to end this war. That's a good thing." Sarah refilled Esther's cup with weak coffee. "At least it's over. Maybe rationing will also be over soon, and I can stop pouring you coffee that looks like gray dishwater. Tastes like it, too, I bet. No sugar, today. Sorry."

"That's okay. I'm starting to get used to no sugar." She took a sip and grimaced. "Or not."

"Maybe with this United Nations, there will be no more wars?" Sarah sipped her glass of milk. "Feh," she said, making a face. She took another sip then pushed it away. "That's also a good thing, no?"

"Yes…maybe…I don't know. Without a war, Hitler would have killed more Jews than he did." Esther thought for a moment. "But Nate would be alive." She flattened the newspaper on the table with the heel of her palm. "I miss him, Sarah. Four years later and I still miss him."

"I know. He was a good kid."

Esther read the article and scanned the rest of the front page. Lots more United Nations news: about Siam being welcomed in and Spain being shut out, and about trusteeships in Africa. France had a new prime minister. A former premier of Alberta had died. The Chicago Bears had beat the New York Giants for the NFL Championship, and two players were said to have been bribed to fix the game. Through all that, all Esther could think about was her brother. "You know," she said, looking up from the paper, "this is a horrible thing to say and God will probably strike me dead when I say it—"

"You wish it was Manny not Nate who got killed at Dieppe."

Esther stared at her friend, speechless.

"Now God can strike me dead instead of you," Sarah continued, "and put me out of my misery." She rubbed her giant belly. "These Kaplan septuplets, or whatever's in there, they're gonna kill me."

"How did you know what I was thinking?" Esther asked.

"I know Manny. I knew Nate. I know you. Manny may be your brother, but he's no mensch. He's a— Well, never mind what he is. Now, Nate…Nate was a mensch."

Nate might have understood about Mac. Manny never could. Never would. He was almost as bad as Sadie, and that was saying a lot. Esther finished her coffee in thoughtful silence then picked up the paper to return it to her coat. That's when she remembered.

"Oy, what a dumkop," she cried. "I forgot the reason I came here, the reason I brought you this paper."

"What? What is it?"

Esther opened the newspaper to page three, waved it in front of Sarah's face, pointing to the headline.

> **Venerable Prince Street Art Gallery to Reopen**
> The Leonowens-Fyshe Gallery, closed since the outbreak of War, is set to open its doors again on New Year's Day, *The Herald* has learned. Renowned for decades across Canada for its traditional oils and watercolors, as well as for its family links to Halifax's own Anna Leonowens, the Leonowens-Fyshe has been shuttered since June 1941. At the time, owner Francis Fyshe told *The Herald* that with Canada engaged in a prolonged war, an exclusive art gallery was a "frivolous indulgence."
>
> The new owners have not identified themselves nor is there any indication whether they will maintain the Prince Street gallery's longstanding focus on classic masterpieces. However, major work underway on the building's interior suggests that major changes may be afoot for the venerable establishment.
>
> All that is known for certain is that the new owners plan to reestablish Mr. Fyshe's longstanding New Year's Day levee and will use that occasion for the gallery's grand reopening, January 1 at one o'clock in the afternoon.

Esther folded the newspaper neatly and set it down next to her coffee cup. "You'll come," she declared. "Today. Now. I can get us a taxi."

"How can we go? It isn't open. The newspaper says New Year's Day."

"New Year's Day will be too late. I'll be back in Montreal, thank

God. Maybe if we go now and knock on the door, they'll let us in to take a look."

"I can't. Look at me." Sarah lifted her feet. Her ankles were more than twice their normal size." I can barely make it across to go the bathroom every five minutes, and you want I should go traipsing all over Halifax? You know I would go if I could. I love Anna as much as you do. More, maybe."

"Please, Sarah," Esther begged. "You have to come with me. If you don't, I'll run into Mac again. I know I will. I always do. Wherever I go, there he is. I can't see him. I can't."

"Just go, Esther. You can't hide in your house forever."

"Only a few more weeks."

"You're going to stay inside under your bed the whole time?"

"If I have to."

"Does this man, this Mac, know you're leaving Halifax?"

Esther ignored the question. "You have to come. You heard what the article said. The gallery's named after Anna. *Leonowens*-Fyshe. It isn't far. It's around the corner from the Carleton. Near Anna's art college."

"I want to come. You know I do." Sarah tried to prize herself up, then collapsed helplessly back onto the chair.

"It's Anna," Esther pleaded.

Sarah shook her head sadly. "You'll have to come back and tell me about it."

23

The squat, two-story building on narrow, sunless Prince Street was tucked behind the Carleton Hotel like an afterthought. It looked nothing like an art gallery; more like the hotel's laundry annex. Only a discreet, yellow-on-burgundy sign hanging by the forbiddingly solid door identified it as the Leonowens-Fyshe Gallery. The building's mullioned bay window with its score of miniature, frosted panes was designed to let light in without revealing anything but a shadowy suggestion of what lay beyond it.

Esther tried the handle. It was locked. She jiggled it again, hoping someone inside might hear and open the door to investigate. Nothing. Then she noticed a tiny card next to a half-hidden doorbell: "Ring for Entry." She rang.

A long moment later, the door opened.

"You," Esther gasped.

"Me," Mac replied, breaking into a boyish grin. It had been nearly a month since he last ran into her. He had begun to fear he might never see her again.

The color drained from Esther's face. "What are you doing here?"

He stepped aside to let her pass. "Come inside and let me show you."

Esther ignored the warning alarm pounding in her head — or was that her heart? — and climbed the single step and over the threshold. She heard Mac close the door behind her, plunging the shadowy entryway into darkness, and felt his hand on the small of her back, pushing her toward a second door. He reached past her and pushed it open.

"Welcome to the new Leonowens-Fyshe Gallery," he said.

Esther stepped into a space two stories high topped by a series of pyramidal skylights. Bright theatrical lights focused on a series of unframed canvases, each a mass of luminous slashes and whorls. Most were already hung. By the far wall, one lay face up on the floor; a second leaned against a padded bench.

"This is brilliant," Mac gushed. "I mean you…here. How did you know I would be here today? No, of course you didn't know. You couldn't."

He leaned in toward her. She edged back a step.

"What are you doing here?" he asked, flustered by Esther's rebuff.

"I-I don't know," Esther stammered, still sensing the heat from his hand on her back, even though it wasn't there anymore."What are you doing here?"

"It's mine."

"The gallery?" she asked in amazement.

"The art."

"It's yours," she repeated dumbly, not fully taking in what he had said.

"Do you like it?"

Esther retrieved the *Herald* from her pocket and thrust it at him. "When I saw the name of the gallery, I had to come."

"Because of Anna."

Esther stepped away from Mac and closer to the paintings. The colors and shapes leapt out at her, almost as if they were alive. She could almost feel the heartbeat in each canvas, and her own heart raced to keep pace. There was nothing conventionally identifiable about what she was looking at, yet she knew exactly what she was seeing. She could feel it, and she could feel Mac in it.

"You could have waited until the grand opening," Mac said, breaking the spell.

"No," she said, her eyes remaining focused on the paintings. She offered no explanation.

Mac watched her, wondering what she was seeing. "Do you like them?" he asked again, not sure he wanted to hear her answer.

Suddenly, it hit her. Yes, Mac said the paintings were his. Yes, she sensed something of him in each one. Still, until this moment, her brain had failed to register the most significant fact of all: Mac was an artist. An *artist*. As crazy as that was, and it was crazier than crazy, his work was hanging in a gallery named after Anna. *Anna!* The room began to sway. She stumbled onto the bench, barely aware enough to avoid the painting it was supporting, certain she was about to faint. Something touched her knee. She squinted through the fog shrouding her vision and saw Mac's hand. He was sitting next to her. She didn't know whether to slide away or move closer. It didn't matter. She doubted that she could move if she wanted to.

"Are you all right?" Mac's voice sounded as though it was coming at her from a long way away.

Esther tilted her head and strained to hear.

"Esther? Queen Esther?"

Esther moved her mouth. Nothing came out.

He reached for her hand. "You need a cup of tea."

Tea? What is it with the British and their tea? Esther knew she needed something. It was not tea.

Ten minutes later, Esther was sipping a manhattan in the restaurant at the Carleton. Mac, nursing an Alpine lager, had chosen the cocktail for her and had chosen well. Esther didn't drink. To be clear, the old Esther didn't drink. This Esther experienced the alien concoction race through her body and was grateful for it. She was even more grateful that a table separated her from Mac. A plate of food sat untouched in front of her. Had she been hungry before she sat down, the four slices of an unidentifiable meat-like substance held in place by two slices of spongey white bread would have dulled her appetite. An identical serving sat by Mac, also ignored. Neither was hungry, but no liquor without food. That was the law. It didn't matter whether you ate the food, as long as you ordered it.

Esther only barely remembered Mac pulling her to her feet and half pushing her out of the gallery, up Prince Street, around the corner into the Carleton, down a long corridor, through a set of curtained French doors and down five steps into the restaurant.

"Do people really eat this drek?" She pushed her plate away, distastefully.

"You look cute when you wrinkle your nose."

"Don't, Mac. Please."

"I'm sorry."

"I shouldn't have come."

"Of course you should. You needed something that wasn't tea."

Esther picked up her cocktail glass and swirled the red liquid around before taking another sip. "Maybe."

"Look, I— Can we start again?"

"What do you mean?"

Smirking, Mac thrust his hand across the table. "Hi. My name is Marc-Allan Cameron. My friends call me Mac."

Esther took it, tentatively.

"I hope you'll call me Mac."

She giggled. "I'm Esther Freed." She tried to pull her hand free. Mac held on.

"I can't help myself," he said.

"What if someone I know were to come in? What if my husband were to come in and see us holding hands?"

"Does your husband ever come here?"

"No," she conceded.

"Do you know anyone else who comes here?"

"No," she replied again. She gave a tug and Mac released her hand.

"Did you know that this is the third-oldest building in Halifax?" he asked. "The other two are churches."

"What are you doing?"

"I'm making neutral conversation. Well, did you?"

"Did I what?"

"Know that you're sipping a cocktail in an important historic building."

Esther shrugged.

"It was built in 1760 by Richard Bulkeley," Mac continued. "He was some kind of high muck-a-muck here in the province before it became a province." He paused. "It became a hotel about a hundred years later." He paused again. "Did you know they expanded the building during the war? I hear it's much bigger than it used to be."

"Really?" Esther tried to stop herself from giggling at Mac's inanity. "I hadn't heard."

"Well, they did—"

"Stop!" Esther burst out laughing. "I give up. I surrender. We can talk about anything you want. Just stop with the boring history."

"What about a boring Scottish artist's history? Would that be more to your taste?"

Esther popped the maraschino cherry from her manhattan into her mouth. "Yes," she said. "I think it would."

For the next two hours, she and Mac talked nonstop, making up for all the words previously left unspoken.

Mac, Esther learned, was also inspired by Anna Leonowens, which was why when the war ended, he came to Halifax from his native Glasgow to study at the Nova Scotia College of Art. It was also why, like Esther, he was at the *Anna and the King of Siam* showing the day it opened and again the day it closed. As for the Leonowens-Fyshe Gallery, one of Mac's monied professors had snapped it up as a showcase for college students when Francis Fyshe died and the family decided to sell rather than reopen. Mac's work would inaugurate the gallery the day after his return from a family Christmas in Scotland. He would be leaving for the UK in less than a week.

Then it was Esther's turn. Fortified by her drink, she shared everything — her family, her less-than-successful marriage, her imminent return to Montreal and, in the end, Baron Byng and her frustrated-artist dreams.

"Did you know that there's an Anne Savage at the Nova Scotia Museum of Fine Art?"

He knows about Anne Savage?

"It has a Lismer, too. *Sunglow.* He painted it right before they made him principal of the art college."

Lismer was here? In Halifax? Miss Savage talked about him all the time. One of her greatest inspirations, she said. How come she never mentioned him being in Halifax at the art college? And he was the principal.

Esther's head was spinning, and it wasn't only the manhattan. It was as though all the ambitions and desires she thought she had left behind in Montreal, left behind for good, had followed her here. Now they stared at her with gold-flecked hazel eyes. She looked away. She had to or she would fall into those eyes and never be able to climb out.

"I-I have to go." She rose unsteadily, though whether from the manhattan or the conversation she couldn't be sure. Probably both. Mac was talking, but she couldn't hear him. Or maybe she didn't dare listen.

"Esther? Queen Esther?" Mac reached for her arm.

She dropped back into her seat and smiled weakly. "I think maybe it was easier when we didn't talk." She pushed herself up again. "I do have to go. Morris will be home soon."

"Will you meet me tomorrow? At the museum? We could look at the Savage and the Lismer, together."

Esther's eyes filled with tears. "I don't think I could face them. Especially Miss Savage. Not after—" She shook her head. "I know I couldn't."

"Why aren't you painting, Esther?" Mac asked so gently and lovingly that the tears she had been holding back started to flow.

Mac held her hands across the table and let her cry, saying nothing. After a few minutes she extricated her hands, retrieved a handkerchief from her purse and flagged the waiter.

"A tea, please."

"Sir?" The waiter looked inquiringly at Mac.

"For two."

"Yes, sir. Anything else?"

They shook their heads and sat in silence, slowly growing back into wordless comfort.

"Meet me tomorrow," he said fifteen minutes later as they passed through the lobby and out onto Argyle Street.

"Not at the museum," she said firmly. "I can't do that."

"I understand. Not at the museum."

They continued around the corner and stopped in front of the gallery. Prince Street was deserted.

"Back at the Public Gardens?" he offered.

"Closed for winter."

Where could they go? More important, where would Esther feel comfortable enough to meet? "We could go to the Capitol. Do you like Humphrey Bogart? *The Big Sleep* is playing."

"Not anymore. It closed on Sunday. *Shadow of a Woman* is playing now."

"And?"

"I saw it yesterday. It's the only movie I have ever walked out on. It was shreklekh."

"Shrek-what?"

Esther grinned. "Shreklekh. It means terrible, horrible, awful."

"I won't make you go back, then." *You aren't making this easy.* He strained for an idea, any idea that she couldn't shoot down. "What about Victoria Park. Across the street from the Public Gardens. It never closes."

"It's December. It's too cold for walking."

"The weather will be perfect tomorrow. I promise."

"You know that? How can you know? How can you promise me something like that?" Her tone was joking but her heart was pounding. "How can you promise me anything?" she wanted to shout. "Better you should promise me that if I snap my fingers you'll disappear and take Arthur Lismer, Anne Savage, Anna Leonowens and all of Halifax with you."

Mac smiled and his whole heart was in that smile. Esther mentally snapped her fingers. He didn't disappear.

"Didn't you know?" he asked. "God is an Englishman."

"And you're a Scot," she countered, grinning back at him in spite of herself. "Do you think he'll listen to you? Anyhow, God is not an Englishman. He's a Jew."

"Good. You have connections." He touched her cheek. "You'll see what you can do?"

"Fine," Esther sighed. "I'll see what I can do." She pulled his hand from her face, held it for a moment then let it go.

"Does that mean that you'll meet me?"

"It means I'll try."

"Three-thirty at Spring Garden Road and South Park Street? By the statue?"

"Three-thirty inside Murray's at the Lord Nelson." That was the safest place Esther could think of. Only the area's WASPy matrons frequented the hotel's coffeeshop on a weekday afternoon. No one she or Morris knew would likely see her there.

"That's in case God decides not to listen to either of us about the weather," she added. Esther spoke calmly, but butterflies had invaded her insides and her head felt like what she imagined it would be like to fly in an airplane: at the same time woozy, buzzing and throbbing. Fearing she might really faint this time, she reached for the building to steady herself. Mac took her arm and pulled her toward him. Their lips were inches apart when, gasping for air, she pushed herself free and half-staggered, half-ran back to the busyness of Argyle Street.

"No," she declared out loud when she turned the corner and both Mac and his gallery were out of view. "Good Jewish girls don't." She hurried up Argyle, away from the Carleton. Half a block later she stopped to catch her breath. To her right were City Hall and the military memorials of the Grand Parade; to her left— *Oh, no!* She had stopped in front of the Nova Scotia College of Art.

"No, no, no, no, no," she shouted. "Good Jewish girls *won't*."

24

"She didn't meet him?" Bernie asked. He threw another log onto the fire. As warm as the evening was, Sarah would not let the fire die out. Along with the faint glow from City Hall, the fire now cast the only light in the living room, and its flicker danced on their faces as they continued working through the bottle of Saint-Émilion.

"Almost," Sarah replied.

"Almost did or almost didn't?"

"Until the last minute, she couldn't decide. The minute Morris left the house the next morning, your mother had me on the phone. She was crying. So hard, she was crying.

"'I can't go,' she said. 'And I can't not go. What do I do, Sarah? What do I do?' Sammy was home, so I had to do more listening than talking."

"She went?"

"First, there was more drama, about what to wear and how to look. Should she dress pretty and look her best? Or should she dress like me?" Sarah laughed. "She was smart. She dressed pretty. Yes, she went."

"To meet Marc-Allan Cameron," Bernie said. "I still can't believe it was Marc-Allan Cameron…the same Marc-Allan Cameron."

Sarah stared into the fire and through the fire into the past — her past, Esther's past, Bernie's past. *So much more you won't believe, boychik. So much more.*

25

Esther sat alone in Murray's, at a table for two that offered all the unobstructed views she sought: of the windows overlooking Spring Garden Road, of the doors to both the street and the Lord Nelson lobby and of the brass-enclosed ship's clock that ticked away the minutes under a carved anchor set into the wall next to her. A mural of Lord Nelson addressing his men aboard the HMS *Victory* filled another wall, and naval knickknacks and Nelson memorabilia were scattered throughout the dining room.

She had arrived at three o'clock — a miracle, given all her fussing — and had ordered a traditional afternoon tea. That's what the other ladies in the dining room were drinking, affluent, self-important woman who were all a generation older than Esther. Not one was Jewish; she was certain of it.

Tea had been something to keep her occupied while she waited. Now, the china pot was cold despite the faded George VI coronation cozy that hugged it tightly. Next to it, her dainty, porcelain cup sat empty in its saucer, and the silver tray of cucumber and watercress sandwiches in the center of the table was limp and soggy. Each time Debbie approached in her blue button-up uniform and crisp white apron, Esther waved her away. She didn't want anything, except maybe to be a thousand miles away, and a twenty-year-old waitress couldn't help her with that.

Outside, the fog hung heavy, wet and gray over the December day, veiling all but the shadowy, raincoat-clad figures with their upturned collars scurrying past the window. Inside, Esther twisted the edge of the starched linen tablecloth with fingers that refused to be stilled, trying to banish from her mind the summer's hit parade sensation. It was playing on the Marconi as she had walked out the door, and the Perry Como in her head continued to refuse to be silenced.

Surrender, I beg you, surrender
How long can your heart resist?

Esther glanced at the clock. One minute to 3:30. Thirty seconds to 3:30. Fifteen seconds after 3:30. One minute past—

A cloaked figure carrying a shoulder satchel emerged damply from the gauzy gloom and pushed through the door. It tinkled gaily in sharp contrast to Esther's mood and the cast of the day. Debbie looked up. The ladies taking tea looked up. Everyone watched the handsome gentleman scan the room. At first he seemed not to find what he was seeking and the hopeful look melted from his eyes. Then he noticed the sad-eyed woman sitting by herself and beamed.

Lucky lady, Debbie thought, thinking of the tiny flat she shared with four other single girls. It's not that there was a lack of available young men in Halifax. More soldiers, seamen and airmen were being demobbed here every day. Still, you didn't often see one like this. There was something about him…not only his Hollywood looks but the way he carried himself. Self-assured yet not cocky. And sweet. Not puppy-dog sweet. Powerful-sweet, like a colt.

Debbie waited until the young man had hung his Mackintosh on a peg and pushed his seat closer to his companion before approaching.

"Can I get you anything, sir?" she asked in her flirtiest voice.

Mac touched the cold teapot and gazed with dismay at the sandwich tray. He smiled up at Debbie. "Take all this away, would you? And bring us fresh?"

"Of course, sir." Debbie smiled, bobbed the subtlest of curtsies and scurried off. When she had set the replacements on the table and moved nearly out of earshot, Mac retrieved a package wrapped in brown paper and string from his bag.

"I brought you something, Queen Esther," he said. "It isn't much, but it's the reason I was late." He handed her the package. "One of the reasons."

"Late? Thirty seconds is late?" All Esther's anxiety melted in Mac's presence, and for the first time that day she was happy. "Can I open it now?"

"Isn't that what you do with presents?"

"It depends who they're from," she replied, recalling the homely, unflattering outfits that Sadie always gave her. Morris had a bit more imagination when it came to gift-giving, but not much.

"What about when they're from me?" Mac asked.

"I don't know. This is the first." She hurriedly untied the string and ripped away the wrapping.

"Oh, Mac!" she cried. It was a pristine copy of Margaret Landon's *Anna and the King of Siam.*

"You told me that you never had your own copy."

"I told you that? When did I tell you that?"

"At the Capitol. While we were waiting for the movie to start."

"I don't remember," she confessed. "I don't remember much." Esther paused. "No, that isn't true. I remember everything, except what we said. That wasn't as important as...as everything else." She stroked the cover, wishing it was Mac's face she was touching, noticed what she was thinking and jerked her hand away. "Look at Anna's dress," she exclaimed instead, trying to conceal her emotion. "It looks like a pineapple."

"Open it, Queen Esther," Mac urged softly.

Torn between anticipation and trepidation, Esther opened the book. As she read the words, written on the flyleaf in a neat, cursive hand, Mac whispered under his breath. "To my Queen Esther: More regal than any monarch, wiser than the wisest schoolteacher, more beautiful than all the beauties in Siam, or anywhere. I love you. Mac. 18th December 1946. Halifax."

Esther must have said something. Mac must have responded. They must have continued to chat amicably over tea and sandwiches. They must have finished, paid, donned their coats and left. But like their conversation in the Capitol, Esther recalled none of it. Next she knew, she and Mac were walking through the mist, past the locked Public Gardens gate and into Victoria Park. *Anna and the King of Siam* was tucked safely inside her coat and Mac's arm was wrapped securely around her waist.

"Do you know Robert Burns?" he asked, stopping by a youthful statue of the Scottish poet, its bronze arms crossed, its bronze eyes gazing unblinkingly back toward the red-brick neo-Georgian hulk that was the Lord Nelson.

"My friend Sarah would know him better," Esther replied. "She's the big reader."

"O, my Love's like a red, red rose," Mac recited. "My Love's like the melody that's sweetly played in tune." He looked up at the statue then back at Esther. "Robbie Burns is writing about you, Queen Esther. For me."

Esther pulled Mac from the statue. "Roses have thorns," a part of her wanted to shout. "Yet they are incomparably beautiful," another part of her countered.

It's not that I don't love this man. I do. That's the problem. That's what terrifies me.

"I don't know what scares me more," she wished she could confess to Mac, "the rose petals or the thorns." Instead, she said nothing and clung more tightly to his hand.

As they did the day they first met, Esther and Mac walked in silence, this time back and forth along the narrow strip of Victoria Park. They passed Robert Burns a second time, then a third and fourth time, featherlike snowflakes dancing in the air around them. When they passed the statue a fifth time, daylight was starting to melt into dusk. Esther shivered.

"Are you cold?" Mac asked.

Esther nodded and hunched her shoulders. Mac hugged her closer to him and she felt his heat seep into her through the heavy cloth of her coat. Or was it her heat she felt, ignited, despite her resistance, by this stranger who was no stranger at all?

As if by silent agreement, they left the park and crossed the road back toward the Lord Nelson Hotel. If her feelings toward him had alarmed her earlier, now they calmed and fortified her. They walked purposefully up the tree-lined drive to the front door, where a liveried doorman ushered them in.

"You booked a room," Esther said matter-of-factly.

"A suite. Do you mind?"

"You know I can't stay the night."

"I know."

"I don't have to rush back, either. Morris is at a meeting. He won't be home until late."

"I wish you could stay forever. I wish you could be my Queen Esther forever."

So do I, Mac. So do I.

They passed through the richly paneled lobby with its massive chandeliers and gold-leaf ceiling, Esther's heels click-clacking on the shiny marble floor as they walked by the registration desk. A hopeful Mac had checked in earlier, overnight bag in hand, to save Esther any possible embarrassment.

"Seventh floor, please," Mac said to the aging, ruddy-faced elevator operator. Despite his naval blues and gold epaulets, he looked like he would have been more at home hauling nets on a Cape Islander than captaining a brass-doored lift in a luxury hotel.

Room 723 was at the end of plush, burgundy-carpeted corridor embellished with white-and-gold patterned wallpaper and hung with lacquer-framed mirrors. The doors were gold-trimmed ebony.

Mac inserted the brass key into the lock, pushed the door open and let Esther step past him into the sumptuous three-room suite.

"It's magnificent," Esther breathed. "Like a palace." She crossed the thick-piled rug to the sitting room's twin windows. The setting sun glinted against the light dusting of snow settling on the Public Gardens.

"A palace for a queen," Mac said, shutting the door.

Esther turned back to face him. That's when she noticed the three cut-glass vases filled with red-roses and the bottle of champagne chilling in a silver ice bucket next to two crystal flutes.

Mac pulled one of the roses from the vase and presented it to Esther. "My love's like a red, red rose," he repeated.

Esther closed her eyes and inhaled the sweet scent. "Mine, too," she murmured too softly for him to hear. "Mine, too."

Still clutching the rose, she explored every inch of each of the three rooms — increasingly incredulous at the suite's lavish extravagance. Morris's family had money, but not this kind.

"Is this the royal suite?" Esther called from the bathroom, marveling at its extra-large tub and gleaming fixtures.

Mac leaned in and kissed the back of her neck. "I couldn't get the royal suite. I tried. It's at the other end of this floor. Frederick Mathers lives in it."

Esther looked up questioningly.

"The old lieutenant governor. He's been there since 1942 when his term was up. They also told me that a judge used to live in this suite. Judge Rankin. He retired a few months ago and moved back to Cape Breton. That's why the other bedroom is more like a study.

They haven't converted it back. They're probably waiting for him to send for his books."

Esther poked her head into the second bedroom. There was no bed. Instead, a giant rolltop desk sat next to the window and bookcases crammed with leather-bound law volumes lined the walls. She pulled a hefty tome from the shelf and flipped through it. "It might as well be Greek," she said.

"Or Gaelic."

"Or that." She followed Mac back out to the sitting room.

"That's why there's a radio," he added. "Apparently, Judge Rankin loved his Canadian Broadcasting."

Esther switched on the Viking console and tuned the dial to 960. Marjorie Hughes backed by Frankie Carle and his Orchestra filled the room from the CHNS studios on nearby Tobin Street.

Rumors are flying
And I'm not denying
That people are sure I'm falling in love with you
'Cause for a change, darling
All the rumors are true

Esther blushed. She was accustomed to the restrained emotions of a distant father and frosty, mother-surrogate sister, not to the more effusive expression she witnessed in her friends' families. Morris, too, was controlled and undemonstrative. Mac, on the other hand, hid none of his feelings and never hesitated to act on any of them. Even as his declarations awakened in her a hunger for more, they overwhelmed and embarrassed her, mostly because she didn't know how to reciprocate.

Her discomfort deepened as one hit song segued into another.

A rose must remain with the sun and the rain
Or its lovely promise won't come true
To each his own, to each his own
And my own is you

Esther lowered the volume on Eddy Howard and his Orchestra and returned the rose to its vase. "This must have cost the world, Mac," she said after an awkward silence. "How did you pay for it? You're just an art student. Is there something you aren't telling me?"

"There is nothing I wouldn't tell you. All you have to do is ask." Mac pulled the champagne bottle from the ice bucket and wrapped it in a towel. "When my parents telegraphed money to get me to Scotland for the holidays, I asked for extra, as a Christmas present. I didn't tell them that you're my Christmas present. No, my Hanukkah present. It is the first night of Hanukkah, isn't it?" He pronounced it with the guttural kh.

Esther smiled. "You say that like a good yiddishe bocher."

"A what?"

"A good Jewish boy. The way you say the 'kh' in Hanukkah." She let the *kh* sound linger in her throat.

"I was a good Scots bairn who went fishing with his dadaidh." He pronounced it "daddy." "On the loch." He mimicked Esther's prolonged kh in "loch."

"At least *we* have our kh's in common," she said.

"We have much more in common than that." Mac pressed his thumbs against the champagne cork. It popped out with a sharp crack and flew across the room, as champagne overflowed onto the rug.

"Oh, no," Esther cried. "Let me clean it up." She started for the bathroom. Mac pulled her back.

"Didn't you know?" he asked as he filled the two champagne flutes. "Bubbles are good for carpets." He passed one of the flutes to Esther and clinked his glass against it. "Happy Hanukkah, Queen Esther."

"Now I know you aren't Jewish," she said after she took her first sip and felt the bubbles tickle her nose and the champagne warm her insides. She had never tasted champagne before.

"Why? Does it matter? What do you mean?"

"You have me in the wrong holiday." She giggled. "Queen Esther is Purim, not Hanukkah." She took another sip, then another and another. She could get used to this.

26

"I need some fresh air," Bernie gasped, wiping away the perspiration dripping down his neck. The air conditioner couldn't stay ahead of the fireplace. "More wine, too." He opened one of the windows and peered down toward the fenced-in lawn-bowling club across the street. "There are benches out there. Can we get in? With our wine?"

Sarah joined him at the window. "Not this time of day. Maybe not any time of day. I'm not a member. Can you see me with all those hoity-toity ladies? Can you see me lawn bowling?"

Bernie shut the window and positioned himself in front of the air conditioner, relishing the chill.

"We could try the roof," Sarah suggested. "Sometimes it's unlocked. No one is supposed to go up, but us old rebels like to break the rules sometimes." She slipped on a pair of shoes and draped a sweater over her shoulders while Bernie poured the last of the wine into two coffee cups.

They said nothing as they exited Sarah's apartment, climbed the back stairs and pushed against the door to the roof. It gave easily.

"Don't go too near the edge," the mother in Sarah warned.

Bernie chuckled. He leaned on the low parapet and let the light breeze riffle through his sweat-soaked shirt. Moist as it was on this sultry evening, the gentle whoosh of air felt refreshing after the stultifying heat of Sarah's living room.

Marc-Allan Cameron. How is it even possible?

Bernie wasn't sure he was ready to find out what happened next in that Halifax hotel suite. He wasn't sure he wanted to know. Instead, he asked, "Did Daddy ever find out about…?"

"I don't think so," she answered tentatively. "No, I'm sure not. Not about this or—" Sarah caught herself.

God help me, Esther, I have to tell him. Not right this minute. Please, not yet. Soon. I'll tell him soon.

"Your mother would never have told," Sarah continued, hoping Bernie had missed her hesitation. "Not Morris, not Gerry, not Harold. Not anyone."

"Only you?"

"Only me."

27

Esther lay in Mac's arms, the satiny sheets in knots at their feet. She had always been self-conscious about her nakedness; not now, not with Mac. At home, she would have made certain that the bedroom lights were switched off and that "the thing," as Morris euphemistically called it, happened in the dark. Here, she welcomed the soft glow created when Mac draped her black-and-gold silk scarf over one of the nightstand lamps. She was grateful to be able to see Mac as well as touch him, grateful, for the first time, to be both seen and touched.

"Was that how it's supposed to be?" she whispered into his neck.

Mac looked down at her anxiously. "I'm not sure I know how to answer. Was it that terrible?"

Esther smiled as she stroked his face, just as she had wanted to do at Murray's. Now she could. Soon she wouldn't be able to again. "No. I'm sorry. It's that…it's that…"

"Maybe this was a mistake." He tried to pull away. Esther stopped him.

"No, no. I've made lots of mistakes in my life, Mac. This was not one of them."

"You're sure?"

She snuggled closer and tilted her head up to meet his. "More sure than I have ever been, about anything." She leaned back, closed her eyes and again felt Mac's hands caressing her body, felt his lips where no one else's lips had ever been. She shuddered with remembered pleasure. "Thank you," she sighed.

"Why are you thanking me? I should be thanking you."

"Morris isn't very good at this. I didn't know that until now.

He's awkward, almost embarrassed. So I was aways embarrassed because he was. But this…you…"

"Were you embarrassed?"

"Only that I wasn't embarrassed…or ashamed. This…you and me…it's so wrong. It should feel wrong, but it doesn't."

"How can it be wrong when two people love each other? You do love me, don't you?"

"If that's what this is," Esther replied, "I've never felt it before. Why haven't I felt it before?"

"Because there was no you and me before now," Mac said. "Now there is."

"I'm married."

"It doesn't matter."

"How can it not matter?"

The Dinning Sisters' harmonies crackled on the radio, washing into the bedroom.

We'll meet again,

Don't know where, don't know when.

But I know we'll meet again some sunny day.

"We will, won't we?" Mac asked.

Esther said nothing. How could they? *In two weeks I will be on a train back to Montreal, for good, and Mac will already be in Scotland. He's coming back to Halifax. I'm not. I can't. Maybe not ever again.* She lay in Mac's arms happier than she had ever been, and sadder.

28

"We're just like a pair of regular English ladies," Sarah said, squirming to fit her growing bulk into the dainty chair. She lifted her pinky as she raised the delicate, art deco-trimmed floral teacup — over her head instead of to her mouth. "Aynsley," she said. "Not bad." She took a sip. "The tea's not so bad, either. At least it's full strength, not like the brown water I get to drink at home. You know," she continued, taking another sip, "we'll have to start going to Eaton's restaurant when we're both back in Montreal, now that we've become so English. The one up there on the ninth floor. That's where all the Westmount ladies go for tea after shopping."

Esther stared out the window, watching cars pull into the drive, some stopping to unload at the Canadian National Railway station next door, some continuing on to the Nova Scotian Hotel, where she and Sarah sat ensconced in a corner of its Ladies' Tea and Lounge Room. A piano tinkled subtly in another corner, accompanied by the soft susurrus of women's voices and the muted clinking of silver spoons against bone china. The third corner was occupied by a giant Kentia palm and the fourth by a tinsel- and garland-decked Christmas tree.

"Esther? Hello, Esther..." Sarah drummed her fingers on the table.

Esther turned away from the view — she would be getting out of one of those cars in less than two weeks. In front of the train station. "What?"

"You get me out of the house when I can barely move. You tell me it's a matter of life and death. You get me to meet you in this fancy schmancy hotel. Now that we're here, you ignore me. What's going on? Has something bad happened? Is Morris okay?"

Esther said nothing.

"Better it should be something good," Sarah continued. "You've got good news, maybe?"

Still, Esther said nothing.

The pianist took a drink of what looked like water but probably wasn't, shuffled his sheet music and started to play "We'll Meet Again."

"I hate that song," Esther said.

Sarah slammed down her cup. Tea sloshed into the saucer. The women at the next table glared at her. Had she been alone, Sarah would have stuck her tongue out at them, but she wasn't. She couldn't have been. She would never come to a place like this by herself. She wouldn't be here at all if Esther had not insisted.

"Esther Freed," she demanded, "what is going on with you?"

Esther's eyes glistened with tears.

"It's that Mac, isn't it?"

"He asked me to stay, here with him in Halifax. He wants me to leave Morris and," she blushed, "be his Queen Esther." Esther spoke softly, almost whispering. "He said he would get me a ticket to go with him on the *Queen Elizabeth* or he would cancel his trip so we could be together here."

"And you," Sarah asked, "what do you want?"

"I want to turn the clock back to before Morris. I want to have met Mac then." Esther gazed out the window again, past the hotel drive and into Cornwallis Park. Governor Edward Cornwallis stared back at her through the bare trees from atop his plinth, motionless as the statue he was. "If I can't have that," she added, "I want to turn the clock back to before *Anna and the King of Siam*, so I wouldn't have gone to the Capitol that day, so I would never have met him."

"I'll call H.G. Wells for you. We can borrow his contraption." Sarah pulled a copy of *The Time Machine* from her purse. There was always a book in her purse. "It's good. You should read it."

"I'm serious."

"I know you are. It's the babies talking. I don't know what's coming out of my mouth most of the time." She stuffed the book back into her bag.

"It's too hard." Esther wiped her eyes.

"I know. But H.G. Wells or no H.G. Wells, you can't go back in time. You can't change what was. You can only do what is, what's now. So what do you want now? Today."

Esther leaned in toward Sarah. "It's not what I want to do anymore. It's what I have to do." She inhaled sharply. "I'm going to have a baby, Sarah."

"You know for sure?"

"Not for sure, but I know. I just know."

"Me, too, I knew," Sarah said. "That farkakte doctor wouldn't believe me when I told him. He wouldn't even test me. I was right, though. He called it a lucky guess. The dumkop. He still wants me to believe I'm only having one. Look at me." She patted her belly. "There's an army in there. So I believe you. It's good news, right?"

But Esther didn't look happy. Sarah could tell that something was troubling her. "The baby. Is it—?"

"It's Morris's," Esther interrupted, a little too insistently. "It has to be. Even if it isn't, it has to be."

Two months later, Esther was no longer pregnant. Climbing the icy steps to their new Montreal apartment building, she slipped and tumbled to the unforgiving pavement.

The doctors said she would never have another child.

29

His mother had an affair, in Nova Scotia of all places. And a miscarriage. Bernie would never have expected her to confess to cheating on his father. But the older sibling he might have had? He wished he could have known about that. Esther spoke little about those few years in Halifax…or about any other part of her past. Whatever Bernie would ask — about the grandmothers he never knew, about Esther's childhood, about Baron Byng and Clark Street, about his Uncle Nate — Esther would shake her head and reply, "It was a long time ago, sweetie. What can matter from so long ago?" After that, she would try to satisfy him with the tiniest insignificant morsel of information and change the subject.

With Halifax, there weren't even morsels. "I wish we had never gone," she would always say, "but we had to go because of your father's job with the government. It was the war. We had no choice." Then with a finality that brooked no followup, "I was glad to get back here. So glad."

"I know she said it wasn't, but was it Mac's?" Bernie asked. "The baby, I mean."

Sarah shrugged. "Maybe. Who knows? It doesn't matter now."

"It does. To me it does."

Sarah looked at Bernie. So tired he looked, like he had aged ten years in this one day. *And there's more. Oy, is there more.* She patted his arm. "I think yes, Bernie. Probably, it was."

Bernie drained the last of his wine, returned to the parapet and stared eastward. The rotating beacon on top of downtown's Place Ville-Marie office tower wheeled around to meet him and he followed its counterclockwise circuit half a revolution until it pointed past Sarah and Esther's old neighborhood and all the way through Quebec, Maine and New Brunswick to Nova Scotia — to the Halifax of Anna Leonowens, Esther Freed, Marc-Allan Cameron and Erik Donnekin.

"I can't believe that this man my mother fell in love with — had an affair with, for God's sake — is the same college art professor that this random artist guy I met tonight studied with in Halifax."

"Maybe not so random," Sarah muttered, half to herself. Aloud, she said, "Carl Jung would have called it synchronicity."

"Meaningful coincidence."

"You know Carl Jung?"

"Bits and pieces." He turned his back on the view. "If any of what has happened today has meaning, God knows what it is. I don't."

"Are you so sure?"

"Not about anything. Not anymore. Maybe I never was." He retrieved his coffee cup. "Are you ready to go back down?"

"Will you call him?" Sarah pushed herself up.

"Who?"

"This random artist boy of yours."

"He isn't mine. And why would I call him?"

"This is Sarah you're talking to. Maybe I don't know from abstract art in a fancy Westmount gallery, but I do know from life. And I know that look."

"What look?"

"That faraway, sick-puppy look you get when you talk about, about…what's his name?"

"Uh, Erik."

"There, you have it again. All you have to do is say his name. It's the same look Esther got when she would talk about Mac."

"Did she talk about him a lot?"

"Not after she left Halifax. Not for a long time after that. Not until Morris died."

Bernie checked his watch as Sarah fumbled with her key. It was nearly midnight.

"You'll stay the night," Sarah said. It wasn't a question.

Even with a cab, Bernie knew that he would not get to bed until well after one. And he was sure that for all her surface devoutness, Auntie

Sadie would have broken shiva long enough to fill his answering machine with increasingly intemperate messages about why he had walked out of the funeral and never turned up at Manny and Dora's.

"There's a sofa bed in the den with fresh linens and there are clean towels in the guest bathroom. I can find you a toothbrush, too, maybe." Sarah shut the door and bustled down the hall. Bernie could hear her poking about in one closet after another. "Ha!" she exclaimed waving a new toothbrush and fresh tube of toothpaste in one hand and a pair of striped pajamas in the other.

"Do you have a boyfriend you aren't telling me about?" Bernie teased.

"Don't be smart. They're Jack's. God knows why I keep them. It isn't like he's going to drop down from heaven some night looking for them." She held the pants up against Bernie's waist. "They're too big in the middle and too short in the legs, like Jack was. So they'll fit on you funny. But a little funny today couldn't hurt."

Bernie took the pajamas.

"Is there anything else you need? A glass of water, maybe, for by your bed?"

"No, I'm good. Thank you, Sarah." He hugged her tightly. "I wouldn't have gotten through today without you."

"Me, too." She stood on tiptoes to kiss him on the cheek. "It's been a day, hasn't it, boychik?"

"It has." He started for the den then turned back. "I'm glad she didn't," he said.

"You're glad who didn't do what?"

"Mom. I'm glad she didn't leave Daddy for Mac."

"Because?"

"Because if she had, we wouldn't be having this conversation."

"I don't understand."

"If she had left Daddy, there would be no me."

Oy. Sarah sighed, loudly. "How tired are you, Bernele?"

"Exhausted. You must be, too. Why?"

"It doesn't matter about me." Sarah lowered herself into one of the armchairs. "Put all that down, get the bottle of Carmel from the fridge and two clean glasses. It isn't your fancy Saint-Émilion, but you're going to want it. There's another story I have to tell you, and it can't wait until morning."

30

"There are some chocolates in the pantry, too," Sarah called after Bernie. "A box of Laura Secord miniatures I've been trying not to eat. Next to the cereal."

Bernie opened the wine then excavated through the chaotic accumulation that was Sarah's food stock. "Got it," he shouted.

"Good." *Those I'm going to need more than the wine. And, boy, am I going to need the wine.*

Sarah pushed the papers cluttering the coffee table onto the floor.

"Are you really going to go through all those papers?" Bernie set down the bottle, glasses and unopened box of chocolates.

"Feh." Sarah flicked her wrist at the papers and sank into the chair, closing her eyes. Her face looked troubled.

"What is it?" Bernie pushed a wine glass into Sarah's hand. "What's so terrible that you need wine and chocolate and have to keep me up past my bedtime?"

Sarah opened her eyes and sat up.

"It's about Mac, isn't it. About Mom and Mac."

Sarah gripped the glass tightly and took a long sip. "I've been trying all day to not tell you this story. Believe me, it isn't a story I want to tell…" She looked up at the ceiling. "Am I doing the right thing, Esther?"

Bernie followed her gaze, half-expecting to see his mother perched, *Bewitched*-like, up in the corner. All he saw was a giant cobweb. Sarah saw it, too.

"You already know I'm the world's worst balabusta, Bernie. What I hope I'm being is the world's best friend to your mother by telling you this. Maybe to you, too." Sarah kicked at the pile of papers by her feet until a leather-handled, stiletto-like letter opener emerged. "Open the chocolates," she ordered.

Bernie sliced open the cellophane, opened the box and held it out to Sarah. With much deliberation, she picked three — a lemon cream, a caramel and a raspberry cream. She pushed the box away and bit into the lemon cream. "Your mother's favorite." She swallowed the rest and looked at the handful of embers in the grate. "Maybe we should light another fire?"

"No fire, Sarah. Just tell me the story. Whatever it is. How bad can it be?"

How bad can it be? Bad enough. Sarah took a gulp of wine. *Or maybe if we're all lucky, not bad at all?*

"It was also an August day, like this one," Sarah began. "Hot, sticky and overcast. You ask me how I remember from twenty-eight years ago? I remember everything about that day. Like it was yesterday, I remember. I even remember what I was wearing. Your mother was supposed to maybe come with me to the Anne Savage art opening at the YWCA that afternoon, and I was supposed to go downtown with her in the morning, to the movie. It didn't work out that way. None of it did."

"The movie?"

"The other Anna movie. *The King and I.* It opened— It's after midnight, yes?"

Bernie nodded.

"It's August 10 now?"

"Uh-huh," Bernie replied tentatively.

Sarah looked up at the ceiling again. "What are you telling me, Esther? You're saying that it's right? That I should go ahead? That I should tell him?"

Now, Bernie was certain that Sarah was crazy. At best, she had drunk too much wine. He knew he had. He started to get up. He would slip off to bed. Sarah would never notice.

She noticed.

"Sit down, Bernie."

He sat.

"I'm not crazy. I know you think I'm meshugena, talking to your dead mother like this. You see, I need her permission to tell you what I think I have to tell you. You'll understand when you hear. I have it now, I think. Her permission." She closed her eyes for a moment. "With the dates lining up like this, I'm sure I do."

31

Esther had planned to get to the Palace Theatre in time for the premiere showing at 9:15. But first Morris was late leaving for work, then she missed her bus. By the time she stepped off the No. 65 at Phillips Square, it was nearly ten. Better to wait a few hours for the next screening than risk walking in after the feature had begun. As anxious as she was to see the movie, there was really no rush. She had the whole day to herself. *Who knows? I might even sit through it twice.*

From Phillips Square and its army of brazen scavenger pigeons, Esther wandered over to Morgan's and Eaton's, stopping to linger in front of the department stores' display windows and admire the latest fall fashions. A smart, chenille two-piece caught her eye. Rose red. Sarah was always trying to get her to wear brighter colors. This was perfect: bright, but not too bright. And that elegant clutch-style coat. She loved its broad, shawl collars, perfect for turning up during cold, blustery weather. Wool, she guessed. Warm, too. Not cheap cloth. No more cloth coats for her since Morris's promotion. And she did need a new coat for the winter. Did she have time to go inside for a closer look? Maybe try something on? Esther looked at her watch. Not now. Maybe after the movie she could come back to do some real shopping. There was time for coffee now, though. She crossed the street to Kresge's and installed herself on a stool at the lunch counter.

If Kresge's was quiet at this hour, St. Catherine Street was not. Day or night, the two-way flow of traffic and pedestrians along Montreal's main shopping thoroughfare never seemed to wane. She could almost be watching a movie, looking out the Kresge's window. Most secretaries and businessmen had settled into their office buildings by now, although a few stragglers still hurried past. But the army of early morning shoppers was already marching on the department stores and specialty shops. Then there were the college students: The more serious-looking ones would be trooping a few blocks north to McGill; the more casual would be ambling westward toward Sir George Williams.

As much as she enjoyed observing the passersby, Esther loved to watch the streetcars. They reminded her of what she liked to think were the simpler times of her childhood, even though she knew they were not simpler at all. So many of the city streetcars had already been replaced by quieter diesel buses and trolleybuses, but St. Catherine Street had kept its clackety tracks and clanging bells, both of which made the street seem more vibrant still. Not that it needed any help. Stores, offices, restaurants, nightclubs, taverns, even churches: They were all here. Whatever you were looking for, whenever you were looking for it, you could find it on St. Catherine Street. At least that's what people said. Esther had never been on St. Catherine Street before dawn or after midnight to find out for herself. Good Jewish girls were home in bed at that hour.

The Kresge's waitress topped up her coffee while Esther eyed the fresh pies in the case. Maybe she would walk the few blocks to Laura Secord after the movie and pick up some chocolates. Pie was almost as good as chocolate. Almost. Sarah was always teasing her about her insatiable craving for chocolate. It was true. She could rarely pass a Laura Secord without going in to buy a box of miniatures, and once she did it was hard for her not to eat half the box in a single sitting. Sarah wasn't much better. That was okay for Sarah. She never had a figure to worry about. *If I don't stop with the chocolate, I'll lose mine, then no chenille two-piece for me. No. No Laura Secord today.*

Why was Sarah not here with her? What with the pregnancy, Sarah had never made it to *Anna and the King of Siam*. Now, it looked like she would miss another *Anna* movie. She was supposed to come but had called early that morning to cancel. All she said was, "Something's come up. Go without me." She hung up before Esther could argue.

A streetcar clattered by. Soon they would all be gone, Montreal's streetcars: Another piece of Esther's past dumped into the garbage can of history. Well, she could think of a few pieces of her past that belonged there. Some, like her time in Halifax, should be more than trashed. They should be incinerated and their ashes scattered somewhere far away. Like South America or the Arctic Circle.

Esther glanced across the street to the theater. *"The King and I* in Cinemascope 55!" the Palace marquee screamed. "Deborah Kerr. Yul Brynner." She could hardly wait to see what Rodgers and Hammerstein had done with the Anna story after *Carousel,* which she had seen at the Palace a few months earlier and loved. She had almost seen Yul Brynner as the King on stage in 1954, on Broadway. Unfortunately, Morris's business trip was postponed at the last minute, and by the time they made it to New York, Yul Brynner had left, taking *The King and I* with him.

It was getting close to showtime, and the line in front of the theater quickly began to swell. Esther dropped three quarters onto the counter and left Kresge's. At the corner, she waited until the white-capped policeman directing traffic whistled the all-clear for her to cross. Then she stepped carefully over the tracks and exposed cobblestone, past the waiting No. 15 streetcars, one on either side of her, and hurriedly joined the movie queue, where she crashed clumsily into a tall, casually dressed man arriving at the same time.

She knew who it was before she saw his face.

"Esther? Queen Esther?"

Mac had barely changed. His hair was a little thinner and some of his auburn curls had begun to silver, but his eyes were as bright as ever, and a decade later his smile was as heart-stoppingly dangerous as ever.

"No. Yes. I have to go." She did have to go. She couldn't stay. She could see *The King and I* another day. Or not ever, if that was the only way to be sure that she would never run into Mac again. Yet when she tried to leave and discovered that Mac's hand was already on her arm, the old electricity surged through her. She couldn't move.

"Why are you here?" She tried to ask it casually, but the words emerged as a hoarse accusation. Suddenly, Esther was back in Halifax, back in front of the Capitol Theatre, experiencing the same depth of emotion for this man that she had sworn she would never feel for him again, feelings she had intentionally left on the platform when the *Ocean Limited* chugged out of Halifax station on the last day of 1946.

Mac jerked his head toward the marquee. "Same reason as you."

Esther shook her head, as much to try clear it as to indicate that that wasn't what she meant. "No. Why are you in Montreal?"

The line started to move. Mac guided her forward, still holding her arm, gently but firmly. Esther moved like an automaton. She felt trapped — by a past that she thought she had escaped and inside a present that terrified her. She willed her hand to open her purse so that Mac couldn't pay for her ticket, again. Like the last time, though, her hand wouldn't cooperate, couldn't act independently, any more than the rest of her body could. Once inside, they climbed the grand staircase to the balcony and for a moment Esther was convinced that it was 1946 all over again, that this was the Capitol and that it was *Anna and the King of Siam* she was seeing…they were seeing.

"For Anne Savage's one-woman show, at the YWCA," Mac said once they had settled into the centermost seats in the front row of the balcony.

"What?" Esther wasn't sure where she was, or when she was. And her mind failed to grasp what Miss Savage could have to do with any of it.

"Why I'm in Montreal."

"Oh." Esther shook her head again, but past stuck to present as though they were glued tightly together. "Yes."

"Did you know about it?"

Esther looked at him stupidly. She felt stupid.

"The Anne Savage show," he said gently.

"Yes. No. I-I don't know." Esther didn't know anymore what she knew or didn't know. Anne Savage? A show at the YWCA? Did she know? She honestly couldn't remember. It was all too much. This was all too much.

"You never said goodbye," Mac said softly as the lights slowly dimmed.

"You were in Scotland," Esther shot back, knowing that that was not what he meant.

Once she had realized that she could not leave Morris, Esther rarely stepped out of the house until she was certain that Mac was safely on his way to Glasgow. She couldn't risk running into him.

Mac leaned forward onto the balcony rail and stared down into the auditorium, unsuccessfully feigning indifference as he studied the shadowy last-minute moviegoers filing into the plush red seats below.

"I'm sorry," Esther said, allowing herself to look directly at him for the first time. It was safe now, with his back to her and the light fading. "It was wrong, I know. I couldn't. I was afraid…"

Mac leaned back into his seat and touched her cheek. "What about now?"

"Now I'm more afraid."

"The vernissage is at five this afternoon, for Anne Savage's show. Will you come with me?"

"With you?" Even as she heard herself silently crying, "Yes, yes. Of course. Anywhere, anytime," the words she spoke were different. "You know I can't," she said.

He looked at her ring. "Still?"

She nodded. "You? Did you ever…?"

"There was always and only one queen for me."

The theater darkened, the heavy scarlet curtain parted and once again, the Twentieth Century-Fox drumroll, fanfare and search-lights filled the screen, this time in DeLuxe color. Mac reached for Esther's hand. She didn't resist.

Two hours later, Esther realized that she was clutching Mac's sopping handkerchief and that she had barely stopped weeping all the way through the movie. She sobbed when the Siamese children marched in — for the child she had almost borne and for the children she now could not bear. She sobbed when Anna sang of her great love for her husband — for the great love she could never feel for Morris. She sobbed at Tuptim's unrequited passion — for the passion she continued to feel for this man sitting next to her, a passion as impossible as Tuptim's. She sobbed when Anna and the King flung themselves across the palace floor in the wild, polka abandon of "Shall We Dance," knowing that she had closed the door on such wild abandon a decade earlier. She was still sobbing at the death of the King — at her unrealized potential as much as at his.

Mac and Esther neither moved nor spoke as the lights came back on and the theater emptied then started to refill for the next showing. Only when the lights again began to dim did they stand and in a further replay of another time, descend to the street and begin to walk hand-in-hand, saying nothing. Three blocks later they turned south toward the trees, grass and relative calm of Dominion Square and to a bench under the watchful gaze of another Robert Burns.

"O, my Love's like a red, red rose," Mac recited again, gazing from statue to Esther.

"Don't." Esther pulled her hand free and stood. "The best laid schemes o' mice an' men gang aft agley," she countered. "I've been reading my Burns." She strode away.

Mac followed after her. "They don't have to," he said. He reached for her hand. She hesitated before reluctantly letting him take it.

"It's too late," she said.

"You're wrong, Queen Esther. It's never too late."

She said nothing. What was there to say? That she wished she could have stayed with him in Halifax all those years ago? That she wished she was the sort of person who could have stayed with him in Halifax all those years ago? That, whatever he thought, it was too late? If it had been too late a decade ago, it was certainly too late now.

They continued walking in silence, past the square's other statuary tributes — to the Montrealers killed in the Boer War, to the country's first French Canadian prime minister, to Queen Victoria's Diamond Jubilee.

"Are you hungry?" Mac asked after a while.

She was, she realized.

"For old time's sake?" he asked, pointing across Dorchester Boulevard to the sky-scraping art moderne Laurentian Hotel and its street-level Murray's restaurant.

Esther had never been inside a Montreal Murray's, even though this was where the chain was headquartered and had most of its outlets. She had purposefully avoided the restaurant since her return from Halifax. Now, in the ongoing replay of a past she had tried so desperately to leave behind, she followed Mac through the trademark revolving door and into the dining room. Instead of naval memorabilia, Murray's in the Laurentian Hotel sported murals depicting Montreal's three hundred-year history and, in keeping with the streamlined look of the hotel, a more contemporary flavor. In most other respects it was eerily identical to the Halifax Murray's, from its dark-stained chairs and paneling to the bow-tied, blue-and-white uniforms of its waitresses.

Esther and Mac ate in silence surrounded by the gentle backwash of late lunchtime conversation — a club sandwich (rebelliously, with bacon) and coffee for her and a cheeseburger and tea for him. Then in yet another replay of that other time and place, Esther followed Mac into the hotel's sleekly modern lobby and up the self-service elevator to the sixteenth floor, whistling under her breath to convince herself that, like the Anna of *The King and I,* she wasn't afraid.

Room 1612 was not a luxury suite, nor were roses or champagne flutes waiting for her. It didn't matter. There was Mac.

The afternoon flew by in a tsunami of uncontrolled passion. It did not seem possible to either of them that their lovemaking could be more overpowering than it had been in that other hotel room all those years before. It was. Esther could rationalize that it wouldn't take much to eclipse Morris's attentions, which had grown increasingly rare and indifferent once her miscarriage destroyed his parental ambitions. She knew different. Never had she achieved orgasm three times in two and a half hours, and in perfect sync with her partner. Never had she experienced such ecstasy and release. Never had she wept so intensely. And as she collapsed into Mac's arms after their third climax, she knew utterly and irrefutably that what could not be possible absolutely was: Despite what the doctors had proclaimed a decade earlier, she would have a child. This child had just now begun its journey to life. This child was Mac's.

32

"That child, Bernie, was you."

Sarah's voice was almost a whisper, but to Bernie it was as loud as the trumpets at Jericho, with similar repercussions. He stood shakily and staggered to the window deaf to whatever else Sarah was saying, bombarded by a barrage of conflicting thoughts, questions and emotions.

Why did he care so much? He had barely known his father…the man he thought was his father. Morris died when he was six. That didn't matter. What mattered is that Morris lay at the root of everything he thought he was. He even worked for the federal government, he realized, because that's what his father had done, if more successfully than Bernie had ever managed.

And now? When Bernie had climbed out of bed that morning, it was with no plan other than to bury his mother, launch his week-long obligation as son-in-mourning, then get back to his life. He had known then who and what he was: dutiful, responsible and conventional, predictable, straitlaced and, well, straight. Maybe a bit boring. Comfortably boring.

Now, eighteen hours later, that certainty was in tatters. His identity was in tatters. How could it not be when his mother was a stranger, and a stranger was his father? How could it not be when it turned out that nothing about the past twenty-seven years was true, when everything that had brought him to this moment was a lie? He was no longer a civil service accountant. He was no longer a heterosexual. He was no longer his father's son. Who was he if he wasn't any of those things? Who was he if he wasn't who he thought he was? Who was Bernard Marc Freed anyway? *Marc? Oh, my God. Not only Marc Chagall; Marc-Allan. Marc-Allan Cameron.*

"Bernie?" Sarah started toward him then faltered. Had she made a mistake? *Esther?*

Again, the rotating beacon on the roof of downtown's Place Ville-Marie caught Bernie's eye. This time, it picked out all the things that had disappeared: Baron Byng, no longer a high school; Anne Savage, no longer alive; the Laurentian Hotel, now a vacant lot; the Palace Theatre, now a cookie-cutter multiplex; Bernard Marc Freed, now an empty shell. Only Dominion Square's Robbie Burns remained, somewhere out there in the impenetrable darkness of a nightmare night, a reminder that everyone's best-laid schemes were most certainly doomed.

Sarah took Bernie's arm and led him back to the sofa. She refilled his glass and pressed it into his hand. Then she poured another for herself. There was more story to tell.

33

Esther studied her reflection in the bathroom mirror. This was not the same woman who had freshened up before joining Mac in bed all those hours ago. Of course she expected to be flushed after a marathon of lovemaking. This was different. She touched her cheek. It was damp and warm, almost feverish, subtler than the high color of physical exertion. She doubted whether anyone else would notice. Well, maybe, Mac would. And Sarah. Sarah would notice.

Esther splashed cold water on her face and patted it dry. Although paler now after the water, her face still bore an almost otherworldly luminescence. Sarah and other of her friends had taken on that glow everyone talked about getting while they were pregnant. This couldn't be it; she was minutes pregnant, not weeks or months.

Whatever it was, she was certain of one thing: She would carry this baby to term, and it would be a boy. It made no sense that she could know this but she did, with more certainty than she had known anything. Ever. She knew, too, more than anything else, that she had to get home. She dressed, ran her fingers through her hair and reapplied her makeup.

"Now, will you come with me to see Anne Savage?" Mac called to her through the bathroom door. When it opened and Esther emerged fully dressed, Mac's face fell. "You're leaving me again, aren't you, Queen Esther?"

He looked like an abandoned puppy and Esther's heart broke, as much for herself as for him. "I have to go, Mac. You know I do."

"Will I see you again?" he asked with whatever optimism he could muster. "My train isn't until Sunday." He wasn't sure whether to say what he was thinking. "I was hoping…" Did he dare say it? He had to. "I was hoping you would be on it with me."

Esther sat on the edge of the bed, left hand folded over right on her lap. She gazed out the window to the sky over Dominion Square, wondering whether, if she looked hard enough, she could see all the way east to Halifax and whether, if she looked harder, she could see back into the past. What would have happened had she chosen differently ten years ago? Could she choose differently now?

Mac slid up behind her and kissed her neck. Esther turned and threw her arms around him, resting her head on his shoulder. She felt his heart pounding through her dress and tears soaked her face. She pulled back so she could see his eyes, also wet with tears. "You will never know," she said, her voice trembling, "all the gifts you have given me. You will never know how grateful I am…how grateful I will always be."

"Then—"

Esther touched her finger to his lips. *If you only knew how much I want to stay. If you only knew how much I wish I could go with you. If you only knew how much I love you.* She stroked his cheek, stood up and, not daring to look back, walked out of Room 1612.

Ten minutes later, Esther was hiding in a stall in the ground floor ladies' room of the Simpson's department store a few blocks away, trying to stifle her wracking sobs.

"Are you okay in there?" A woman's voice and a sharp rap on the stall door.

Esther swallowed hard. "Yes, thank you," she choked out.

"Are you sure?" The voice didn't sound convinced.

"Yes. Really. I'm fine."

Esther held her breath until the restroom door slammed shut. When she tried to get up, the flood of tears returned, more forcefully than before.

Finally, when she had no tears left and could compose herself, she washed her face, touched up her makeup and smoothed her dress. Then she took the elevator to the fifth floor.

When the doors opened to The Platters singing "My Prayer," she almost couldn't get out.

My prayer is to linger with you
At the end of the day in a dream that's divine

Biting her lip to keep from crying again, she forced herself to follow the music to the record department and its movie-soundtrack bin. Then with *The King and I* tucked in a paper bag under her arm, she returned to the ground floor and picked out the most revealingly alluring lingerie she could find.

Tonight, she would seduce Morris.

34

"You have to realize," Sarah said, "that you were a miracle child." The bottle of Carmel was empty, as was the box of chocolates. Sarah and Bernie now drank coffee, a muddy instant brew whose only purpose was to keep them both awake and that was rendered drinkable only when heaping spoons of sugar were stirred into it. "Esther wanted so badly to have children," she continued, watching Bernie closely. Whatever he was thinking, he wasn't showing it. "When she lost that first baby, she was heartbroken, a wreck. She didn't leave the house for weeks. She wouldn't eat. She couldn't sleep. All she did was cry and cry and cry.

"She gave up her art and always said it was too late to get it back. After that, she gave up the only man she ever really loved and said it was too late to get him back. Then she lost her only child and was told she could never have another.

"Morris thought maybe they should adopt. She refused. Later, when she thought she might be ready for adoption, Morris wasn't interested anymore. All her friends had children. She had nothing. Until *The King and I*. Until Mac."

"Mom always called me her miracle child," Bernie said, staring into his coffee cup. "I never knew why."

"Now you know."

He looked up. "A whole lot more than that."

"Are you sorry I told you?"

"No. Of course not," he replied unconvincingly.

"So you see, there would have been a you, even if your mother had run off with Mac." She paused, waiting for a response. None came. "Now, Mac has come into your life, because of this random artist boy, like you called him. This Erik. Now that's a nes, a miracle."

Was it a miracle? Bernie didn't know. Whatever it was, it was certainly freaky. "Does Mac know about me?" he asked.

"After that day, your mother never saw him again. Never spoke to him again. So, no. How could he? She didn't forget about him, though. I know that."

"How? How do you know that?"

Sarah tried to push herself out of the armchair. "Help me up." Before Bernie could move, she dropped back down again. *Too much wine and not enough sleep.* "Never mind. I don't know if I can even walk." She waved toward the den. "There's an old Birks box on the top shelf in the closet. Don't open it. Just bring it here."

The familiar blue box from Montreal's premier jeweler was where Sarah said it would be. Bernie resisted the temptation to peek inside and carried it back to the living room.

"When your mother knew she was going into the hospital, maybe for the last time, she asked me to look after this. She didn't want Sadie poking around and maybe finding it."

Sarah lifted the lid with great tenderness. Individually wrapped in pink tissue were *The King and I* soundtrack album, its cardboard frayed from frequent handling, sealed VHS recordings of *Anna and the King of Siam* and *The King and I*, and a yellowing *Weekend* magazine feature profiling Canada's brilliant new abstract artist, Marc-Allan Cameron, complete with pictures of him and of several of his canvases. Wrapped in a black-and-gold silk scarf at the bottom was a pristine copy of a book: *Anna and the King of Siam.*

Bernie opened the book. "To my Queen Esther," he read aloud. "More regal than any monarch, wiser than the wisest schoolteacher, more beautiful than all the beauties in Siam, or anywhere. I love you. Mac." He tried to imagine the woman those words were written for that day in 1946, tried to imagine the man who wrote them.

"Did you ever meet him?" Bernie asked.

"Meet him? No. I saw him, that night, though. At the YWCA."

"You went to the art show, not to the movie? How come?"

Sarah picked up the picture of Jack and addressed it instead of Bernie. "Sammy stopped me from leaving the house. He hid my wallet and purse, so I had no money for carfare, let alone a movie."

Bernie said nothing until Sarah put the photo back down. "I'm sorry," he said.

"It was a long time ago." She picked up her coffee cup. It was empty. "Get me a glass of water, would you, Bernie? Please?"

When Bernie returned with two glasses, Sarah drank hers all the way down. Then she drank his, too. She sighed and continued her story. "I looked all morning for that wallet. If I hadn't found it I might have walked the whole way downtown, that's how bad I wanted to go to Miss Savage's opening. I swore that Sammy wouldn't stop me twice in one day.

"After he went out, I eventually found them, my purse and my wallet. They were at the back of the freezer. Behind a pot roast. He never had much imagination, my Sammy."

"So you went."

"I left Morty with a neighbor and took the bus downtown. Funny thing, I probably missed your mother by just a few minutes. I was at Murray's, too. What would have been different, I wonder, if I had run into her?" She considered the possibilities. "Nothing, probably. It might have been awkward is all. I might have tried to talk her into running away with Mac. I don't think she would have listened. And Mac or no Mac, I don't think she would have come with me to the Y. Your mother always believed that Miss Savage thought less of her because she walked away from her art. She wouldn't have. Miss Savage didn't judge. She wasn't like that. Your mother, of course, wasn't so sure." She picked up her coffee cup, remembered that it was empty and put it down again.

"You want more?"

"Maybe." She yawned. "Yes."

Bernie returned from the kitchen with two steaming mugs. "It's possible, maybe, she would have changed her mind and gone to the show," Sarah continued, "but after what happened at the hotel…"

Sarah closed her eyes, conjuring up that long-ago evening. "I got to the Y early, right at five, so I could say hi to Miss Savage…not that I was sure she would remember me." Sarah smiled at the memory. "Anne Savage was as wonderful as ever. If she didn't remember me, she pretended that she did. She was the same with all her students that showed up. What a mensch."

"Mac?"

"Of course. Mac. When he came in right after me, I thought he was maybe one of Miss Savage's students. A very polite student. He stood to the side, waiting until I was finished. Not like a Baron Byng boy at all." She laughed. "So I didn't meet him, like I said. But when I heard him say his name to Miss Savage, I nearly platzed. 'Wait till I tell Esther,' I said to myself. I almost looked for a phone booth right then and there."

"What was he like?"

"He was real handsome, like your mother always said. It was his eyes I saw first. They were so sad, and red. Like maybe he'd been crying. Like maybe he'd lost his best friend. He had, with your mother, right before. I didn't know. I couldn't know.

"I wish I'd had the nerve to go up and introduce myself. But what would I have said? 'Hi, Mac. I'm Sarah, the best friend of the woman you loved who walked out on you in Halifax?' So I watched him instead. I watched him and I liked him.

"Your mother was a good actress when she wanted to be. A regular Sarah Bernhardt, she was. I called her the next morning and told her what I saw. She pretended like it didn't matter, like she had no interest in seeing Mac again. She didn't tell me they had already met...more than met. Not until later. That didn't stop me from opening my big mouth." She yawned, then giggled. "See? I do have a big mouth. Sometimes too big. Like tonight, maybe?"

Bernie hadn't decided whether or not he was happy about Sarah's big mouth. He took another sip of coffee and waited.

Sarah watched him for a few minutes before continuing. "I told your mother that I didn't believe her that she didn't care that Mac was in town. I told her that she was a fool all those years ago for not going off with him. Not that I would have had the chutzpah if I was her. Not me. But your mother could be bahartst. Brave like a Maccabee. About all the wrong things. Instead of leaving Morris to be with Mac and their baby, she made sure Morris thought the miracle baby was his."

"Maybe she loved Daddy more?" Bernie asked doubtfully.

"Is that what you think?"

Bernie didn't know what to think, only what he wanted to think.

Sarah picked up the magazine clipping and studied Marc-Allan Cameron's face. The family resemblance was subtle but definitely there. Not the nose. That was Esther's. But the eyes and the mouth. And the forehead. Those were Mac's. "I don't think your mother ever loved Morris, even if she thought she did," she said. "When Esther married him, she was head-over-heels infatuated, not head-over-heels in love. How could she be? She didn't know what love was until she met your father. Your real father." *Me, neither. I didn't know until I met my Jack.*

Bernie took the clipping from Sarah and looked closely at the photo of this stranger who was his father. "Do you think he would want to hear from me?" he whispered.

"Why wouldn't he? Of course he would. I know he would. Even if you weren't his son, he would want to meet Queen Esther's prince."

Queen Esther's prince? Bernie smiled in spite of himself. Suddenly, he was serious again. "What if after…after…you know. What if he got married? What if he has a family?"

"What if?"

"Maybe he wouldn't want me, this ghost from his past, to turn up out of the blue. I don't know that I would."

"Don't you?"

Bernie stared at the man who had given him life, who had burst out of obscurity and who, with Erik Donnekin, had turned his life upside down. "Yes," he said at last. "Yes, I would."

35

Esther and Sarah stamped the snow off their boots and brushed the dusting of flakes from their hats and coats before they pushed open the door into Stella's Lunch. A cluster of tiny bells jingled as they walked in, and a jukebox started playing the week's unlikely top song, The Singing Nun's "Dominique," under a swell of dissonant chatter and clinking crockery.

Even before draping her coat over an empty chair at their favorite table, Sarah tugged a napkin from the dispenser and wiped the condensation from her glasses. Then she pulled out another and cleared a peephole view through the window. Sherbrooke Street was already looking Christmasy in this first week of December, with garlands wrapped around bow-trimmed lamp standards and fairy lights blinking from many store windows. While most holiday shoppers had converged on the downtown stores, enough stayed behind to populate Westmount's main street with a colorfully festive assemblage of bobbing hats and bulging shopping bags.

Esther and Sarah had barely settled into their seats when Stella rushed over. She knelt next to Esther and clasped both her hands. "Poor Morris. It was sudden? It must have been. You would have told me if he was sick, wouldn't you?"

It was two days after the end of the shiva and Esther's first chance to escape the house since the funeral. Sadie would not approve of her being in a restaurant during the shloshim, the thirty-day mourning period after the burial. After a week of Sadie's rigorous do's and don'ts — mostly don'ts — Esther didn't care. She needed to be in the world again, among ordinary people doing ordinary things, like shopping and sitting around in coffeeshops.

"Thank you, Stella. Yes, it was sudden."

"What happened, if it's okay me asking?" Stella stood but kept her attention focused on Esther, ignoring the many customers clamoring for her attention.

"No, of course not." Esther sighed. She had told the story so many times over the past ten days that she wished she could record it onto an LP and never have to tell it again. "It was a massive heart attack," she repeated. "There was no warning. Nothing. One minute, we're watching TV. The next, he falls forward. Just collapsed. By the time the ambulance came, he was gone."

"At least he didn't suffer. It's not a lot, but it's something." Stella gazed across her restaurant to the black-framed photo that occupied a place of honor by the register. "First President Kennedy," she said, "then your husband. Both the same week. Both so young."

"Forty-six," Sarah said.

"Like the President."

Esther nodded yes, suddenly so tired that she could barely hold her head up. *Maybe coming out here today wasn't the smartest thing I could have done.*

"And your little boy?" Stella asked.

"Six." Esther's eyelids drooped shut.

"Here I am going on and on and on. I'm so sorry. I— Let me get you some tea, okay?"

Esther nodded again.

"Anything else?"

"No, Stella. Just the tea. Thank you."

Stella turned to Sarah.

"Me, too, Stella. The usual."

Stella disappeared behind the counter.

When Esther opened her eyes, Sarah was biting her lip and staring intensely at her.

"I know what you're thinking, Sarah Kaplan. Don't say it," Esther warned.

"But—"

"Morris just died."

"Exactly."

Esther waited until Stella had served their tea and moved on to attend to other customers. "I won't chase after Mac," she insisted. "I don't know where he is. Anyhow, he's probably married."

"You could find out if you wanted to. You could find him if you wanted to."

"I don't want to." Esther avoided Sarah's eyes and spooned sugar into her tea.

"You don't take sugar."

"I do now," Esther snapped.

"You're lying."

Esther looked up sharply. "I take sugar in my tea," she said through clenched teeth.

"Fine. You take sugar in your tea."

Sarah waited. Esther said nothing.

"Bernie is going to need a father," she added softly.

"He has me. Manny's a good uncle. He'll help."

"Manny's a putz. Anyhow, Bernie has a father."

"Morris was his father."

"Esther…"

"Okay." Esther's voice dropped to almost a whisper. "Mac is Bernie's father."

"So?"

"So even if I knew where to find him," she began, "and I don't," she added defiantly. "Even if I knew where Mac was, how could I face him? I wouldn't go with him when he wanted me to. Twice, I wouldn't go. I can't chase after him now. I can't, Sarah. You know I can't."

"And he isn't Jewish."

"No, he isn't Jewish."

"Look around you, Esther. It isn't 1939 anymore."

"Some things never change, Sarah."

Sarah knew better than to argue. "Everything changes," she wanted to say. "Too much, sometimes." Instead, she asked, "What about Bernie?"

"That's the other reason. The big reason. My family would turn their backs on us if I went with Mac, especially if they found out that Mac is really Bernie's father. People would talk. They would say mean things. Horrible things. Cruel things. Those names would follow Bernie for the rest of his life. It's better he grows up proud of himself and proud of his parents, not ashamed."

"This is 1963, Esther. Almost 1964."

Esther shrugged. "Like I said: Some things don't change." She sipped her tea, grimaced and pushed it away. "No. It's better for Bernie if everyone keeps thinking that the 'Marc' in Bernard Marc is 'Marc Chagall,' like I said when he was born."

"Okay," she said. It wasn't her life. She reached across the table and squeezed Esther's hand.

36

"That's why she never did anything," Sarah said, picking up her latest cup of instant coffee, already cold.

"Not even after she threw Harold out?" Bernie asked.

"Not even then. Or said anything to you. More than anything, she was afraid you would think she was a bad person for what she'd done. She'd lost so much, your mother had. She couldn't risk losing you, too."

"Is that what she said?"

"She didn't have to say. I knew her more than fifty years. I knew." Sarah wiped her eyes. "I know." She drank the last of the coffee and shuddered. "Shreklekh. How can I drink such garbage? How can you?"

Bernie laughed.

"It's good to hear you laugh. It hasn't been much of a day for laughter." Sarah patted Bernie's arm. "Go to bed. Me, too, I'm going to bed. What time is it? Two in the morning?"

"Something like that." He stood, and his whole body ached. "Can I help you clean all this up first?" he asked.

"No, no." She pushed the Birks box at Bernie. "Take it."

He reached for it, then pulled back. "She left it with you."

"So it could tell you what she couldn't. Of course, it's yours."

"Thank you." He hugged it to his chest.

"Wait. I have something else that belongs in there." She picked up the old photo of her and Esther in Stella's and handed it to Bernie.

"I can't. That one's yours for sure."

"It's yours now," she insisted. "I don't know why, but I know you have to have it. Take it."

Bernie lifted the lid and Sarah slid the photo into the box under

The King and I. He pulled out the LP. "Do you have a stereo?"

"In the closet there's a fancy stereo I don't know how to use. In your room, in the den, there's an old Fleetwood hifi, almost as old as you. That one I figured out, so for sure you can make it work."

Bernie started for the den but stopped after a few steps. "Can I read your story?"

"My story?"

"Good Jewish Girls Don't."

Sarah rummaged at her feet for the manuscript. "You don't want to read this, Bernie. It's from a long time ago. It's probably as shreklekh as the coffee." She thumbed through the pages and shook her head. "Maybe after I read it all the way through again, I'll let you…if I think it's any good."

Bernie reached for the sheaf of papers in her hand. "Give, Sarah. You will never think it's good enough for me to read."

Sarah tightened her grip on it. "Maybe for a fifteen-year-old in English class it's good. But today? Fifty years later?"

"It's not fifty years yet. It's what? Forty-seven? Forty-eight?"

"Such a comedian. Who knew you were such a comedian?"

He grabbed a corner of the stapled sheets and tugged gently. "Will you let me read it?"

"You're pushier than your mother."

"Will you?"

"Will you tell me what you really think of it?"

"Do you want me to?"

Sarah thought for a minute. "Only if it's good."

Bernie chuckled.

"Take it before I change my mind." She released the papers into his hand. "Only if it's good. Okay?"

"It's good."

"How do you know, Mr. Smarty Pants?"

"I'm like my mother and my father. Like both of them. Between the Jewish God and the English God, I got it covered."

Sarah rolled her eyes. "Go to bed, you." She watched Bernie disappear into the den.

A few minutes more and I'll get up.

She heard him fumble with the hifi, then heard the opening measures of *The King and I* overture.

Just this one song. A few more minutes…

Sarah's eyes drifted shut, her chin fell to her chest and soft snores thrummed in counterpoint to Anna and her King.

37

"Shall we dance? On a bright cloud of music shall we fly?"

Yul Brynner as the King and Deborah Kerr as Anna fling each other around Siam's gilded royal palace to the orchestra's rich swell, wheeling and twirling so quickly it's like they are flying. Faster and faster they whirl until their faces blur.

"Shall we still be together, with our arms around each other? And shall you be my new romance?"

The music slows, and so do the dancers. As they do, Anna is no longer portrayed by Deborah Kerr but by Esther Freed, and Marc-Allan Cameron is the King. As for the palace, its opulent embellishments have dissolved, leaving a celestial ballroom where dozens of glittering chandeliers hang from a hazy nothingness and waltzing tendrils of milky mist make up the walls and floors.

Suddenly, The Wizard of Oz's Almira Gulch bicycles in, carrying Bernie's copper-colored cocker-terrier, Tik-Tok, in her basket. She circles counterclockwise around the dancing couple, gaining in speed. The faster she cycles, the more quickly the mist spins out into mini-tornadoes that darken from white to gray to black and thicken from wispy threads to sticky, molasses-like globs

Now, Almira Gulch morphs into her Wicked Witch of the West alter ego, her bicycle has become a broomstick and Tik-Tok is Gerry as a leering flying monkey. Gerry leaps up, grabs Mac by the neck and takes off, leaving Esther alone with the witch…who is no longer acted by Margaret Hamilton. She is Auntie Sadie.

"I'll get you, my pretty," Sadie screeches and aims her broomstick, with its flickering, green pinpoint-light tip, at Esther.

"Sadie, no!" Esther shrieks and shields her face with her arms…only Esther is now Bernie and it's Bernie who's screaming.

"Sadie, no!" Bernie opened his eyes. A sweat-soaked sheet covered his face. He threw off the tangled shroud and sat up. For a moment, he wasn't sure where he was, was terrified that the pinpoint of green light was doing more than flashing at him through the darkness. It was coming for him. Then he remembered. He was in Sarah's den. The green light was the hifi console.

He switched off the Fleetwood and padded into the kitchen for a glass of water, pausing on the way to cover Sarah with a blanket he found in the linen closet. There, he also collected fresh linens for his sofa bed and another pair of ill-fitting pajamas for himself.

Sleep eluded him for hours. Every time he was about to drift off, Sadie's witch-green face thrust itself at him and his eyes shot open. In the end, he banished Sadie the same way he had banished his nighttime monsters as a child: He switched on the bedside lamp.

His nightmares, however, would not be driven away as easily…

Bernie skips along a yellow brick road, singing "We're off to see the wizard, the wonderful wizard of art." Accompanying him on a honky-tonk upright and dressed like a Munchkin is Bubbie Ruth. Only it's not the Emerald City Bernie sees in the distance. It's the Montreal skyline, dominated by the beacon-topped cruciform tower that is Place Ville-Marie.

The beacon gyrates wildly out of control until all four beams converge to pick him out, pick him up and transport him to the art room at Baron Byng High School. There Anne Savage, outfitted as Oz's Good Witch Glinda, hands him her wand. At first Bernie doesn't know what to do with it. Then a blank canvas materializes in front of him, unsupported by any easel. He taps the wand three times against the edge of the canvas and a completed painting instantly takes shape. It's a highly stylized, almost abstract rendering of the vintage photo of Esther and Sarah at Stella's Lunch.

Strangely, he isn't surprised. It's almost as though he was expecting the painting to paint itself for him. Now, Erik Donnekin is standing next to him, admiring his painting and giving him a thumbs up. Before Bernie can acknowledge Erik, all the art room's windows implode and the glass fragments re-form as a squadron of Harold-like flying monkeys directed by wicked witch Sadie. Two of the monkeys seize Bernie and fly him to a vast, bullpen office occupied by an army of King *and* I-*styled slaves dressed in identical suits and ties and toiling at endless rows of identical desks. The monkeys drop Bernie at the only vacant desk in the array and speed away.*

Panicked, Bernie tries to escape. He can't. His leg is manacled to his desk, his arm to a giant adding machine bolted to the desk. He tugs and tugs and tugs and finally jerks free, only to find himself falling, falling, falling…

Bernie dropped with a bone-jarring thud to the uncarpeted floor as dawn's earliest rays of sunlight poked through the blinds. He sat up, again soaked in perspiration. This time he was also sobbing.

38

Sarah was asleep on the sofa when Bernie emerged into the living room dressed in his rumpled funeral suit. She had kicked off the blanket but otherwise lay in the same awkward position in which Bernie had found her in the middle of the night. He covered her and finding nothing breakfastable in either fridge or pantry, jotted her a quick note and tiptoed out of the apartment, carrying Esther's Birks box under his arm. To its existing treasures Bernie had added Sarah's story and his Anne Savage and Marc Chagall library books.

"Meet me at Dominique's at 1:30," his note read. He didn't know how he would spend the next six hours or where he would go. All he knew was that the only way to clear his mind of the nightmares and confusion of the previous twenty-four hours was to get out and get moving.

The early morning air, as he stepped out of The Whitehall, was sweet and refreshing, its cool moistness a pleasant contrast to the night's jarring battle between air conditioner and fireplace in Sarah's apartment. In a few hours, cool-and-moist would turn disagreeably close. For now, it felt light and delicious, enfolding him in the fresh scent of trees, flowers and grass.

A light trickle of pre-rush hour traffic greeted him as he turned onto Sherbrooke. A block to the west, he noticed a dozen men climbing the Shaar Hashomayim steps into the synagogue building on Metcalfe. *Morning services.* He followed them inside and installed himself in a worn wooden pew at the back of the chapel until it was time to rise for the Mourner's Kaddish, until it was time to complete on his own what he had not been able to finish at the cemetery.

Oseh shalom bim'romav hu ya'aseh shalom. Aleinu v'al kol Yis'ra'el v'im'ru—

Instead of sitting down after the congregational "amen," Bernie slipped out.

It was hours too early to get back into the conservatory, Bernie's preferred option. Instead, he continued west to Dominique's for a takeout coffee then looped back to the bench outside Galérie Cinq Arts. The art hadn't changed, yet something in him must have, for none of it appeared as intimidating as it had the previous day. Even Erik's painting, barely visible from the street, seemed less alien. To his surprise, he almost liked it, almost liked everything he saw. One canvas in particular stood out, occupying a place of honor in the window. No. It can't be. It was the painting of his suddenly remembered nightmare: a brilliantly colored Expressionist rendering of Sarah and his mother as teenagers at Stella's Lunch. Bernie stared at it in unblinking incredulity. Every detail was exactly as he had dreamed it…until the flying monkeys snatched him away, that is. He shuddered at the memory.

I'm imagining it. I must be. Bernie squeezed his eyes shut and counted to ten. He counted ten more to twenty. When he opened his eyes, tentatively, he was relieved to discover that his dream painting was gone. "Not enough sleep," he muttered. He downed the rest of his coffee and hailed a cab.

"Ville Mont-Royal, centre-ville," he told the cabbie. "Laird and Sherwood Crescent." He leaned back into the seat, shut his eyes and immediately dropped into a mercifully dreamless sleep.

It seemed only minutes later when the Diamond taxi jerked to a stop, startling Bernie awake. This was not his apartment building. It wasn't anywhere near his apartment. Was he still asleep? Was he having another nightmare?

"Édifice Sun Youth," the driver announced. "Jeunesse au Soleil."

"But—"

"Monsieur?"

"Never mind." Bernie thrust a few bills into the front seat, grabbed his Birks box and stepped out onto St. Urbain Street. In front of him rose a bleak, bricked, three-story building. Set into the wall above the recessed doors was a bas-relief slab fancifully scripted with "Baron Byng High School." Above it, an electric sign spelled out "Jeunesse au Soleil / Sun Youth" in chunky black letters on a yellow-and-white background. *I must be dreaming. Maybe I'm still asleep at Sarah's.*

Bernie tried the front door. It was unlocked. When he stepped inside he was greeted by an eight-foot-high mural of a fire-breathing dragon. Grime and neglect may have dulled its colors, but the image remained striking. As he continued undisturbed along the corridor, mural after mural brightened the old school's doleful demeanor. If it were not for the muffled clacking of IBM Selectrics and the electronic chirping of modern telephones, he could almost imagine himself back in the 1930s, as armies of students, paintbrushes in hand, tarted up Baron Byng's dull institutional interior under the creative generalship of Anne Savage. Here was a farm scene, not unlike Savage's own *Quebec Farm.* And here, a clown. Next to it, a painting of Baron Byng itself, looking more animated on this decades-old representation than it did today.

He scanned the signatures of the teenagers of long ago whose nascent talents this astounding woman had believed in, fought for and nurtured. Some, he recognized: Mordecai Richler, Freda Kimmel, Alfred Pinsky, Leah Sherman, Irving Layton, William Shatner. This school had produced more than its share of luminaries. What about the rest? He knew what had happened to Sarah Schumacher. What about Sylvia Kornbluth, Doris Rosen and Edith Plotnick? What about Sophie Benjamin, Anna Paretsky and Sara Soicher?

He strolled farther along the hall to another mural, a fanciful, multihued representation of a flock of Canada geese in flight. This was more to his mother's taste. She had loved birds, especially Canada geese. If Bernie half-closed his eyes, he could almost see a fifteen-year-old Esther Finkel, her face screwed up in concentration, daubing a bit of scarlet here, a bit of violet there. He knelt and hunted for the signature. It was hard to find, camouflaged in the tall grasses at the lower right, but there it was: a less mature version of the careful signature he had come to know through years of letters, postcards, school notes and permission slips. Only the family name had changed.

In that instant everything that Sarah had said to him about his mother's artistic dreams became real. In that instant he saw his mother as the artist she could have been, the artist she wouldn't let herself become, and he felt an indescribable sadness — for himself as much as for her.

Bernie wiped his eyes dry when he noticed a young woman in her early twenties coming toward him from the other end of the corridor. She had wavy ash-blonde hair that fell to just below her shoulders and wore a white, loose-fitting, off-the-shoulder top, high-waist Guess jeans and red stiletto heels. "Puis-je vous aider, monsieur?" she asked. "Can I help you?"

Bernie stabbed his finger at the mural. "My mother," he stammered. "She—"

"Painted this?" the young woman asked. This was not the first Baron Byng son or daughter who had wandered in to Sun Youth only to be rendered speechless by a parent's long-ago artwork.

Bernie touched Esther's name.

"C'est une belle peinture," she offered, smiling. "I always liked this one."

"Is it okay if I look around?"

"Of course. The murals are everywhere. Take your time." She pointed to a door two rooms down. "I'm in there if you have any questions. I'm Simone."

Yet Bernie had already forgotten about Simone and was again fully focused on his mother's mural. Simone shrugged and disappeared into her office.

Two hours, three more coffees and a scalding shower later, Bernie left his Town of Mount Royal apartment. Now, he was more comfortably dressed — in khakis and a blue button-down shirt, open at the neck. He still carried his mother's Birks box, now more conveniently in an Eaton's shopping bag, as he strolled across Connaught Park to the local Royal LePage real estate office. He scanned the listings in the window then went inside.

He emerged forty-five minutes later, found a cab at the nearby commuter train station and directed the driver to his mother's house a few miles away. Then while the taxi idled at the curb, Bernie ran up the half dozen steps to the front door.

For a moment he was ten again, racing home for dinner — to his mother's famous meatloaf with mashed potatoes and corn, if he was lucky. All washed down with a glass of milk: Esther's was never a kosher household. The moment passed, and it was 1984 again. Bernie closed his eyes and ran his fingers over the familiar door. It awakened no other memories. His mother was gone and his childhood home felt just as dead.

He didn't bother to ring the bell. There was no point. Sadie would have left for the second day of shiva at Uncle Manny's and the house would be empty. Unfolding the note he had written and rewritten multiple times before leaving his apartment, he gave it one final read.

> Dear Auntie Sadie,
>
> I won't be joining you this week at Uncle Manny's. I know Mom would want me to mourn her in my own way, so that's what I'm going to do. I'm grateful for all your help over the months and for taking care of things here at the house while Mom was in the hospital. Now that she's gone, there's no reason for me to keep the house. So I'm selling. The listing doesn't take effect until the 29th, to give you a couple of weeks after the shiva to move back into your apartment.
>
> Bernie

He stared at the note, wondering whether he should give Sadie more time or whether he should change "Bernie" to "Love, Bernie."
No.
He slid the note through the letter box.
Halfway down the stairs, Bernie pulled his mother's house key from his pocket. Should he retrieve the note and rip it up? He thought about it for a second or two. But only for a second or two.

39

Bernie checked the time. He had an hour to kill before he had to meet Sarah. Instead of continuing to Dominique's, he asked the driver to drop him a few blocks east, in front of Librairie Westmount.

The window hadn't changed since the day before, and Bernie again stared at the mountain of books with their rainbow-colored, Star of David cover motif. "I don't know," he murmured to the giant photo of their author.

"Sure you do," he swore he heard Ray David Blackman counter in reply.

Beyond the window display, floor-to-ceiling wooden shelves sagging under the weight of books new and used filled the musty store, a Sherbrooke Street fixture for decades. Westmount Books when Hugh Vickers opened it, the bookstore's signage had followed the trajectory of Quebec's controversial language laws through the years, becoming Librairie Westmount Books in 1974 and Librairie Westmount three years later. The name over the door was irrelevant. Most of the shop's titles had always been in English and to most locals and the irascible Vickers, it would always be Westmount Books, no matter what the store's government-mandated sign said.

Vickers squinted over the top of his reading glasses and over the wobbly tower of books on his desk as Bernie walked in. He was eighty-three, with a snowy mane of hair and a full white beard that set off his dark eyes and florid complexion. *The Gazette*'s police reporter in the forties and fifties when Montreal was Canada's Sin City, Vickers quit when a new firebrand mayor launched a crime-busting crusade to clean up the rampant municipal corruption and, as Vickers put it, "took all the fun out of my job."

"Hey, Mr. Vickers." Bernie waved at the old man. Bernie had been coming into the store since he was little — first with Esther, when they would occasionally stop in between library and Stella's on the way home from visiting his grandfather in the hospital, and later on his own, during his reflective visits to the Westmount conservatory. When Bernie was a kid, Vickers let him ride on the sliding wooden ladders that offered access to the uppermost shelves — when Esther wasn't looking, of course. Bernie gave one of the ladders a gentle push and the childhood thrill returned as it coasted smoothly along the wall.

"Bernie, my boy," Vickers shouted back. Hugh always shouted, more loudly with each passing year. It didn't matter whether you were standing next to him, at the other end of the store or across the street. It was a byproduct of a worsening deafness he refused to acknowledge. "Where's your pretty young friend?" he bellowed.

"My pretty young friend?" The man was getting crazier by the day.

"I saw you with her yesterday, when you walked by the store."

"It can't have been me. It must have been someone else." Bernie replayed his Thursday, which already felt as though it must have been years in the past. *He can't mean Sarah.*

"Of course I mean Sarah. Who else? She's a hot one."

Bernie grinned. "Bad luck, old man. She's mine."

Vickers guffawed. "The hell she is." He turned serious. "Your mom. How is she?"

Bernie shook his head and said nothing.

Vickers raised a bushy eyebrow inquiringly.

"Tuesday night. The funeral was yesterday."

Vickers extricated himself from his fortress of books, seized Bernie's hand in both of his and shook it warmly. "I'm so sorry, my boy," he said with genuine affection. "She was a wonderful woman, your mother. A mensch. Isn't that what you people say?"

"Yes. Thank you," Bernie replied awkwardly, trying not to bridle at Vickers's "you people."

Hugh waved him off. He had picked up on the awkwardness, though not the reason, and he assumed that Bernie was uncomfortable talking about his mother. "You're here to look at books not gossip with an old man," he said, returning to his desk. "Let me know if you need help finding anything."

Half an hour later, Bernie emerged from the labyrinthine stacks, his arms full: a box set of illustrated *Wizard of Oz* books, *MAC: A Cameron Retrospective*, a gift for Sarah and, after much wavering, a copy of *A Blessing on My Head: Gay, Jewish and Proud.*

Vickers eyed Bernie curiously as he slid the final title into a recycled Provigo grocery bag. "He's local, you know. He lives a few blocks over, on Lansdowne. That's the reason I featured his book in the window." He paused. "One of the reasons."

40

"You didn't!" Sarah was laughing so hard she was crying. She wiped her eyes with a napkin and blew her nose loudly, ignoring the disapproving glares from neighboring tables.

"I did," Bernie said, "and it took every ounce of will power I could muster not to add a PS telling Sadie not only what I think of her but letting her know her that I'm having the locks changed on the thirtieth."

"You're having the locks changed? Not really."

"Damn right." Bernie speared a forkful of ketchup- and vinegar-soaked french fries and washed them down with a gulp of Coke. "So she better make sure she's out."

"Good for you. Tell me, can you sell that fast? Legally, I mean."

"Mom put the house in my name a couple of months ago. I asked her not to. Now I'm grateful she insisted."

"A smart cookie, your mother," Sarah said. "About some things." She picked out the green peppers and red onions from her salad and deposited them distastefully on her bread plate. "If Dominique was here today, she'd know I can't eat those," she said.

"Is that her daughter?" Bernie indicated the twenty-year-old disappearing into the kitchen.

"Sylvie. Yes. She's working here for the summer."

"You're going to have to train her in your little eccentricities," Bernie teased.

"I have too many, and there isn't time. She's gone in a month, back to Concordia." Sarah paused for dramatic effect. "She's studying art."

Bernie groaned. "Of course she is."

"She—" Sarah started then stopped. "Sadie," she sputtered.

"What about Sadie?"

"Does she know?" Sarah stabbed her fork at Bernie. "That you own the house?"

"If she doesn't, she will pretty soon. I bet she'll call the notary the minute shiva's over, if she waits that long. She might call as soon as she sees my note."

Sarah skewered a tomato. "I wish I could see her face when she finds out."

Bernie laughed. "You are a mean one, Sarah Swartz."

"Not half as mean as you, it looks like. Good job." She stuffed the tomato into her mouth then nudged a black olive up to the rim of her bowl, where it teetered precariously. "Dominique knows I only eat green olives," she explained. "The ones stuffed with pimentos." She drilled down into her salad, excavating for more interlopers. "You've had a busy morning, boychik," she added as she prodded another culprit up the side of her bowl. It tumbled onto the table and fell to the floor. She kicked it out of sight.

"More than you know." Bernie told Sarah about his unexplainable taxi ride to Baron Byng. "I know I gave him my address," he said. "I swear I did."

"Esther," Sarah said.

"What?"

"Your mother. She's tidying up loose ends before she goes off to wherever she's going."

Bernie focused on his lunch. It was easy to do. Other than four cups of coffee, this was his first meal of the day, and he was ravenous.

"I see you ignoring me, Bernie Freed. You think that's more craziness from me? You think that's the mishigas of an old lady?"

It was tempting to look at it that way. However, as Bernie reflected on everything that had happened to him since the funeral, it dawned on him that if Sarah was crazy, he must be, too. Maybe his mother was upstairs somewhere, directing this farce. Maybe—

"I'm an idiot," he exclaimed, his mouth full. He wiped his greasy fingers on a napkin and pulled Sarah's story from his Eaton's bag. "I totally forgot about this." He unfolded and smoothed the eight typed sheets and pushed them across the table. Sarah glanced down at them but kept her hands folded on her lap.

"So?" she asked when all Bernie offered was a silly grin.

"It's good," he said. "Really good."

Sarah ran her fingers lightly across the letters typed on the title page. *"Good Jewish Girls Don't* by Sarah Swartz," she half-whispered. "You think?" she asked in full voice. "You aren't just saying that?"

"I'm not just saying that. Do you want me to say it again?"

"Sure."

"Okay. It's really, really, really, really good. So good that I read it twice. I would have read it a third time if I'd had more time."

Sarah turned to the first page. "Autumn was already dying into winter," she read aloud, "when Sarah Birnbaum and Esther Mutter strode up to Paul Epstein and announced, 'We've come to play.' The thirteen-year-old boy could not believe his ears. 'No way,' he exclaimed and turned his back on them, but not before he sneered, 'Good Jewish girls don't play street hockey.' The bells of St. Jude's clanged mockingly—" She stopped and looked up. "That's good?"

"It's better than good. It's pie-worthy." He signaled to Sylvie.

The young woman smiled and sauntered over. She had reddish-brown hair styled into a boyish pixie cut, a naturally luminous complexion and brown, Bette Davis eyes. Unlike her ultra-tall mother, Sylvie was leprechaun-like at barely five feet. "Mom knew you'd be wanting pie today," she said. "She baked one especially for you this morning. She told me not to serve it to anyone else."

"Peach, right?" Sarah asked.

"First one of the season. For two, with ice cream and coffee?" Sylvie asked.

"Yes, dear," Sarah replied. "For me, tea. With lemon."

"Coming right up." Sylvie returned a few minutes later, expertly balancing the tray on one hand. "On the house," she said. "Mom's orders."

Sarah sipped her tea and gazed thoughtfully at her manuscript. Maybe it wasn't too late. Maybe she could be a writer…was already a writer…was still a writer.

"I brought you something," Bernie said, reaching into the Provigo bag at his feet. "You probably don't need this, not after what you've written, but it kind of leapt off the shelf when I walked by, so I had to get it for you." He slid the book out. "By the way, Mr. Vickers called you 'my pretty young friend.'"

"The dirty old devil." Sarah chuckled. "I don't think I'm his type. Boy, is he not mine." She put on her glasses and took the oversize paperback from Bernie. "*Writing the Natural Way: Using Right-Brain Techniques to Release Your Expressive Powers,*" she read aloud and riffled through the pages. "'A mind without story is a mind without meaning.' Someone named Renee Fuller said that. Do you know this Renee Fuller?"

"I don't know anything about the book," Bernie replied, "but maybe it will help you find more of your stories. I'm sure you have lots." He tapped Sarah's manuscript. "I bet *Good Jewish Girls Don't* is just one of them."

"You think?"

"Of course I think. You've been telling me stories nonstop since yesterday morning."

"That's different. Stories I can tell. Writing them good is something else. Writing them *well.*" Sarah leaned across the table and kissed him. "This means a lot. Everything, it means." She slipped her manuscript inside the book and reached for a plastic bag at her feet. "Me, too, I've been shopping."

"Le Boulevard des Arts?" Bernie asked when he saw the bag. "I don't understand."

"Open the bag, Bernie. Then you'll understand."

Bernie laid his palms flat on the bag, concealing the store name. "You're already a writer, Sarah. Your story proves it. You've been writing since high school. But I'm no painter. I'm not any kind of an artist."

"You're still saying that?" Sarah raised her eyes heavenward. "After your mother and your father and this Erik boy, you're still saying you're no painter? You think that's only coincidence? Remember Carl Jung? Remember synchronicity?"

"Six words: Mr. Buchanan. Mount Royal High art class."

"That's seven words, but never mind. Look, Bernie. Not everyone can have an Anne Savage. We were lucky. Luckier than most. But even a Miss Savage guarantees nothing. Gornisht. Look at your mother." She gave the bag a nudge. "Open it."

Bernie shook his head.

"You're scared."

"I'm scared." Bernie slid the bag toward Sarah. Sarah pushed it back. Bernie stopped it mid-table.

"What are you scared of," he asked, "about your writing?"

"That's easy. That I can't. That even if I can, I'm no good. That even if maybe I'm good, no one else will think I am."

"Exactly."

"Forget 'exactly.' What kind of talk is that? You're smarter than that." She laid her hands over Bernie's. "Open the bag, Bernie. Please. What's inside isn't going to kill you."

Maybe not. But it will change me. It will change everything.

"It's too late," an inner voice countered. "Everything has already changed. Open the damn bag."

Bernie slipped his hand inside and groped around. There was a book and another, larger package: a wooden box with hinges and a metal clasp. He slid out the book. Somehow, that felt safer. When he saw the title, he laughed. "Okay. You win." It was like the book he had bought for Sarah, only for artists: *Drawing on the Right Side of the Brain: A Course in Enhancing Creativity and Artistic Confidence.* He laid the book aside and pulled out the wooden box. It was an artist's starter kit, containing a sketch pad and a selection of brushes, pencils and charcoals, as well as a rainbow of colored oils, pastels and watercolors.

"See?" Sarah poked him. "Nothing happened. You're still alive. You aren't dead."

Bernie felt a frisson of excitement even as his stomach contracted in terror.

"It's time you did something artistic with those artist's hands of yours," she added gently.

What would he do with all this? What could he do with it? Nothing. That's what.

"The only pencil these hands know what to do with is an accountant's pencil, and the only painting I will ever do is the walls of my apartment. Probably not even that." Bernie shoved box and book back into their bag and, with fists clenched, again pushed it toward Sarah. "Thank you, but you are confusing me with my mother."

Sarah took Bernie's hands and pried his fingers free. So much like his mother's, yet so different. "No," she said. "I don't think so."

Bernie extricated his hands from Sarah's and studied them. His fingers were long and slender like his mother's, only bonier at the knuckles. Esther had wanted him to learn to play the piano. He didn't know at the time that his grandmother had played as a child, back in Russia. His grandfather told him once, in the hospital. "She was a prodigy," he said. "She could have been something if the sewing machines didn't ruin her fingers. Not that anyone ever had money for a piano. Then she died."

"Then she died" was Zeyda Max's signal that all discussion about Bubbie Ruth was over and that the subject was closed. His grandfather had talked less about the past than his mother did.

Bernie's experience with piano lessons lasted only slightly longer than had his foray into the world of scouting. Two weeks longer: After five lessons, Bernie determined that little in the world could be more tedious than practicing the same piece over and over and that nothing could be more boring than scales.

The piano, which once belonged to Gerry's first wife, Greta, had not been played in years, not since that final lesson. Bernie always thought it strange that it didn't get sold after his stepfather went to prison, when Esther was selling off bits of the household to raise money. Maybe she hoped he would take it up again. He never did or would. Always polished to a mirror-like finish, the mahogany upright stood in its original spot by the living room window. Not for long. Bernie had told the realtor to sell the house furnished if she could. He would hold back a few meaningful keepsakes. The piano would not be one of them.

"Oh," groaned Bernie, covering his face with his hands. "Oh, no."

"What is it? What's wrong?"

Bernie peeked out through his fingers. Thinking about the piano and Bubbie Ruth had reminded him of the previous night's dreams. "I never told you why I left so early this morning," he said.

"You couldn't sleep? The bed wasn't comfortable? You didn't have enough blankets? You didn't like the pillow?"

Bernie laughed. "Stop playing the guilty Jewish mother. It had nothing to do with you." He told her what he remembered of his nightmares.

"You see!" she exclaimed exultantly. "You're already an artist in your dreams." Sarah retrieved the art box from the Boulevard des Arts bag and pushed it at him. "Go," she said, pointing to the far end of the café. "Go play with your new toys back there in the corner. Sylvie won't mind. You won't mind, will you, Sylvie," she called across to the young woman, who was sitting by the kitchen folding napkins, "if Bernie sits at one of those tables?"

Sylvie shrugged and returned to her napkins. Dominique's had already emptied of its lunchtime crowd. Tables would not be at a premium again for a few more hours.

"I had a magic wand in the dream," Bernie argued weakly.

"This box, it's full of magic wands. All different kinds. All different colors. Take them and go make magic." She opened *Writing the Natural Way* and feigned total absorption, all the while peering over the top of the book at Bernie. He opened his mouth to debate the point then changed his mind. Instead, he groaned, cursed, seized the box with both hands and exiled himself to an empty, distant table.

Bernie opened the box and stared impotently at its overwhelming array of tools. Not sure what to do, he rose and returned to Sarah. When she saw him coming, she plopped her purse on his chair. "So sorry, sir," she said solemnly. "This seat is taken."

"Coffee," Bernie snarled and grabbed his half-empty mug. He stopped for a refill from an amused Sylvie before returning to his art supplies.

For ten minutes, he glowered at the blank page. Then some unseen force impelled him to pick up one of the pastel pencils. "Crimson lake," its label read.

As soon as Bernie touched the pencil's tip to the page, he lost all awareness of where he was and what he was doing. It was as though the pastels *were* magic, as though they possessed wills of their own and his hand's only job was to hold them up while they sketched. Only once in the midst of his ninety minutes of frenzied drawing did Bernie's mind try to butt in with harsh judgment of what was taking shape on the page. The pencils quickly silenced it.

Unfortunately, their mystical power over him ended the minute he signed his name. "It's crap," he growled when he returned to Sarah, sketch pad under his arm. "Move your damn purse."

Sarah obeyed, her eyes twinkling. "What you got there, Van Gogh?"

"Shouldn't it be Chagall?" Bernie harrumphed. "Or Cameron?"

"What about Freed?"

Bernie rolled his eyes and thrust the pad at her. "I hope the store will take back the art box. If not, I can take it to Sun Youth or donate it somewhere else. Unless you want it. I'm done with it."

Sarah flipped open the pad to a rough sketch of the painting in Bernie's dream. Rough, yes, though not so rough that she could not recognize a long-ago Sarah and Esther perched on stools at the counter at Stella's Lunch. She was stunned. As passionately as she had been urging Bernie to explore his creativity, she couldn't know if he really was his mother's son. Looking at this drawing, she knew he was. Absolutely. With practice and a bit of guidance, he might even be as good as his father one day.

"It's good," she breathed. "Really good. Really, really good."

"You're making fun of me."

"No, boychik. It absolutely is good. Amazing good."

"It's just a scribble."

"Like Picasso is just a scribble."

"Now you are making fun of me."

"I wouldn't. Not about this. I swear."

"What have you got there?" Sylvie stood over Sarah's shoulder. "Is that what all the fuss and fighting is about?" She turned to Bernie. "Is that what you were doing over there?"

Bernie pushed his chair back and stood up. "I think it's time to go," he announced.

"Sit down," Sarah and Sylvie barked in unison. They looked at each other in astonishment then burst out laughing.

"Now I know for sure you're making fun of me. Both of you."

"No, Bernele. Sylvie?"

"If you let me have this," she said, "your lunch is on the house."

"You're joking."

"Dinner, too. Wait till Mom sees it. I bet she'll want to frame it and hang it here in the restaurant."

"You can't be serious. You really like it?"

"Do you know that modern artist who does all those crazy abstracts? Cameron something. No, something Cameron."

"Marc-Allen Cameron," Bernie whispered.

"Yeah, that's the one. There was a big article about him in *Maclean's* a couple of weeks ago. You must have read it."

Sarah and Bernie shook their heads.

"It might be in the back, if you want to see it."

Sarah shouted yes at the same time as Bernie muttered no.

"I'll find it for you before you leave. Can I?" She scooped up the pad without waiting for Bernie's answer. "I know this isn't abstract, and I know it's rough. Still, there's something about it that reminds me of his stuff. I know it doesn't look anything like a Cameron. It *feels* like it. Maybe it's the lines. Or the use of color. Or maybe I'm crazy. But I know it's good. Really good."

"See? You don't have to believe me. I know nothing from art. Sylvie does. Don't you, Sylvie?"

"A bit."

"A bit, she says. Like I said, Sylvie is studying art. An M-something."

"MFA. Master of Fine Art in art history. I don't know the contemporary stuff as well as I know the classics."

"What did I tell you? A master? You don't believe a master?"

"So what do you say, Bernie?" Sylvie asked. "Can I have it?"

"An original Freed?" Sarah snorted. "I don't think so, missy. Anyhow, he's going to need that sketch. Aren't you, Bernie? For the big painting you're going to paint from it."

41

Sarah and Bernie walked back toward The Whitehall in silence, each carrying thoughts much more burdensome than their respective shopping bags.

Sarah moved slowly, leaning heavily into her cane and pushing against a viscous August humidity that felt impenetrable, like the decision she was almost ready to make. Almost. She was already sixty-one. What business did she have picking up at her age what she had dropped more than forty years earlier? For Bernie it was different. He had forty, fifty, maybe sixty years in front of him — more life ahead than behind. *But me? How many good years, healthy years, do I have left? To write a book, maybe? It's craziness. What would I write about? What would I write about that anyone would want to read? Even if 'Good Jewish Girls Don't' is good — and that's a big "if" — I wrote that a long time ago. A lifetime ago.*

Sarah's pace slowed. She looked down at her feet, which did not seem to be able to keep up with the rest of her. *See? I am getting old. Never mind "getting." But Bernie? Bernie has a gift. What a gift. I owe it to Esther to nag him into seeing it…into doing something about it.*

Sarah looked up. They were passing Galérie Cinq Arts. *We should go in. Bernie should talk to that young man. I'd like to meet him, this boy who knows art and knows Mac.* She willed her feet to stop. They kept plodding on, paying her no heed. She sighed. *Maybe it's for the best. Bernie doesn't want an old lady with him when he talks to his young man. Yes, his young man. How could he not be?*

Bernie snuck a peek into Galérie Cinq Arts. He longed to go in yet didn't dare go in, all at the same time. What if Erik was there? What if he wasn't? From the sidewalk he glimpsed a corner of Erik's painting and was about to point it out to Sarah. *No. What if she wants to go in? What if she doesn't like Erik's painting? What if she doesn't like Erik? What if she does and embarrasses me like only a Jewish mother can?* He kept moving.

The bag from Le Boulevard des Arts felt like it would drag his arm to the pavement, it was so heavy. If he could, he would take the bag and chuck it and everything in it — including the Marc-Allan Cameron magazine profile that Sylvie had found for him — into the next trashcan and never look back. He stopped, letting his two shopping bags drop gently to the pavement, and shook out his arms. Then he picked up the two bags and continued forward. If anything, they felt heavier now. It was like he was carrying rocks. Rocks. That's what Sarah and Sylvie must have in their heads if they thought he could draw.

Me, an artist? How ludicrous is that? That was only a silly scribble back there in Dominique's. And Sylvie comparing me to Marc-Allan Cameron? That's just weird. Creepy, even. Does Sylvie know? Sylvie can't know. How could she know? Did Mom tell Dominique about Mac? No, that's crazier than the thought of me as an artist. Is it even true? About Mac, I mean. It's definitely not true about me being an artist. It's different for Sarah. She is a writer. A good writer. She has boxes of writings. She was writing in high school. In high school, I was being humiliated for my so-called art. I'm not an artist. I'm an accountant. Maybe I'm not an artist's son. Maybe I'm a lawyer's son after all. Maybe Sarah made up the story about Mom and Cameron. Writers make up things. No, not even a writer could make that up.

Bernie slowed his gait to match Sarah's. She was moving so slowly, like she had weights in her shoes. "It's hard walking in this heat," he said as they approached the library. "Do you want to go inside for a bit? It would be good to sit down and cool off."

Sarah started to shake her head but her no turned into a silent head-nodding yes. They crossed Sherbrooke's early rush-hour traffic, passed through the library and returned to their old oasis by the conservatory fountain.

The gentle, burbling splash of the fountain smoothed out the jaggedness of the day and calmed their edgy insecurities.

Sarah breathed out a noisy sigh and chuckled. "I thought yesterday was crazy. I didn't think anything could be crazier than yesterday."

"Then today happened," Bernie said.

"Then today happened."

"You know," they both started at the same time.

"You first," Sarah said.

"No, you."

"Okay. Me." Sarah gathered her thoughts, which, she realized, had never settled since the funeral…maybe not since Esther's death. "This is going to sound selfish, I know. But when your mother died, it felt like she took my life with her. For fifty years, half a century, more than half a century, we were like Siamese twins. Not joined physically." She touched her heart. "Here. Heart to heart. Only that one thing we never shared — her about Harold and me about Sammy. But everything else. A long time ago, we shared our dreams and almost as long a time ago, I'm ashamed to say, we both walked away from them. Now she's gone and it's like my compass has lost its needle. No, that isn't true. That's what it felt like until we sat down here, until we sat down here in this place that was so much a part of our lives, that was so much a part of those dreams. Those lost dreams. Now I know something, Bernie, something I didn't know before now. It's true for me and maybe, also, it's true for you."

Bernie looked at Sarah. He thought he knew what she was going to say. He hoped he knew. He was also afraid he knew. He waited.

"Esther's dying, your mother's dying, didn't take my life away. It gave it back to me. To you, too, maybe."

Bernie's eyes welled up with tears. He looked away.

"To you, too, maybe," she repeated.

"Me, too, maybe," he whispered.

"I have to be that writer," she said with sudden force. "If not for me, then for her. I have to live what she couldn't. I don't know that I have enough time left. That doesn't matter. I have to try." She wiped her eyes. "What about you?"

"Me, too." He knelt, dipped his finger in the water and drew a stick figure on the tile. "I'm scared," he said. "Yesterday morning I was an accountant going to his mother's funeral. This afternoon, I don't know who the hell I am. All I know is that I can't be that accountant anymore. I'm not sure if I'm an artist. It's hard to believe that could be possible. I have to try, though. Like you, I have to try."

Bernie pulled Esther's Birks box from its shopping bag, set it on his lap and lifted the lid. One by one, he lifted out its treasures, holding each for a few moments before placing it on the bench next to him. The last was *Anna and the King of Siam*, still enclosed in his mother's scarf. He unwrapped the book, turned to the flyleaf and silently reread Mac's inscription.

She gave up so much. Maybe she didn't have to, and maybe she gave up the wrong things, but so much of what she did she did for me.

He shut the book and carefully returned everything to the box, keeping it open on his lap. "I have to try," he said, "for Mom and maybe even for this Marc-Allan Cameron, this Mac who is my father. Mostly, I have to try for me."

Sarah took Bernie's hand. "I'm proud of you, Bernele. I know your mother would be, too. Maybe your father, also. Your fathers. Both of them." She hesitated before continuing. "Morris was a good man, Bernie. Not like those mamzers, Gerry and Harold. He was a good man and in his own way he was as much your father as Mac was… as Mac is. Morris was kind to your mother and to you. He loved you and your mother both. Mac wasn't his fault. Mac wasn't your mother's fault, either. He just was. It's good he was, or you wouldn't be here. If that was Mac's only gift, what a gift.

"Listen, Bernie. I know you don't think you're an artist. Like I don't think I'm much of a writer. But with parents like Esther and Mac, how could you not be?"

Bernie could not hold back the tears. He sobbed noisy wracking sobs, not caring if anyone saw or heard him. He wept for the mother who had given him life, for the mother who had been taken from him, for the mother who had been too frightened in life to follow her passions and for the mother who had now gifted him with a new life.

"Do you want me to call Freda Kimmel at Concordia for you?" Sarah asked when Bernie's tears finally subsided. "You could talk to her and maybe she could get you some classes or something. I know she would want to help if she can, for Esther as much as for you."

"Maybe," Bernie replied uncertainly. "I'm not sure. I'm not sure of anything right now." Then he was sure, of everything. "No. Not Freda Kimmel. I'm going to talk to my father. I'm going to talk to Mac. I'm going to ask him for help." He would call Revenue Canada on Monday and ask his boss to extend his compassionate leave. When the shiva was over and the house was ready to be shown, he would fly to Halifax and find Marc-Allan Cameron. He would find his father.

"Do you remember the vow your mother and I made?" Sarah asked.

"That you would be the first great Jewish Canadian woman author and she would be the first great Jewish Canadian woman artist."

"It's too late for that now. But it isn't too late for you and me to make a different kind of vow, to each other."

"What do you mean?"

"You're scared, right?"

"Right."

"And I'm scared. Right?"

"If you say so."

"I am. So scared I don't have words for it, not a good thing for a writer." She laughed nervously. "Here's the thing. I know I can't be the first great Jewish Canadian woman author. That's already happened for somebody else. But I can still be a Jewish Canadian woman author. Maybe a good one."

"Maybe a great one."

"We'll see about that. And you…"

"What about me?"

"I promise to write if you promise to do your art. You're good. Even if you don't believe you're good, you're good."

"Ditto."

"Okay," Sarah conceded. "Ditto."

"Okay, I promise." Bernie deliberated for a moment. "I'll give it a year."

"How about you give it three."

"Three?"

"It takes time to write a book, and it takes time to become an artist. A real artist."

Bernie stood and slowly circled the fountain. For a year, he probably could have taken a leave of absence from work. Not three years. They would never give him three years. He stopped and stared at the water bubbling out of the cherub perched on a ball in the center of the pool. What would that little angel tell him if it could talk? It would tell him to trust. And that meant…

Okay. To hell with it and to hell with Revenue Canada. I'm going to quit. I'm going to go in Monday morning and quit. I hate the damn job, anyway.

If he was careful, he could easily manage for three years on his savings, the money his mother had left him and the sale of her house.

Careful? To hell with that, too. I've been too careful too long.

"Here's the deal." He sat back down next to Sarah." Did you ever see that movie *Same Time Next Year?*"

"About the once-a-year affair, with that boy from *MASH*? What's his name?"

"Alan Alda."

"Yeah, that's the one. Sure, I saw the movie."

"Here's my version. Tell me what you think. After I walk out of here in a couple of minutes, I won't call you or get in touch with you for a year, unless it's some kind of emergency. Same for you. No calling, no contact. Next year, on the anniversary of Mom's funeral, I'll meet you here— No. Back at the cemetery, at Mom's grave. At eleven in the morning. Same time we were graveside at the funeral. Same time I walked out on it all. We'll meet there and you can tell me what you've written and I can tell you what I've drawn."

"That's crazy."

"You started this."

"I did. No, I didn't. Your mother did."

"You're splitting hairs. Even if Mom started it, it's up to us to finish it. What do you say?"

"A year, you said?"

"A year."

Could she do it? Could she at least start a book and have written enough in a year that she would have something to report to Bernie? Well, she would just have to. "Okay," she said at last.

"There's more."

"More? What more could there be?"

"We only show up at the cemetery if we have done something worth sharing. Or if we've given up. But we are not going to give up. Neither of us. So forget that."

"So what happens if I show up and you don't?"

Bernie thought. "If I don't show up, you keep coming back every year for those three years until I do. And vice versa. Deal?" Bernie stuck out his hand.

"How many years do you think I have left?"

"Enough. More than enough."

Sarah said nothing. *This is crazy. Crazier than crazy.*

"Deal?" Bernie waved his hand in Sarah's face.

She ignored it. Instead, she retrieved *Good Jewish Girls Don't* from her bookstore bag, reread the opening sentence three times then, turned to the final sentence. She tried to imagine writing a book. A whole book. Pages and pages and pages. Then more pages. Then more pages still. She couldn't imagine it. She couldn't imagine it, but that didn't mean she couldn't do it. She would have to do it. For Esther. For Bernie. For herself. "It's meshugena. It's more meshugena than meshugena." She took Bernie's hand and shook, hard. "Okay, mister. It's a deal."

"Awesome!" Bernie leapt to his feet again. "Wait here. I'll be right back." He dashed up the stairs into the library, nearly colliding with Evelyn Waugh.

"You've come back, Mr. Freed Bernie Freed," she said. "Did you read the—"

"Yes— No. Not yet. I— Do you have some Scotch tape I can borrow?"

"Scotch tape? Yes, of course. I must." Bernie followed Evelyn to the circulation desk where she rummaged through drawer after cluttered drawer, while Bernie drummed his fingers impatiently on the counter. "What do you need tape for all of a sudden that's so important?" she asked as she slammed the third drawer shut without finding the roll of tape.

"It's a long story," Bernie replied absentmindedly. "I'll tell you someday." *When one of my paintings is up on the well next to Anne Savage's and Freda Kimmel's.* While Evelyn continued looking, he pulled eight pieces of ripped card stock from his wallet and arranged and rearranged their jigsaw pieces on the counter.

"Here it is," Evelyn said, brandishing it like a trophy. "Isn't it always the last place you look?"

"Always," Bernie replied. He ripped the roll from Evelyn's hand, carefully taped Erik's business card back into a single piece and slipped it into his shirt pocket.

Rebirth

42

Sarah stuffed the ream of dog-eared pages into a Steinberg's shopping bag and rested it against the front door. It would not do to leave it behind. She stared glumly into her bedroom closet. *What does a writer wear?* She chose and rejected a half-dozen outfits, settling in the end for navy summer slacks, a white blouse, a tan cardigan and, most important of all, the "sensible" walking shoes that always made her feel so old. At least she didn't need the cane anymore. She suffered only the occasional twinge of arthritis now, not the constant, throbbing ache that had kept her limping for nearly a decade. One final stop: the bathroom mirror. She attacked her untamable mass of thick gray curls with a giant comb then gave up in disgust. "It's the artistic look," she offered her reflection skeptically.

The intercom buzzed gratingly. "Right down," Sarah called back to the staticky voice that crackled at her through the grille.

Thirty minutes later the Lasalle taxi deposited her at the front gate of the cemetery as the bells of St. Luc's began their eleven o'clock toll.

The problem with cemeteries, she thought as she struggled to remember the way to Esther's grave, is that people continue to insist on dying. There were many more headstones than there had been the year before and it took Sarah ten panicked minutes to navigate her way to Esther's marker. She was expecting to find Bernie waiting for her in his new artist persona, tapping his feet with mock impatience. But he was later than she was. Sarah didn't mind. It would give her a few minutes to catch her breath and visit with Esther.

"I'm writing, Esther," she said, placing a pebble on top of the grave marker. "Me. A book, I'm writing." She touched a finger to her lips and pressed it against Esther's name.

This was her first time seeing the basic granite slab with its simple inscription: "Esther Finkel Freed. 1923-1984. Beloved mother, wife and friend." It had seemed wise to avoid the stone's unveiling the month before. Esther didn't need her there and after her most recent conversations with Sadie, Sarah preferred to avoid as much contact with the family as possible.

First, the instant the sun had set on the final day of shiva a year before, Sadie called her in a rage. "I don't even know where to begin about that boy," Sadie railed, finding no difficulty at all in beginning her rant. "His mother, my poor sister, barely cold in her grave. Such disrespect. Such insensitivity. He's throwing me out. Did you hear what I said? Throwing me out. Out of my own sister's house. Can he do that? What kind of boy would do that? I shouldn't say this, Sarah, but it's good for Esther that she's gone, God rest her soul. It would kill her to see how that boy has turned out. She should never have left Harold. Harold would have turned that faygele into a man, a man who would respect his mother and his aunt."

Sarah had listened patiently, doing her best to hold her tongue and offer little in return, and expressing silent gratitude when Sadie finally kvetched herself out.

By the next call a day later, Sadie had transferred her enmity from son to mother. "That ungrateful bitch," she spat. Sadie had just learned that Bernie already owned her sister's house. She had also learned the terms of Esther's will, which left everything to Bernie unconditionally and which stated in language that brooked no misinterpretation that her gravestone was to include only her maiden and first married name. There would be no "Coopersmith" on her stone, even if Harold was still Esther's legal husband.

This time, Sarah hung up on her, though not before issuing this icy warning: "If I ever hear that you have made any trouble for Bernie, any trouble at all, or that you have gone against Esther's wishes in any way, Sadie Finkel, I will make it my business to make your life a living hell."

She never heard from Sadie again.

Now Sarah wondered whether she would ever hear from Bernie again. It was noon according to St. Luc's, and there was no sign of him. Had he given up? Or did he have nothing new to report? Sarah waited fifteen minutes longer. Then she picked up her purse and shopping bag and trudged back to the cemetery gate, keeping an eye out all the while for Bernie.

In the weeks that followed, Sarah picked up the phone a dozen times to call Bernie. Each time she hung up before dialing. She knew that Esther's house had sold, and quickly. That's all she knew. Dominique hadn't seen him, Hugh Vickers hadn't seen him, and Sarah's covert glances into Galérie Cinq Arts also revealed no sign of him.

After two months she stopped wondering whether she would run into him. After three, she settled back into her writing.

43

There was no manuscript for Sarah to stuff into a shopping bag this August morning as she prepared for her *Same Time Next Year* pilgrimage to Esther's grave. Instead she switched off the radio, slipped a neatly typed letter on buff stationary into her purse, locked her front door and stepped into the elevator.

Sarah had still heard nothing from Bernie, or about him, since they parted in the Westmount conservatory that Friday afternoon two years before. It was like he had disappeared off the face of the earth.

"Please God he shows up," she said in silent prayer as, once more, a Lasalle taxi sped up the Décarie Expressway to carry her to the cemetery.

"Please God he's all right," she repeated, this time to Esther as, once more an hour later, she began her trek back to the street.

44

"I have to go," Sarah insisted, staring glumly at the tangle of plastic tubes pumping drugs into her arm.

"You are not going anywhere, Mrs. Swartz," Dr. Morgan snapped, her voice raised over the tinny voices emanating from the portable radio on Sarah's nightstand.

"You don't understand," Sarah argued, trying to push herself up. "I have to. It's a matter of life and death."

Dr. Morgan scrutinized the array of monitors by Sarah's bed, compared what she saw with what was on the chart in her hands and scratched a few hieroglyphic additions. She then focused her sternest gaze on Sarah. Elizabeth Morgan, MD may have been twenty years Sarah's junior, but on the fifth floor of the north wing of the Royal Victoria Hospital, she was God. Woe betide the nurse, intern, orderly or patient who defied her.

"I have told you before, Mrs. Swartz, and I will tell you again. It will be *your* death if I let you walk out of here before next week. Not that you could walk anywhere today. Whatever is so important will have to wait until you are well again. Until I say you are well."

When Dr. Morgan shut the door behind her a few minutes later, Sarah stared out her window at the summer-green slopes of Mount Royal and burst into tears.

That evening, she asked the orderly to retrieve her purse from the locker. Buried at the bottom was her address book, as old and frayed as she felt. She found Bernie's number under the B's, not, as she expected, under the F's. Her finger hovered over the phone uncertainly. She dialed. In the instant the call connected, she was tempted to hang up. But it was not Bernie's voice that greeted her. Instead, an anonymous Bell Canada recording picked up: "Je régrette, mais il ne y'a pas de service au numéro que vous avez composez," the voice intoned. "I'm sorry, but there is no service at the number you have dialed."

Bernie must have moved. Somewhere cheaper, maybe? He wasn't collecting a civil service salary anymore. She dialed 411. The operator was as sorry as the recording had been: There was no Bernard Freed on Laird Boulevard…or anywhere else in the metropolitan area.

Where are you, Bernie Freed?

45

In the days leading up to the fourth anniversary of their vow, Sarah debated whether she should return to the cemetery. It seemed pointless. Bernie had missed the first two years. She had missed the third. They had made no commitment beyond that.

"Let's face it," she said to the photograph of Jack on the mantelpiece, "he's gone, vanished. Kaput." She shook her head sadly. "What's the point?"

Yet the moment she woke up on August 10, before she opened her eyes, she knew she had to go. "It will be good to visit with Esther," she told herself to justify the outing, even as she prayed that Bernie would show up.

"Why am I dressing up?" she asked herself in the mirror as she slipped on a rare pair of pantyhose and her favorite red-and-black summer print. "No," she said to her walking shoes. "Not today." She reached instead for a pair of low heels. "I know we're going to regret this," she said to her feet as she slipped on the shoes and tentatively crossed her bedroom rug.

Her hair was as hopeless as ever, despite the previous week's salon visit. She ran a comb through it anyhow. *Just because.*

Before heading downstairs to the waiting cab, she slipped one last item into her purse.

46

Bernie's back was to Sarah as she approached Esther's grave to the sound of St. Luc's final eleven o'clock chime. She stepped out of view next to a mature oak and paused, as much to spy on Bernie as to compose herself. Using the tree for support, she lifted one complaining foot, then the other.

Although Sarah could not see Bernie's face, she could see that he carried himself differently now. There was a self-assurance about his posture that she had never known in him before. A maturity, too. And he was dressed, well, artistically. Not like a government accountant at all. He wore a black leather jacket, with jeans and sneakers. A canvas messenger bag sat on the ground by his feet. Bernie bowed his head, then knelt to pick up a pebble and add it to Sarah's several atop the gravestone.

Sarah waited a few minutes more before continuing toward him, her feet aching in shoes that crunched against the gravel path.

Bernie swiveled around at the sound and smiled warmly when he saw her.

"Your beard," Sarah said. "It's gone. What happened?"

"I was afraid I would grow up to look like Hugh Vickers." He chuckled. "I'm happy you made it."

"You think I wouldn't?" Sarah asked as Bernie leaned down to kiss her.

"Four years is a long time, longer than we planned for."

"What? You think I would have joined your mother by now?" Sarah's eyes twinkled behind her sunglasses. She touched the top of Esther's gravestone reverently.

"No. No—"

"I know what you meant. Maybe it's good we waited four years. I didn't have this the other years." She reached into her purse, as commodious as ever. "I brought you something. A present." Sarah pulled out a book and handed it to Bernie.

Bernie looked from book cover to Sarah and back again. "It's you."

"It's me."

"*Sara's Year*," Bernie read aloud, "by Sara Shumacher." He looked up. "Sara-without-an-h Shumacher. You dropped the 'h.'"

"I dropped the 'h.'"

He opened the flyleaf. "You didn't sign it to me," he teased.

"I will if you want me to," she said. "Maybe you should read it first before you decide. You're in it, you know."

"Will I have to sue you for libel?"

"You'll tell me after you read it."

"I'll read it after you sign it."

"Are you sure? It's a risk."

"I'm a risk-taker now." He pirouetted awkwardly. "Do I look the part?"

"Whatever you look, boychik, you look good." She removed her sunglasses. Her eyes were wet. "What about you? Who are you four years later?"

Bernie grabbed Sarah's hand and shook it heartily. "Bernard Marc Freed. Good to meet you." He released her hand. "That's Marc with a 'c.'"

Sarah laughed. "Of course it is."

"I have something for you, too." He pulled an oversize postcard from his bag. "It's tonight. I made sure it would be. Will you come?"

"What is it?" Sarah rummaged through her purse for her reading glasses. They weren't there. "An art opening?" She held the postcard up to her face. "Bernard Marc Freed," she read. "It's you!" She examined the reproduction that illustrated the invitation. "Gott in himmel!" she cried. "It's me!" The signature piece illustrating the gala vernissage was Bernie's sketch of her and Esther at Stella's Lunch. Only it was no longer a rough sketch. It was a textured, brilliantly colored, full-size acrylic. "The shoes! I love the shoes." Esther wore Dorothy's ruby slippers from *The Wizard of Oz*.

Bernie smiled. "You didn't answer. Will you come? It's downtown, at the Klinkhoff."

"The Klinkhoff? Anne Savage's gallery."

"So, will you come?" he asked again.

"He asks, 'Will I come?'" Sarah said to Esther's gravestone. "I'm the glamorous model in the picture. Of course, I'll come. Do we have time for lunch first? Dominique's. My treat."

"I love Dominique's and I can't wait to go back for her peach pie. But this is bigger than Dominique's. It's bigger than Westmount. It's so big, it's Ritz-Carlton big. So I already made reservations there, with champagne. And it's my treat."

"Champagne? At lunch? With what? You're an artist now, not a fancy accountant."

"I was never a 'fancy' accountant. Just a civil service grunt. Anyhow, even artists deserve lunch at the Ritz now and again." He grinned. "Authors, too. Anyhow, it's a big day. For all of us."

"All of us, Bernie? What all of us?"

Bernie slipped his bag over his shoulder and took Sarah's arm. "You and me, of course. And Mom and Anne Savage."

"And who? And what? There's something you are not telling me Bernie— Bernard Marc Freed."

"Haven't you always wanted to meet a certain famous Canadian artist? He's been written up in *Maclean's* and everything."

"You don't mean— Mac? Mac will be there?"

"Yup. And not only Mac." Bernie waved at a bench a few paths away. A young man stood, waved back and began walking toward them. Bernie steered Sarah in the young man's direction. Even from this distance, Sarah could make out the man's chiseled features and tawny hair. What struck her more than anything was the radiant, love-filled smile he directed at Bernie.

They had almost reached Erik when Sarah stopped. "Wait," she said. "I forgot something. Something important."

"What?"

Sarah said nothing. Bernie watched her as she returned to Esther's grave and added one last pebble to the top of the granite marker. She pulled two cards from her purse, the invitation to Bernie's art opening and the publication announcement for *Sara's Year*. She looked at each in turn, then leaned them both against the foot of Esther's gravestone, side by side.

"Thank you, Esther," Sara whispered. "Thank you."

Sara's Yiddish Glossary

Alevasholem (ah-*LEY*-vah *SHOW*-lem) — May he rest in peace
Alte moyd (*AL*-teh *MOYD*) — Old maid
Alteh machashaifeh (*AL*-teh makha-*SHAY*-feh) — Old witch
Bahartst (bah-*HARTZT*) — Brave
Balabusta (bah-lah-*BOOS*-tah) — Exemplary mistress of the household, good cook and housekeeper
Batamt (ba-*TAMT*) — Delicious
Bilder (*BILL*-der) — Pictures, paintings
Boychik (*BOY*-chick) — Term of endearment; literally young boy
Bubbie (*BUH*-bee) — Grandmother
Chazerai (khazer-*EYE*) — Junk, garbage
Chutzpah (*KHOOTZ*-pah) — Nerve, gall
Drek (*DRECK*) — Garbage, dirt, manure
Dumkop (*DOOM*-kohp) — Dunce
Farkakte (far-*KAK*-teh) — Lousy
Faygele (*FAY*-geh-leh) — Gay, often derogatory. Literally, little bird
Gonif (*GOH*-niff) — Thief
Gornisht (*GORE*-nisht) — Nothing
Gott in himmel (gohtt een *HIMM*-el) — Exclamation of shock. Literally, God in heaven
Gott tsu danken (gohtt tzu *DUNK*-ehn) — Thank God
Goyim (*GOY*-im) — Non-Jews
Kvetch (*KVETCH*) — Complain
Mamzer (*MUM*-zer) — Bastard
Mazel tov (*MAH*-zel tov) — Literally, good luck. Used most often to convey congratulations
Mensch (*MENCH*) — A good person
Meshugena (meh-*SHOO*-ghe-nah) — Crazy
Mishigas (mih-shih-*GUSS*) — Craziness
Mieskeit (*MEES*-kite) — Ugly, misfit
Mishpochah (meesh-*POH*-khah) — Family

Narishkeit (*NAHR*-eesh-kite) — Foolishness
Nes (*NESS*) — Miracle
Platz (*PLUTZ*) — Burst with emotion
Putz (*PUTZ*) — Derogatory. Literally, a prick.
Schmatta (*SHMAH*-tah) — Literally, rag, but refers to the clothing trade
Shabbas (*SHAH*-buss) — The Jewish Sabbath, celebrated from sunset Friday to sunset Saturday
Shaineh maidel (*SHAY*-nuh *MAY*-d'l) — Term of endearment. Literally, pretty young girl
Shiksa (*SHICK*-suh) — Non-Jewish woman; often derogatory
Shiva (*SHIH*-vuh) — The traditional seven-day mourning period that follows a Jewish funeral
Shloshim (*SHLOW*-sheem) — The traditional thirty-day mourning period that follows a Jewish funeral
Shreklekh (*SHREK*-leckh) — Horrible
Shtupping (sh-*TOO*-ping) — Having sexual intercourse
Tsuris (*TSOO*-riss) — Troubles
Yiddishe bocher (*YIH*-dish-eh *BOH*-kher) — Jewish boy
Zeyda (*ZAY*-dah) — Grandfather

Mourner's Kaddish Selections

Yis'gadal v'yis'kadash sh'mei raba (*YEES*-gah-dal vih-*YEES*-kah-dash sh-*MAY* rah-*BAH*)
B'al'ma di v'ra khir'usei, v'yam'likh mal'khu'say (be-*AHL*-mah *DEE*-vrah khee-roo-*SAY* vih-*YUM*-likh mull-khoo-*SAY*)
B'chayeikhon uv'yomeikhon (b'*KHY*-ay-khown uv'*YOM*-ay khown)
Oseh shalom bim'romav, hu ya'aseh shalom (*OH*-seh *SHAH*-lom beem-roh-*MUV,* hoo *YAH*-ah-seh *SHAH*-lom
Aleinu v'al kol Yis'ra'el v'im'ru amen (ah-*LEY*-noo vih-ul-*KOHL* yis-rah-el vih-*EEM*-roo ah-*MEN*)

*** Yiddish pronunciations can vary widely and there is no universal standard for transliteration.*

The *Sara's Year* Saga

It's March 2014 and I'm doing a radio interview to promote the recent paperback release of *The StarQuest* and *The SunQuest*, the sequels to my first novel, *The MoonQuest*. "Any plans to write a fourth novel?" the host asks as the show draws to a close.

With no ideas for another novel and no conscious desire to write one, I reply, "Sure, if inspiration strikes." Under my breath I add, "Some time in the *distant* future."

A few months pass and I find myself in the midst of a series of health scares. As I deal with my anxiety, one of the questions I know I must answer is, "If I'm to die sooner rather than later, what is it I want to make sure I do before I go?" To my surprise the first response that bubbles up from somewhere deep within is, "Write another novel."

I'm in the midst of preparing for a business trip to Los Angeles when this happens, so I promise to think about it when I get back. That, however, is not good enough for my Muse, that disembodied creative source that is the wisest expression of my unconscious mind: "The time for a new novel is *now*," it insists. "Start it when you get to LA."

So one evening after the day's obligations have been met, I park myself at a Santa Monica Starbucks (where else?), switch on my laptop and begin to write. I know nothing of the story I am being called to. All I have is a vague notion for an opening scene.

Eight months pass. My health concerns resolve themselves and my focus turns to a different book, *Birthing Your Book...Even If You Don't Know What It's About*. Little do I realize, as I move forward with *Birthing Your Book*, that I am writing it at least as much for me as for other writers: I am writing it to help me birth a novel that I still know little about.

Not long after *Birthing Your Book's* release, I find myself back in

LA, this time to sign books at the Conscious Life Expo. It is there on the second day of the event that a stranger marches up to my table, scrutinizes me and my book display, and with a gaze of alarming intensity, asks me for my rising sign.

"Virgo," I tell him.

"When do you normally write?" he asks next.

There's little you can call "normal" about my work habits. One draft or book might write itself more easily in the morning, another in the afternoon, another late at night. That's what I tell him.

"You need to be writing two hours before dawn," he declares, backing it up with a complex astrological explanation that I pretend to understand.

"Not going to happen," I mutter as he leaves. I am barely functional two hours after dawn, let alone two hours before. Yet when the next morning I awake spontaneously at 4:30, I decide to put my mystery man's theory to the test. I find the few pages of my barely started novel on my laptop and pick up where I left off.

Through the months that follow that peculiar encounter (though rarely before dawn), Esther, Bernie, Mac and Sarah's story reveals itself to me with a speed and clarity I have rarely before experienced in my writing, often through the meaningful coincidences that Carl Jung termed "synchronicities" and that I can only describe as Muse-inspired miracles.

Despite all that, I still have bouts of resistance, as I often do when launching a new project. But as with every other of my books, I find ways to surrender to the greater wisdom of the story, and in so doing write my way through and past my apprehension.

The result is *Sara's Year*, a story I am profoundly grateful to have written. May it have touched, inspired and entertained you in reading it as much as it did me in writing it. And may you, through it, come to remember that it's never too late to live your passion.

Mark David Gerson
October 3, 2015

Author's Note

Sara's Year is a work of fiction, and like all works of fiction grounded in a real time and place, it contains a blend of true-life and make-believe. I have done my best to paint Montreal and Halifax and the time periods portrayed as accurately possible, but the needs of the story and its characters have always trumped historical exactitude.

Speaking of the story's characters, only one is based on an actual person: Anne Savage was a well-known Canadian artist and a legendary teacher at the very real Baron Byng High School on Montreal's St. Urbain Street. Even as my Anne Savage may bear a vague similarity to her flesh-and-blood counterpart, she is, like all my other characters, a creation of my imagination, and all resemblances are either coincidental or convenient, rather than intentionally factual.

Without cataloguing all the other times and places where I have strayed from verifiable fact, allow me to note several.

If there is a Jewish cemetery anywhere in the world that exists in the shadow of a Catholic church, I am not aware of it. There certainly isn't one in Montreal, at least not to the best of my knowledge. Speaking of cemeteries, even though Esther and Sarah never learn that it's there, Anna Leonowens's grave is in Montreal's Mount Royal Cemetery. The real-life heroine of *Anna and the King of Siam* and *The King and I* died in the city in 1915. She moved there from Halifax, where she was active in the women's suffrage movement and founded what is now NSCAD University. However, the Leonowens-Fyshe Gallery is my own creation, its name borrowed from Anna's son-in-law, Thomas Fyshe, who was a Halifax banker not an art dealer. The current Anna Leonowens Gallery, part of NSCAD, was established long after Esther left the city.

Most other landmark buildings mentioned in *Sara's Year* are real — or at least were when they show up in the story. Some like Kresge's, the Laurentian Hotel and the Capitol and Palace theaters disappeared long ago. Others, like the Westmount Public Library and its conservatory, continue to stand as cherished architectural jewels, although Anne Savage's *Quebec Farm* does not hang in any of them. The Eaton's and Simpsons department stores, once venerable Canadian retail establishments, are gone. Fortunately, their buildings have been repurposed. Morgan's stands, now a Hudson's Bay Company store, as does the Carleton in Halifax, now a popular live-music venue.

There was a Murray's restaurant in each of the Lord Nelson and Laurentian hotels, although not necessarily during the story's time frame. Murray's, too, is now a piece of Canadian history: The last restaurant in the chain closed in Montreal in 2009, ironically, a few blocks from where I grew up.

Discovering that Murray's was the coffeeshop in two of my story's principal hotels was only one of the many remarkable coincidences that showed up while I was writing *Sara's Year*. Another was finding statues of Robert Burns in both Dominion Square (now Dorchester Square) in Montreal and Victoria Park in Halifax.

As noted in the story, *The King and I* premiered in Montreal at the Palace Theatre on August 10, 1956. Anne Savage did have a one-woman show at the downtown YWCA that year, but I could not verify whether it coincided with the movie opening.

Finally, the student murals at Baron Byng High School: They existed (if not as I have described them), created under the stewardship of the real Anne Savage, who did not initiate the project in reaction to a stultifying curriculum. Rather, Baron Byng seems to have been a lively, progressive school, with library shelves far better stocked than my fictional Elaina Drew would have you believe. Did William Shatner, Mordecai Richler and Irving Layton ever sign their names to Baron Byng murals? I don't know. I do know that, along with many other Canadian cultural and political luminaries, they attended the school, as did my mother, whose signature, I am proud to say, appeared on at least one mural.

Gratitude

Sarah mentions Carl Jung's concept of synchronicity to Bernie in Chapters 29 and 40, and given all the meaningful coincidences that both contributed to this project and that occur to Sarah, Bernie, Esther and Mac throughout the story, perhaps I should first acknowledge Jung. Years ago, his work helped awaken much within me that would ultimately find its way into all my books, including this one. A similar tribute must be paid to Carole H. Leckner, whose long-ago mentorship helped me to recognize and value the synchronicities in my life and to trust them enough to pay attention to them.

My sister, Susan Gerson, was responsible for the story's most significant synchronicity: When I started the first draft of *Sara's Year*, Esther was not an artist manqué, Baron Byng was merely a conveniently located Montreal high school, and I had never heard of Anne Savage. Yet not long after Susan mentioned the school's wall art and our mother's 1930s contributions to it, Anne Savage and the murals transformed themselves into key fictionalized players in my unfolding novel.

For insight into the real Anne Savage, I am grateful to her niece Anne McDougall for her engaging blend of biography and memoir in *Anne Savage: The Story of a Canadian Painter*, now sadly out-of-print. I am also grateful to Dr. Janice Anderson at Concordia University's Canadian Women Artists History Initiative for her assistance with my Anne Savage research.

For an appreciation of postwar Halifax, I must thank Graeme F. Duffus and his book *Carleton House: Living History in Halifax*, along with author/historian Blair Beed. Also in Halifax, I relied heavily on members of Facebook's "Vintage Postcards and Photos of Halifax and Nova Scotia," who searched out tidbits from the internet and their own lives to help me with many of my questions. Special thanks in particular to Alice Giddy, John S. Gray, Chris

Johnson, Eileen Kelly, Linda Curry Little, Darlene Morrison and Jay Wesley. And a particular shoutout to Garland Brooks who visited the Westin Nova Scotian on my behalf and grilled current staffers about features and facilities that vanished from the building more than half a century ago.

Members of another Facebook group, "Montreal Then and Now," helped out with aspects of my Montreal research, among them Hugh Brodie, Gabriel Jacob and Christian Paquin. Much gratitude, too, to Ken Brownridge, Carolyn Flower and Danuta Gajewski who went above and beyond to answer some of my other Montreal-based questions. Additional thanks in Montreal to columnist Mike Cohen and Sun Youth's Johanne Saltarelli.

I am always grateful for the online encouragement I get for my work from my social media family. On this project, the enthusiasm was more effusive than ever and helped spur me on to not only meet but beat my deadlines.

To the anonymous astrologer who cornered me at the Conscious Life Expo in Los Angeles: Although you were wrong when you insisted that my best writing time was well before dawn, it was your intervention that resurrected a *Sara's Year* that had sat neglected for eight months. Thank you!

The original edition of Gabrielle Rico's *Writing the Natural Way* was published in 1983, a year before Bernie gifts a copy to Sarah in Chapter 40. When I discovered the book a decade later, it helped dissolve many of my longstanding creative blocks. So it is with great affection and much gratitude that I include Rico's book in my story.

If you have read the acknowledgments in any of my other books or follow me on Facebook, you know that I spend a lot of my writing time in coffee shops and cafés. It was no less true with this book. I am particularly grateful, for their creativity-enhancing ambiance, to the Santa Monica Starbucks where *Sara's Year* was born and to the half-dozen outlets in Albuquerque where many of this book's scenes were composed and revised, as well as to their baristas. I'd like to offer a special shoutout to the manager and staff at Albuquerque's NM 528 Starbucks for their warmth and good humor.

Music plays a significant role in my writing process, and while it would be impossible to acknowledge all the music that kept me motivated and inspired, I will mention some. In addition to the songs and artists included in the story and other recordings of Esther's and Sarah's years, the Barra MacNeils, Mary Black, the Celtic Tenors, Celtic Thunder, Josh Groban, the Irish Descendants, Natalie Mac-Master, Rita MacNeil and Loreena McKennitt seem to have had the most play during this novel's inception and creation.

I'm also grateful to the two cities that, along with Esther, Sarah, Bernie and Mac, are key characters in this story. As my hometown, Montreal still lives powerfully within me more than thirty years after my departure. There could be no *Sara's Year* without it. As for Halifax, I feel obliged to make it clear that I do not share Esther's antipathy toward this jewel of a city. Perhaps if Esther could have experienced Halifax decades later, as I did, she might have revised her opinion.

Sara's Year would not likely exist without the encouragement of Kathleen Messmer, who has unfailingly believed in me and my work and who has demonstrated that support most generously over the years. I am grateful, too, to Adam Bereki not only for his friendship but for his morale-boosting pep talks at some of my lowest moments on this project.

I must also thank my mother, Sophie Katz and Sara Metalin — in whatever realm they now reside — for their unwitting contributions to the story.

The genesis of *Sara's Year* was the opening visual of a single scene. It grabbed on to me a few years ago and refused to let go until I began to set it to paper. Where did that image come from? Harlan Ellison used to joke that he got his ideas from a mail-order house in Schenectady. Mine come from my Muse, that imaginative/creative aspect of my unconscious mind that plants ideas into my head and doesn't stop pushing, poking and prodding until I act on them, sometimes with great reluctance. To that part of me that is wiser, cannier, braver and more audacious than the rest of me, I express my deepest, heartfelt gratitude, for there could be no stories without it.

After Sara's Year

The Sara Stories

Marc-Allan Cameron hasn't felt alive in thirty years. For Sadie Finkel, it has been more than fifty. When life comes knocking, will they let it in?

THE EMMELINE PAPERS

The Sara Stories

When Emmeline Mandeville spends the final months of her ninety-third year reflecting on her eccentric past, she can't know how profoundly her reminiscences will weave through Bernie, Erik, Sadie, Sara and Mac's lives fifteen years later.

www.ingramcontent.com/pod-product-compliance
Lightning Source LLC
Chambersburg PA
CBHW050357190726
48284CB00007BB/2331